THE PROFESSOR
&
A BRIGHT STAR

A novel

For Rahel,

I truly hope you'll enjoy this book.

With love

Mariana

M. R. KAJUE

Edited by Anne Gillion

Cover design by Rebecca-Ira

ISBN 978-1-7395231-0-7

Dedicated firstly to my father, James Kajue. I love you eternally and may you rest in perfect peace. Thank you also to my parents, Mariama & Ibrahim Bakarr for all your love.

Then, most importantly, to my very own Bright Star, Ezekiel. You are my world, and the world is yours, always. This is for you!

A GIRL,
THE PROFESSOR
&
A BRIGHT STAR

1

"The black man is a fool!

"He humours me," proclaimed the blue-eyed, blonde-haired, twenty-five-year-old professor, Matthew Wylde - conviction burning inside his arctic stare, as if his words were gospel.

Silent gasps of horror pervaded the air.

It was the first time a speech/lecture at Harvard's Sanders Theatre had been given the go-ahead to be broadcast on television - CNN deeming it necessary that the debate on race relations, most notably in America, be given centre stage. Many well-known names had been considered to head the debate, but only the British professor had enough balls to tell the Americans the ugly truth.

It was the seemingly unprovoked and lawless deaths of three unarmed black boys by white police officers in the space of a week that prompted the urgency for the once brushed-under-the-carpet covert prejudices of America to be torchlit and shown for what they truly were.

"Most especially with his inaction, which can only be translated as stupidity and lack of intellect," Matthew continued, much to the apparent disgust of the distinguished crowd, made up of academics, students, and public alike.

Yet, he, Professor Wylde did not acknowledge their revulsion; he refused to. Nonetheless, he felt it - their permeable horror and shock - and it excited him like a gazelle would a lion.

Love, hope, compassion are things that move most people. Not him. Not Matthew Wylde. Fear, anguish, and trepidation were the things that stirred him; they attracted him and kept him ticking.

Like wildfire, his words raged through the crowd, engulfing them in flames of confusion, fury, and perhaps humour itself. The professor's views had always been polarising, borderline absurd, but no one had expected that he'd be bold enough to touch on this sensitive topic with such a firm hand.

His words were arrogant, brutal, cold, and incendiary, just like the man himself.

"He is garrulous, but profoundly lacking in substance ... No. No! Be sharp, not serrated, damn it," he demanded of the black man, saliva spewing out of his mouth like drops of poison, while his fist, which was covered with green and purple veins, slammed, and cracked open the tense air.

White people snaked uncomfortably in their seats, even the ones who harboured seething contempt for those whose skin the sun worshipped. Some hid their faces, presumably unsettled that their own kind would voice such racially bigoted views publicly.

The black audience, however, remained steadfast. They refused to waver or quiver while the flames of his words scorched their flesh.

They watched the white man, his eyes dead, as he prowled the room like a lion seeking to devour, his cold blue eyes static and focused like the tip of a gun, aiming to maim or kill.

Professor Wylde presented himself as a merchant of hate, selling his speech like milk to a baby.

His statements, though antagonistic were not facile,

they seldom were, and even those that did not want to accept them, knew it. Which was why everyone remained in their seats, hating the man, but intrigued by his words. Perhaps the same things that moved Matthew Wylde also moved the crowd!

His ethos, though damning, perhaps had some truth in it. If not, why else would he be saying them?

A faint, yet sinister smile etched across his face, as though he acquired pleasure from torturing the black and white crowd.

"He is a philistine, unappreciative of the finer things in life ..." he said, his well-spoken snobbery exquisite – if a redeeming factor was to be considered.

"Fuck you, n*gger," interrupted an irate black student, incensed by the sheer disrespect of the professor. The crowd watched the student, secretly elated that someone had the balls to say something, anything.

But their joy was short-lived, with the professor's retort. "I believe it is you, not me, my friend, who is the you-know-what," he corrected briskly.

The crowd, encapsulated in disbelief and awe at the same time, stayed silent. No one, black or white was audacious enough to defend the black man from the lone white crusader. Enraged by the professor, the young man got up, fuming, his body burning inside out ready to leave, but as he did so, the professor said something that both triggered and persuaded him to stay.

"He is a coward, and I hate him for that," said the professor solemnly, as though he were disappointed with the black man for his timidity. "Even his so-called president, the half-black is a ... coward." He paused, the enormity of his statement sweeping like a gargantuan wave into the audience, including the millions at home glued to their television screens.

The cameras hurriedly zoomed in on the professor's face. But his glacial stare gave nothing away.

His speech was as horrific as it was scintillating. The crowd were ashamedly ensnared in his web.

* * * *

The current president was in the last months of his final term – the 'great black president' *Time* magazine had once called him. He had done well; great even. But in line with the custom to vilify black men, it was predicated that in the end, they would discredit him. And discredit they did!

It wasn't just the professor who voiced negative opinions of the president.

At the end of his reign, the media would fail to illuminate the fact that it was this mixed-race president who had turned the desperately failing economy around. It was he who had brought to life the dying American healthcare through the Affordable Care Act, 2013. Yet they were not to sing his glory but rather his political requiem as though it wasn't he who had removed the mighty United States from the flames and brought it to cooler ground. A feat no one black, white or otherwise could have achieved.

* * * *

In the theatre, Professor Wylde knew his earlier statement would warrant problems beyond his imagination, but he had gone too far to care about the potential repercussions for insulting the most powerful man in the world.

"The half-black ..." he jeered, his words moulded with slabs of ignorance, ambiguity, and ingenuity. A wicked laugh escaped his mouth. "What a funny man he is. I suppose you believe him to be your hero, a saviour, the one seated in the Oval Office to save blacks from evil crackers and their injustices. Right?

"Nope! I'm afraid he is not. He's merely a business strategy. America is not a country. It is a business. And that business needed someone that was black, not fully black, but still black," he said, briefly looking into the crowd and then away. He wondered if he should say what he was about to say next ... He stopped. After all, he was British, and it was in their nature to keep the impolitically correct parts of their views hidden. Nevertheless, he had gone too far, and he was not a man who looked back. So, forward he went with his tirade.

"The black president is not a hero."

A deluge of deafening 'boos' drowned him.

He paused, ever so briefly. Perhaps he had gone too far. Yes, he had gone too far. However, he had gone too far to stop. There were no detours in his route.

"Turn off the cameras, turn them off!" shrieked the CNN producer, almost tripping over two cameramen, fearful that the professor had gone too far.

"Why?" asked the professor, much alert to his surroundings. His words were met with silence.

Needless to say, the cameras kept rolling. Because madmen who spewed chaos were always TV gold.

The world was watching, America was incensed, and that was exactly what he wanted. The professor had finally struck a chord with white America.

The majority of the room stared at him repulsively.

Needing to place the crowd's anger elsewhere, Matthew inserted, "anything that the white man gives the black man is bad. They gave you slavery, prisons, and now they give you a mixed-race president. What does that tell you? There is a reason why the white man calls the half-black, black. If he saw any good in him, do you think he would call him that?

"The black president does not care about the milieu of the black man, because if he did, he would not incessantly and continuously keep telling you to protest peacefully while you're being killed like flies in front of our very eyes by men in blue," he said to the audience, his eyes burning with something that resembled pain.

Could it be that the professor felt the grievances of black Americans?

Suddenly the crowd fell deathly silent.

The United States was going through an elevated reality of some sort. All its old demons were returning, but it appeared that the powers that be were collectively turning a blind eye. It was like *The Birth of a Nation* all over again.

"You're all fools, and fools deserve what they get," continued Matthew Wylde, as the entire crowd simultaneously listened in further disbelief.

How could he say that the oppressed were allowing their own oppression? Surely the mad professor had become even madder, thought the crowd. Nevertheless, the professor refused to mince his words. Like daggers, he threw them at the crowd; the white folks dodged, but the rest were directly hit.

Professor Wylde was impassioned with something; a purpose perhaps, but only he knew what his motivation was. The crowd were simply lost, yet somehow hoped that in the end they would find themselves inside his maddening diatribe.

Every so often, Matthew's stare would focus on the back of the theatre as if he were speaking directly to someone. As if the words he spoke were for no one else but them. As if the sole purpose of his tirade was to petition a reaction from them.

"This is a crusade. Not between Muslims and Christians, but between blacks and whites," he maintained.

The young black man, who had earlier taken offence, was no longer filled with rage.

Perhaps the professor did have a point after all.

He listened attentively, almost as though the professor could be redeeming himself.

"How many of your brothers and sisters will you let die in vain before you realise that the crusade started the moment your ancestors stepped off those ships? Three teens killed by those ordered to protect. Now tell me, could three white boys be killed so recklessly?"

Silence.

Disquieted eyes watched him. He watched them back, as the answer to his question revealed itself on every face in the room. "This is a game, and four hundred years later you still refuse to learn how to play! So, you see you cannot blame anyone but yourselves when the opposition takes advantage because you refuse to learn the rules," he said, the reactions of the crowd more subdued than before, as they finally began to take in the profoundness of his words.

That's when it dawned upon the crowd. The professor was not generalising the black man. However, he was pinpointing the ones who were always straddling the fence between blackness and trying to please whiteness. How can black boys be getting killed at such a high rate without any justice or consequence for the perpetuators? This wouldn't be a question white Americans would ask as justice would've immediately been meted out with impunity. Why then, were black leaders not asking this question? For he knew that the black man was great. Possibly the greatest of man. For who else could the world so relentlessly try to bring down again, and again, and again ... yet still he rose over, and over, and over again.

The black man was not a fool. Rather, it was the black men placed inside the game with the power to change the rules but who chose not to, who were the fools, the cowards, and the philistines.

"Some were made to lead, but the black man chooses to follow, to be demeaned, stereotyped, and subjugated ... Why?" he shouted, his words falling angrily on the crowd.

His eyes wandered through the sea of faces.

He saw none, except one. She was sat next to a man with ginger hair. Perhaps the anger in his words had materialised in her body because she was filled with a rage so potent his body began to break out in goosebumps.

Her skin was dipped in bronze and highlighted with gold. Her eyes were black like magic, as if the tales of a thousand wicked nights were shrouded inside. She shone as if the sun itself had given birth to her.

She was perfect.

Her blackness almost offensive to his whiteness. But such beauty could never be offensive to anything.

He did not want to behold her as the otherworldly beauty that she was. Her cavernous ire which was targeted at him was supposed to enrage him, disgust him, and repel the tiniest iota of desire, yet his entire being could not refrain itself from admiring her. Camus was most certainly right in *The First Man*, when he said, "We all have a weakness for beauty."

His heart stopped as her gaze met his: dark, brutal,

and enflamed with fury.

He quickly looked away, as though he had peered into the eye of the devil. She terrified him, perplexed him, but most of all excited him. She evoked and awoke something in the bosom of his being.

He tried to repel it by refocusing on his lecture, but that proved futile. She shook him off balance, unsettled him, and almost made him look like a fool. Something he had maintained that a man like him was incapable of.

Struggling to maintain composure, he said, "Perhaps, I've dwelled on truths that are ubiquitous ..." The crowd bemused and perhaps perplexed at his almost inconspicuous change in demeanour kept their gaze on him. Their eyes felt like ants crawling all over him. The desperate urge to scratch twitched between his fingers.

Erratically, he exhaled then rustled his fingers through his hair, somehow managing to lay to waste the desire to scratch.

In the distance, she watched him.

"Let me further elaborate by dwelling on academic truths," he said, trying to diffuse his passion.

"Truths, you say?" exclaimed an angry voice from the audience.

All eyes turned to her, the singular black entity in the penultimate row. The cameras rushed to capture her, and silence fell upon the crowd as they anticipated her contribution.

"Do you mean the truths of Hume who said, 'I am apt to suspect the Negroes to be naturally inferior to the whites. There scarcely ever was a civilised nation of that complexion; nor even any individual eminent in action or speculation.'?" she huffed. The room began to buzz, and before he could quieten the sounds, she interjected, "Or perhaps Kant who said, 'This man was black from head to toes and this is a clear proof that what he said was stupid.'" She puffed. "Are those the fucking truths you mean?" she shouted, her voice oozing with venom. Much to the livid complexion of the professor, she added: "I cannot relay my critical thought to such narrow-minded and incompetent truths and suppositions, Matthew Wylde," she concluded, her words spitting poison bang in the face of the professor.

The crowd, finally satisfied that someone had been able to cut the Brit down to size, stood as elation and applause burst through the air like fireworks on the Fourth of July.

She had unhinged the professor, taken him off balance, and made him feel like a mere mortal, where he once felt invincible. She had penetrated his core, and for a mere second the world saw it, but he quickly hid it, almost as if his infallibility had never existed.

Her eyes like two balls of fire had burned him.

He wanted to break her just as she had almost broken him, but he felt pity for her, and he couldn't recall why. Yet the more he stared into her dark and hollow eyes, the more he saw the flames. They were burning her, not him.

The resemblance was so uncanny it frightened him, and that was when he realised who she was.

Bridget White.

Cousin of Tariq White. The last of the black boys murdered that week.

2

Five Years Later

WEDNESDAY, MARCH 18, 2020

I deserve kisses and breakfast in bed, but I am a sociopath and I push all the good men off the cliff, read the mantra inscribed with blood-red ink on the fluorescent green Post-it note wedged inside my laptop. The truth of it all raised a succinct and scathing laugh from my throat.

I suppose it was quite humorous, the audacity to acknowledge one's own sociopathy.

It was doomsday (even though I did not know it yet): March 18, 2020.

The third doomsday.

The first was the day my bright star Tariq was murdered. The second was that fateful day five years back on American soil when Professor Matthew Wylde and I crossed paths. I hope such a day never arises in my life again. The same way I had buried Tariq, I had also buried the professor and his derogatory ethos about my people in the land of the unfree, the land of the shackled, and the land of the slavers and their slaves.

Nonetheless, I could not help but think about the professor most days and nights. Even though I lived in London, sometimes I wished we would cross paths again ... I wondered what he would look like. How would he sound? And would he still be filled with the same arrogance he exhibited in America?

Do not relive the past, do not relive the past, repeated the voice in my head that I seldom listened to.

My thoughts fell upon the image of David, my ex. The blonde-haired, blue-eyed art of a man, who once upon a time made love to me as though the world were on fire, prowled through the arterial labyrinths inside my mind. I tried to vanquish him, but the devil does not die easy.

In front of me, the pernicious eye of my laptop glared with malice as if pre-empting bad news. I tried to call its bluff, but it did not blink, not once, not ever! It maintained the perfect poker face.

My throat expelled an almost imperceptible sigh, "Oh, piss off," before shoving the electronic device to the side.

My physical being was encased inside a tiny suffocating cell - alias, the English office. It was a grey unassuming box littered with worn-out books, computers that creaked, and an uncanny poster at the top of the dilapidated brown door that read, "I See You!"

A face did not accompany the poster, yet I always felt paranoid as if its eyes were walking on me, around me and over me.

Such a room clearly said, "NOT FOR THE FAINT OF HEART," however, it was my only sanctuary. A place for self-preservation, a place where I hid from all the wolves in sheep's clothing that lurked in the corridors of Lady Liberty High. I was the only English trainee teacher. The other had quit because, and I repeat verbatim, "I fucking hate this shithole and its bloody principal."

I should have followed suit, since the principal was more a foe of mine, but I did not like leaving things half-done.

In this box, as opposed to outside it, I did not need to conform or suppress myself at the whim or comfort of others. I was cocooned from the relentless and inescapable gazes that labelled me foreign, for more reasons than one, even though I was homegrown.

The cell was mine, unfrequented by actual teachers. Being a trainee did not afford me the luxury of a classroom that was wholly mine. My teaching space was rented, and each time the bell rang I gave the keys to the landlord who also happened to be my mentor. She was a slight, pale woman with wandering eyes that always searched for problems rather than solutions. Her apathy and disdain for the world was universal. So, I took no offence whenever her dark hollowed gaze glazed over me as if I did not exist.

Most days I imagined the forthcoming freedom of June 19, the last day of placement. The sun would blaze, birds would sing as if honey were dripping off their beaks, and my shackles would come undone.

But fate was a trickster. He had other plans. Plans, if I may add, that I did not agree to.

I had chosen to teach because of Tariq. He had not said the exact words, "You need to be a teacher." But he had said, "You know, I think you'll make a fine teacher, Bridge." I think he was joking; surely, like Mother, he had higher aspirations than that for me. But he was dead and that was the only profession he had spoken about to me, even if as a joke. Furthermore, Mother enraged me at times, and I wanted to do something that didn't fit with her high-flying expectations of me. And if I'm being honest, the bug of teaching did catch me at one point in London. That combined with Tariq's joke had landed me as an unqualified teacher, stuck in a school I neither liked nor despised.

It was 8.23 am, twenty-seven minutes before my

presence was required in class for registration. The sun had carved a fiery path in the clouds, smashed its way through the window, and crashed on my flesh as if to expose me. For what, I was unsure.

As I slumped by the desk in the far corner, a cold chill kissed me, disintegrating the ferocity of the heat that once was.

My undying foe, the one that qualified teachers referred to as "vampire" since he was born before time immemorial, was near. The long bony nose of Principal Greaves entered through the door and sniffed feverishly trying to inhale the scent of my arrival. But I had masked the odour. His ice-cold, dead grey eyes tried to cut me down, but I had donned my armour, so his attack was deflected. His elongated skeletal finger tapped the door and every time it did, it felt like a needle jabbing my eardrums. An ungodly smirk wriggled across his lips before he disappeared down the corridor.

It always perplexed me that the principal interacted with me as if I were a contagion. As if I grew up in Peckham when it was riddled with tower blocks and poor folks with nappy hair and deeply tanned complexions. Though it could not be further from the truth, I sometimes felt myself shrinking and painted red with offence under his gaze. I wanted to know more about him. What pit of hell had he sprung from? And what gave him the audacity to inspect me with such incivility?

One day I will find out, I told myself.

With the principal gone, I was looking forward to the rest of the day, even though the room had suddenly turned cold and unwelcoming.

The sun had somehow fled. Lodged itself under a duvet of clouds.

I looked back at the laptop screen.

The screen saver was my baby cousin, Tariq White. Moisture quietly settled in my eyes while they watched his cheeky smile on the screen. My heart ached. The fact that I would never again get to see him, kiss him, or tell him I loved him ripped apart the strings in my heart.

Sometimes ... No, most times I wished I could rip the beating heart out of the bastard who killed him. But he was a phantom. No one knew him. Yet everyone felt he was a police officer as that was what the professor had confessed that day at Harvard. He had unwaveringly said Tariq's killer was a police officer, to which someone had asked how he knew. His reply? "I just do." The police department had released multiple statements denouncing such claims. They upheld that it was officers who'd killed the other two boys for fear of their own lives. But Tariq, they had claimed, was killed by gangs or something of the sort. Nonetheless, the professor was adamant it was an officer. And in my heart, I too felt it was a police officer.

Despite this, five years have passed, and his killer has never been found. Someone was lying. I hated to admit it, but it seemed the liar was Matthew Wylde.

My finger clicked the email tab. Like magic, all my mails appeared. At the very top with a red exclamation mark to show superiority in rank was an email with the subject line: *Temporary cessation of Initial Teacher Education studies.* The words stared at me with wanton malice, knowing that its content would inflict injury upon opening. I did not want to enter, but the screen hypnotised me and said, *hey you, come on in ... you know you want to ... after all, it is your future not mine that is held inside.* So, I entered ... at my own peril.

The floodgates which were disguised as a PDF file flew open. Submerging me. It read: Due to the VIRUS we have decided to suspend PGCE Secondary ITE school placements, with the students' last day effective today!

The news was abrupt. It felt as if a freight train had just rammed into me and left me mangled on the tracks.

There I was, Bridget White, twenty-five years old, a trainee teacher, a single parent, a woman and worse still, the underachieving daughter of two exceptionally brilliant medical consultants!

* * * *

What do you do when your world breaks in half thrice in the space of five years?

Why would the Department for Education topple the tower I was building? How could they be so cruel as to not consult with me regarding my own future? Who gave them the authority to make decisions on my behalf? Did they not consider the fact that they would leave me to the ungodly elements of ridicule, mockery, and castigation with no pity whatsoever in sight? How could they plan my future without consulting me? How could they? I almost felt myself crying.

Mother!

I needed to call my mum. My fingers shakily dialled her number. The line trilled violently before she answered.

"Hi, baby," her warm voice sang.

I fell silent. Tears begged to be released from their cage, but my pride locked them in and threw away the keys. Gently, I exhaled and loosely held together my fractured pieces. "Hi, Mum."

"How are you, my love, is everything alright?" she asked, her tone wrung with concern. She knew me. She knew me more than I knew myself sometimes.

"Uni-is-stopping-my-course," choked my voice, the words heavy on my bloated tongue.

It was her turn to fall silent.

Trepidation slithered through the line and tried to wring itself around my neck.

I hoped Mother would say words that would console me, but her anger, unlike mine, had not yet fermented. “It’ll all be well, baby ... you can always defer to next term, or better still you can choose a different course,” she cooed, her words, which confirmed my failure at being a teacher, landing on me like missiles.

“There is nothing idyllic about failure, Mother,” I hissed, the soft and caring tone in her voice boiling my blood and prickling my ears. I needed her fury to be set ablaze alongside mine. But she refused. Instead, her words dripped with consideration. Why wasn’t smoke pouring from her ears and nose like mine was? Why?

I recalled red hives prickling her skin the one time I got an A-minus. I needed her to match that same energy. Instead, she said once more, “It will be alright, darling.” I slammed down the phone and imagined stomping on it till the niceties in her voice turned to swirling and whirling tornadoes of anger and rage.

Tensions were high and I was at an impasse with my mum, the DfE. Everyone! I tried to unpack the silence that had enveloped the room, but it refused to be tamed. It was raging like a lion, violent in its quiet. I sighed angrily and placed the phone back to my ear. Mother’s breath was low and monotone. “I’ll talk to you later.” And before she could reply the phone slammed off.

3

My eyes rested back on the laptop. I did not know that by choosing to teach I was attaching my career to a lost cause. Was I to be another statistic: a single black mother who did not, or could not complete university? Surely, the critics would profess from their rooftops that I was a failure, while they jeered and sneered and smote me. They would hiss like serpents and spit their venom as they threw stones, berating my name. I bowed my head and sighed, deeply. *Why would the Department for Education do this to me?* the voice in my head screamed in anguish yet again. I was hurtling down an endless abyss and it was by fate that Caroline came in and snapped me back to reality.

Caroline was the head of the English department. She had ginger hair, which in the correct light appeared blood-red, pale amber eyes that once in a while showcased their crisscrossing talent by flying in multiple directions and throwing one off balance, and freckles that scattered all over her face like grains of sand and tiny pebbles. Other than that, her face was featureless, her chin blending into her neck, the skin pale and bland and her lips, two sharp cuts in a thin line.

Her voice, sharp and excited, split the silence in two. "Hiii," she yelped. I wanted to prod what seemed like an armour of delight and say, "You can be yourself, you know," but my mother always said to let people dance in their happiness, even if it was a mask that concealed their sadness. It was not my place to switch off the music that played in her head.

I gave a dry laugh. "Hi, Miss."

“Hello, doll.” Her voice like a hyena cackled in my ear. I looked up and she beamed, her face changing into different shapes of giddiness. I smiled. Caroline was forty-three with the bubbliness of a twenty-three-year-old. Whenever I saw her, she was so animated, it was as if a character had sprung alive and just bounced right out of Cartoon Network. She was wacky but she was my favourite person in the school.

“Good morning, Miss.” I waved, this time with more enthusiasm. Caroline had been the first person to truly welcome me to the school. Perhaps it was the fact that we both had a tiny human at home. Hers was a four-year-old girl, and mine was an almost three-year-old boy with a most gargantuan name: Winner. Caroline and I never interacted outside of school, but in school we were pseudo-besties. And that was enough for me. There were many things I admired about her, but the most significant of all was the way she smiled, and her red hair would turn into blood, while her amber eyes bloomed with delight when deriding others. It was a skill that I did not possess and, try as I might, I could not master it. It always astonished and perplexed me, as it would a child watching a magician pull a rabbit out of a hat, how one could have two faces at the same time. I suppose it was an art form practised only by her kind. I once asked her, “How do you do it?”

“Do what?” she had said while gently wriggling my braid around her fingers, saying with a radiant smile, “You people have such wonderful hairstyles,” as if I had just landed from Venus and was not human. She saw me as ‘other’ with my lips that were “soo big” and skin that was “soo chocolate”, which she would say as if they were compliments. Nonetheless, I liked her. Perhaps she meant to offend others, but when it came to me, I went with the assertion that ignorance was bliss. Whether it was my ignorance or hers, I was not sure. As I pondered over those thoughts, Caroline cut in, "So sorry ..." she smiled sadly, her darkened eyes assessing my fragility, "to hear about the cessation of your course."

"Don't worry about it," I said with lightning speed, because had I said it any slower, tears would have burst forth and run freely down my face. I was not sure whether her voice was riddled with insincerity, perhaps it was my imagination, but I could almost hear her laughing at me. Surely not; Caroline was my friend. She liked me, she told everyone she liked me and that I was the best PGCE English student the school had ever had. Surely, she was not just saying those things out of political correctness where it was decreed that one had to be nice to the other because their hair was kinky and their skin had been a little over-indulged by the sun.

"Anyway, if it's any consolation, you can always come back next year."

I wanted to say, "fuck you", but instead I said, "thank you" and bared my teeth into what I hoped she interpreted as a smile.

* * * *

After Caroline left, I crawled back into the dense forest of doubt which I had planted inside my mind, with its endless labyrinths and weeds and creepy crawlies that lurked at every corner, burrowing deep inside my psyche.

I was lost in the forest.

Get out! Run! screamed the voice within. So, I groaned and tilted my head back, my neck exposed, as the guillotine of rationality dropped and chopped down the forest.

The first words of the email: *Dear Bridget White ...* floated in my head. Yes, Bridget White. That is my name. A pro-black woman with an anti-black last name. My parents must have been intoxicated when they christened me.

I kid!

The sun snuck back in through the blinds and gently rested on my chocolate skin which was infused with caramel and accents of gold. Black people called me brown skin and white people called me black. I preferred the latter. I am black! Being brown separated me from being black. It hung me on a wall along with dark skin and light skin that said shades of black as if we were colours of paint. Where were the shades of white? They did not exist because the white people concluded that there were no shades of white. White was white, a simple yet ingenious fact. And I wanted to participate in such a clever notion, so to me, black was black.

I was still in the small English office. It was 8.42 am, eighteen minutes before class started. I had disposed of my forest of unsureness, but the root of scepticism still lingered.

I tried to equate my achievements to that of my friends. Friends who were either doctors like Camilla, lawyers like Alison, or artists like Lisa or in tech, which for some inexplicable reason happened to be the coolest and most lucrative job around. Perhaps I should have studied business or software development. But no, I had studied English.

Who the hell studies English at university?

Me!

I was the fool who did! Needless to say, Mother howled like a rabid dog, insisting I drop my preference and pluck something shinier and more appealing. How could I, her only child, whom she and Father had spent hundreds of thousands of pounds on in private school, decide to study English? Black upper-middle-class children did not choose English as a subject at university. They chose the subjects that swaggered with vigour and rigour, demanding and commanding that you admire their beauty and the filthy rich bounty they were to amass at the end.

Mother's friend put it down to a lack of ambition, laziness, and even stupidity on my behalf.

So, the more I sat in that room, my future in tatters, the more I wondered if Mother's friends had been right. Did I lack ambition? Was I lazy or perhaps stupid to have gone into English and teaching as a career choice? Surely, I must have been, because teachers were fleeing the classrooms as if they were warzones, and there I was, willingly going into the line of fire like a mad woman.

Ironically, it now seemed, I even had the audacity to be mad at a silver lining that had been placed on the cloud in my path. Because that was what my mother had insinuated in that phone call. I was already the proud owner of a first-class BA from UCL. So, two years spent completing a Master's in Business was not intangible. All I needed to do was apply and I would join the league of distinguished upper-middle-class children who did not disappoint their parents like a wet Wednesday evening in February.

But I liked teaching. Mainly because of Tariq and the fact that he thought I could make things make sense to anyone. I wanted to remove dogma from the curriculum, to show that Achebe was just as valiant as Shakespeare in the literary Olympics or that religion and science were not heaven and hell but rather earth. To show that the views of King and X were just as philosophic as Plato and Socrates. I wanted to show that intellectual independence was not limited to a certain few but available to all. I wanted to help every child see his or her true potential. I wanted to help my students have purpose.

Yes, stupid; I know.

Nonetheless, those were my dreams. But The Virus, like a masked crusader, came to turn dreams into nightmares. It was adamant that dreams were to be put on hold, along with the Mercedes Benz I was planning to get on hire purchase, since I did not want it as a handout from my millionaire parents.

4

Taking the final sip of my coffee, I made my way to the first class of my last day at school. My feet were stomping, my breathing heavy and my eyes blazing, burning a path all the way to the classroom.

The virus had declared war and the Department for Education had laid down its arms and surrendered. But I did not want to surrender.

Why would the DfE surrender on my behalf? I fumed. Nonetheless, I was determined to enjoy my students.

First period was with the unpalatable Year 10s. They started filing in like a pack of bees, buzzing for no apparent reason. Many were late as is the usual routine, and as always, for the umpteenth time, I told them, "I will not tolerate lateness in my class."

"Okay, Miss," they grumbled, knowing damn well I would have to repeat myself if I were there the following day. They were studying *Great Expectations* by Dickens, and no one hated it more than a pupil named Tanika.

"Oh, for fuck's sake," she groaned, while her bag sluggishly dragged behind her.

Her eyes were dark like half of her ancestors and her skin pale like the others. The binary undertones and overtones of her physicality were equal. For everything that was black, there was also something white to contradict it. And perhaps that was where her confusion lay. She did not know if she wanted to be nice or rude, good or bad, clever or stupid and, ultimately, black or white.

My aunty whom everyone knew could not be truly black but professed and confessed to anyone who would listen that "I am wholly black", always said, "mixed people are confused". And I, at times, believed her because she was a paradigm of her own words.

"I hate this bloody class," Tanika fumed, her mouth a leaking tap. Just spilling and spilling and spilling ... till I had to take a bucket and place it to stop the venom from desecrating our classroom.

She was insolent. Effing and blinding till her bottom hit the seat.

I watched her. "Are we done?" I questioned, my voice using all its resistance to not say, "Shut the hell up, you little shit."

She kissed her teeth. "Whatever man." Her bubble gum popped in the air, before she spat it out with a snide smirk on her face. "I'm done," she giggled, her eyes wandering around the class for some adulation.

Even so, her attention-seeking was ill-equipped to match the disregard that the class fired her way. I knew her blood was raging, and though I was the teacher and was supposed to be the bigger person, I was elated. That little pest was finally being fumigated and her silent screams were big, bold, beautiful symphonies to my ears.

Grateful for the few seconds of silence the class afforded me, I went straight to the starter activity on the smart board. "Alright, today we are—"

Someone cut me off.

It was Tyrone. "Miss, did you know that black boys get marked down disproportionately by their own teachers? Their own teachers!" he fumed, kissing his teeth at the treachery of it all.

At first, I was offended by his rudeness, but the anger in his voice told me he had just discovered this fact and couldn't contain his disdain any longer.

"You won't mark me down if I don't deserve it will you?" He tried to smile. His big brown puppy-dog eyes trying to pry into my conscience. I looked away while his question stabbed me.

The eyes of the class fell on me, even Tanika's.

"Well ... go on, answer him, Miss White," said a student

Another agreed. "Yes, Miss, will you?"

"Of course she will. She's just like the rest of them, they don't care about us," added Tanika, her animus towards me a living, breathing thing.

I looked at Tyrone. In front of me sat a black boy who was six feet tall, with the stature of a man, but still only just a boy. One who could not tell if I were his ally or his enemy though our skin was formed from similar shades of the same colour.

"Miss Wilson always says," his fingers pointing and shaking in imitation, "you won't amount to nothing, you'll be lucky to end up a cleaner ..." He stopped before emotion spilled out of his voice. I could feel my heart breaking. My voice wished to console him and tell him that Miss Wilson was wrong and that her words had no relevance to him. But if I did that, it meant I was going against my superior, as she was the head of Year 10.

Perhaps Miss Wilson was spewing negativity out of frustration. Teenagers are an aggravating bunch. But she was wrong. Would she tell a white kid that? Possibly not.

I did not see his anger as simply a boy aggrieved by his teacher treating him poorly. I saw it as a systemic issue that meant even black teachers were included in the oppression of black kids. The demonisation of black kids. They too were in the whirlpool of stereotyping blackness. The same way my son Winner's nursery headmistress had stereotyped him. So, it was that closeness that made my heart break as I saw Winner in Tyrone and vice versa.

"Firstly, Miss Wilson has no right to say that to you, or anyone else for that matter." My eyes went around the room, the eager faces of my students watching me back with some type of reverence. "And, no. I will never mark you down if your work isn't deserving of being marked down, Tyrone." I threw Tanika an angry glare.

"Do you think she's lying?" whispered a student to her peer.

"No, I think she means it."

"Maybe you're right," the student replied.

I wanted to say *I am standing right here guys*, but I allowed them to have their little debate.

Tyrone appeared half-believing and half-doubtful. It was evident the words of Miss Wilson had wounded him. He wasn't stupid, but he made no effort to work hard. So, maybe the words of the head of Year 10, compounded by the fact that some teachers did indeed mark students down unwarrantedly, made him believe he did not have material access to changing the forecast for the future that Miss Wilson had predicted for him. I hated the fact that at such an age his views of his adult self were pessimistic.

So, I assured him, "You can be whatever you want, once you study hard. Miss Wilson has no say in your future – you do," I smiled.

He smiled back then muttered, "Thanks, Miss, you're not that bad you know."

"I know," I teased while the class laughed.

While I tried to go back to the lesson, my mind

wandered to the day I heard another teacher, whose skin hid from the sun, say in the staff room, "That boy Tyrone is a tyrant," because he had brought weed to school, but when strawberry blonde Thomas brought a knife and cocaine to school, that same teacher had said, "He's just a misguided little boy." Both kids were wrong. Nonetheless, one was allowed to keep his childhood innocence, while the other was judged as an adult.

The sounds of feverish giggling brought my attention back to the classroom. Tanika and some other students were hovering above the head of a boy named Michael and peering inside his bag.

"Sit!" I roared as they all scuttled to their seats. "I give you an inch but you always take a mile." *You little shits*, I thought.

My feet stormed towards Michael; I snatched his bag, which contained, I suspected, books that were not for reading in the classroom.

Miss, it's not that deep" he hissed. A colloquialism for it's not that serious. But I'll be damned because it was that serious.

"Are you kidding me?" I stood before him, eyes blazing.

"Sorry, Miss," he mumbled, pacified by my rage.

"You guys have no manners though I try to treat you with respect."

"Miss, that's cap," the other student next to Michael said. A further colloquialism for lies or fake, depending on context. I was damn tired of all the new phrases. But I matched his energy.

"No Ollie, it's not cap. It's bloody true."

"Whatever," he retorted, under his breath.

In the distance, Tanika sniggered. "Miss is such an opps. She's even left-handed." They laughed as though it were a disability. I ignored her ignorance.

"Everyone is Tanika's opps," jeered a girl who didn't seem to like Tanika much. The class laughed. However, I found no humour in the chaos.

Opps, the noun, I came to realise, meant opposition. A colloquial term used by teens.

"Shut up, you idiot," retorted Tanika, "Michael doesn't even like you. He thinks you're ugly." She stuck out her tongue.

"Ohhh," returned the class in unison. An action that inflicted the other girl's face with varied shades of crimson.

Tanika was being a tyrant to her fellow human, and she needed a good telling-off on my watch.

"For the life of me, Tanika Jones, if you do not stop right this instance, I will remove you from my class for the rest of the term," I shouted, though it was my last day.

Tanika watched me, gauging me, pondering if she should fire back. I dared her.

She did not, all she did was give me a smile that said *bitch.*

Sometimes I wondered why she acted the way she did. In order to avoid putting in an effort, she behaved as though her elevator did not reach the top floor when answering questions, with terms like "erm, yeah, duh ..." However, I refused to believe she was completely stupid. It bothered me why she acted semi-literate.

Then I recalled that she had been through hell and back. Care home after care home, and more. The world had never shown her tenderness. So now *she's* incapable of giving it. Later that day we'll meet at the gates. And she'll hug me saying, "I know we don't get along but you're one of the few teachers who treats me like the child I am rather than the adult I'm not." That day I told her the world could be hers, and somehow, I felt she believed me.

"Miss, I'm going to the toilet. Need to change my tampon."

"Eww," moaned the boys. "Can we have a trigger warning before you say that shit?"

"Okay ... trigger warning," she smiled devilishly, her dark-green eyes blooming with glee in their direction, "my vagina Is bleeding and I need to cover the wound again."

The faces of all the boys distorted in pain and disgust.

She was a trip. But somehow her torturing the male snowflakes in the class made her a little bit more palatable.

All the same, before Tanika could go, the bell rang, and they fled the room before the ringing finished, much to my delight.

Perhaps, leaving such a school was not going to be so bad after all – I managed a chuckle to myself.

* * * *

My other mentor, a stern-faced man with salt and pepper stubble, stormed into my class and said, "I need to talk to you in the staff room now!"

My heart drummed.

I flew up the flight of stairs, and by the time I reached the staff room, it felt like I had run a mini-marathon.

"Surprise!" shouted a myriad of voices including my female mentor as I opened the door. My hands touched my chest as a show of gratitude. "Thank you," I said as everyone cheered for me. There was a cake that one of the Design and Tech teachers had made. She excitedly walked up to me, gave me a slice, and hugged me. "Thank you," I said devouring the chocolate dessert.

Peter the perv, as the female teachers called him, came and hugged me. "You're such a wonderful teacher," he said in his fake posh accent as his hand almost slipped down my butt. But I was ready so I caught his falling hand before it could land on its target. He smiled ... awkwardly ... and I gave him dagger eyes which was his cue to get the heck away from me. My colleagues congratulated me, wished me luck, and made me, for a brief moment, forget. Forget that my life might be going to shit.

A few hours later, the day had come to an end. With my head slumped on the desk, the feeling of failure and hopelessness arrested me once more.

Today was going to be my last day at school. In contrast to the movies, I was not going to ride off into the clouds; nor was I to head into the arms of a six-foot-two lover who gave five orgasms in one session. No. Teachers, let alone trainee teachers, were not that fortunate. I had been unceremoniously thrown to the wolves and it was time for me to face my fate.

Packing my belongings in a small brown box, it felt like someone had died and I was the undertaker disposing of all evidence that they had once lived in the school.

The image of me slumming it at the Jobcentre and my mum falling over in a frenzy, drew a hard and gravelled chuckle from my throat. I tried to rewind the morning and undo my misfortune but the days of turning back time had long since died. So, I got up and injected myself with doses of confidence and positivity, even though they were as fragile as snowflakes.

Peter the perv who wore cheap cologne that prickled your nose before and after inhaling was lurking around the corner. I could sense his beady eyes watching me. Well, my butt to be specific.

On my way through the corridors, I bumped into

him. A look of pained compassion moved inside his eyes. Maybe he was not so bad after all. However, the jury was still out on whether he was a perv.

"Good luck," he smiled.

"Thank you, Pete," I returned.

My feet dragged on the floor. I did not wish to leave, but I had no choice.

On opening the gate, as I had done many times before, there was a finality to it that forced goosebumps to surface on my skin. It was as if I was stepping out into exile - banished to never return.

Suddenly, I felt the urge to stay. Crazy right? Perhaps I had been institutionalised. This was a school I half-hated and barely tolerated. The principal was borderline anti-black. Peter was a perv and the kids were real-life devils. Even so, there I was outside its gates, banished and vying to be accepted back in. So much for "I can't wait to leave this bloody place". My heart ripped open, provoking hot wet liquid to gingerly linger inside my puffy eyes. *Hold on to your pride, princess,* my father's voice said. *I do not know how,* I said to his voice which spoke in my head. *Oh, but you do, because this black girl will not crumble. Not today.*

Not today, I repeated as me and my broken pieces left Lady Liberty High.

5

The long road you wind down before reaching my flat was adorned with cafés, boutiques, restaurants, and a barber shop that everyone, including Winner, went to for a shape-up.

The barber shouted, "Hey, Bridge!" at me from inside the glass wall. He was busy trying to pin down a young boy, who refused to be tamed. I giggled because that is exactly how Winner is. He hated the barbers with a passion that no child should possess. Perhaps it was the buzzing of the clippers, which sounded like a colony of bees, or maybe it was the barber's cape which coiled around his neck like a serpent and gathered the remnants of his fallen hair. Whatever it was, he did not like it. And he made it known, loud and clear, until the barber had no choice but to resort ashamedly to bribing him with a packet of the mighty and life-saving lollypop to distract his attention. Something I suspected he was going to do anyway with the boy currently sitting in his chair.

I waved back at the barber. "Hello, Matt," I called and continued down the road.

The streets of Hackney, which were once notorious for violent acts, were filled with a myriad of blacks and whites and hippies who advocated cannabis as love. Gentrification had raised the once-fallen price of real estate and turned the town's fortunes around. The monied lot were taking over, and I, for one, did not mind the eclectic mix of bodies that flowed past me as I walked towards my flat. To show just how much gentrification had spread, Waitrose and M&S were the only supermarkets on my road. In an area of London where Lidl was once considered too much, Waitrose had proven itself king.

Down the road, right turn, then left, then straight down and, finally, right - remnants of the ghetto that once was Hackney still existed. Nonetheless, it no longer gleamed with prominence. It was no longer proud of its current state. Instead, it cowered in shame as if to say: "Turn your gaze away from me. For I am not worthy to be an occupant existing in this newly refurbished estate that once used to be my home." People who knew nothing of the ghetto spoke of it in the same way as someone would speak of Iraq or Syria; a far-away land that humans who despised war zones mustn't frequent.

So, though I've heard of it. I've never been there myself.

An old white man in a top hat with a strong cockney accent strutted past me, the scent of his musky cologne lingering behind. Then, a young lady, aged about thirty-two, with a tamed afro and wearing a pencil dress spoke in legal jargon with her colleague. I smiled: *You go, girl!* Pride tickled me whenever I saw a black woman blooming like a flower.

The town of Hackney was alive and kicking like a new-born child.

In the distance, a baby cried in its buggy, and the mother bent down to comfort her offspring. Across the road from me, a bunch of school kids with boxes of chicken and chips in their hands chanted, "Yes, school is closing." They erupted into excited fits of giddiness, some hugging each other, while some punched the air as if their favourite team had just won the Champions League. Seeing those teens, especially the boys, enjoying youth with such delight made me sad. My bright star Tariq could've been one of them. He should've been one of them revelling in the sunshine, eating chicken and chips and being a child. But he was six feet under, inside the deep, dark earth, rotting away because an unknown assailant decided it was okay to kill him. My eyes moistened. *Do not cry, Bridge, do not.* So I did not. I pulled myself together and continued down the road.

As I made my way, a car playing drill music zoomed past me, the school kids rapping the words as it fled past them. I looked back and some were even dancing as the traffic lights killed the speed of the car and stopped it dead in its tracks.

I bumped into someone. "Oh, I'm so sorry," I said, trying to regain my balance while I stumbled back.

He gently pulled me in to stop me from falling backwards. "It's alright," he smiled, his eyes like a hawk falling on mine. I felt myself drowning in two spherical balls of miles and miles of sultry brown. He reminded me of David.

"Erm," I murmured looking at his hand, which was around me.

"Oh, sorry, sorry," he said as he quickly removed it from my body and raised his hands to show no offence. He had my heart pounding like a drum, and his eyes almost held me in a trance. "I'm ..."

"Sorry, I have to go," I interrupted as I broke the trance and fled from him.

"Mark. I'm Mark," he shouted in the distance. I smiled and quickened my steps for fear that his sultry voice would catch up with me.

A safe distance away from Mark, the old feeling of despair began to creep up from behind me. *Go away,* I found myself whispering out loud.

As I entered the Waitrose by my home, the stench of despair stabbed me in the gut. The silence was loud. Booming like a drum inside my head and thus inducing a headache of giant proportions.

Thanks to the virus, you are to perpetually remain an unqualified teacher, snapped the voice in my head. *Oh, your mother would be so proud*, it continued, forcing my head to droop. "Shut up," I shouted as it kept reading aloud from a sheet of my inadequacies. An African uncle watched me, bemused. *He thinks I'm crazy* ... perhaps I was.

As an upper-middle-class child, it was without question that I was a thorn, a vast desert of disappointment. Even if not to my family but to the wider upper-middle-class society. "Evolution is a prerequisite for life, darling; why don't you change to law or medicine?" One of Mother's friends had suggested this during one of those suffocating brunches where they compared me to their children who were ... yes, you guessed it, lawyers and doctors. The idea of me evolving into a lawyer or a doctor was embryonic, but I knew that Mother could envision it growing into a full-blown body of work. Sometimes Mother's envy of the successes of her friends' children, compared to me, was so apparent she was damn-near green.

Mother had not said it outright, yet it was evident she felt the cessation of my PGCE was my manna from heaven. "Being a trainee teacher is like being on probation. The irony being that if you're well-behaved during that period, your reward will be prison. Where you'll be teaching a bunch of delinquents," my mother had said when I first told her I'd be pursuing a career in teaching. I laughed. But in the back of my mind, I was apprehensive. Inner London schools did exhibit prison-like traits. In essence, Mother was insinuating that I'd be entertaining the chronically miseducated or, at best, undereducated. She sure knew how to make things appealing, I mused, walking to the ice cream section of Waitrose.

I held my phone in front of me. A fleet of missed calls and text messages ran down the screen. The only name missing from this list was my mother's. However, I knew that Mother would call. She always did.

As I anticipated her call I wondered if I should lie and state that "all is well" when she called. Suddenly, I felt ensnared in a spiralling crisis. I was confined in a moral quagmire. My conscience sought honesty, but my pride said, "Lie, damn it." Yes, I was going to lie to my mother. For both our sakes, especially mine. I was in no mood to discuss why I didn't want to be a doctor. A question I always felt my mother asking without words. Surely, I couldn't tell her that I harboured a fear of not being good enough. Nor could I admit that a part of me just wanted to spite her for expecting too much from me. I could not give her the pleasure or lack thereof of admitting that I, Bridget her golden child, had chosen a less-than-shiny route because I feared failure in the path she would have chosen for me.

Though I may never admit it to her, I knew that it was out of love and legacy that Mother placed me on a pedestal. She simply wanted the best for me and for her family name. However, I felt pressured, and pressure breaks diamonds. So, I broke and went against the grain. The truth of the matter, however, was that I was interested in medicine when younger. I wanted to be as revered as my parents were. I wanted to emulate their every step. However, Mother's unbearable taunts and talks swayed me otherwise. It was as if the better I did at school, the more she expected, the more she taunted me, the more she made me feel inferior - though I was superior to my peers. According to Mother, I had to be better, then some more, than my peers and that was as draining as a parasite sucking the life, the blood, the bone, and the marrow out of me.

The only way to pay her back for her crimes against

me was to rebel. And rebel I did. I told her, "I am going to teach."

To which she replied, "As a professor?"

"No, as a schoolteacher," I answered.

Since then, we've had a love-hate relationship.

Also, if I am being extra honest, perhaps a very tiny part of me had the baby to spite Mother. A defiant *I am going to be a plethora of things you despise, Mother!* As for David, it was more of ... Actually, I do not know what it was for David.

If I had to guess, I would say it was a concoction of love and hate. Though everyone who knows me would say I did it because I loved David.

* * * *

Friends and family were sceptical about me having Winner. "Babies cry infinitely," said Alison. "They shit and it stinks," added Camilla. "They pick their noses. And they will bleed you poor. Don't do it," demanded Melissa.

My pregnancy had happened by accident. I was twenty-two. David was elated. I was mortified. Mother had not said it out loud. However, she may have implied that she was not ready for me to have a child.

My best friend Alison would joke: "Children are parasites, they will suck the life blood off you." I would laugh raucously and wave her off like a fly. "Be gone she-devil," I'd hiss while we both chuckled. Then she'd stop and look me in the eye. "Seriously, babies aren't easy to have. Are you sure you want to do this?" Sometimes I would say yes and sometimes I would refuse to answer. But I never said no.

I wasn't foolish. To a degree, I was aware that being a single parent meant dysfunction, insecurity and, at times, resentment towards the baby and his father. "We don't want that for you, darling," Mother insisted. But my mind was resolute up until the day of delivery.

With the baby bag on my shoulder, my mother and father on both sides of me, I set forth to the labour ward on the adventure or misadventures of parenthood.

I had heard that pain during childbirth was inevitable, yet it was so much more gutting when it reached its apex than I had expected; my insides being cracked, ripped and pulled like pork. The kind of pain so ungodly, it muted my screams, tears welled stagnantly inside my eyes and the sinister laughter of delirium kicked in.

Madness!

Growing and birthing a human did indeed induce madness. I refuse to believe otherwise.

During Winner's birth, I unravelled like an onion, exposing raw and tearful emotions. All the same, Mother, who was known to be my nemesis at times, was on every occasion my beadswoman whenever I was straddling the thin line between life and death. Even though she had rebuked my choices, I knew she was praying feverishly for me and her grandchild's safety. Which was the first time I knew that though she hated my choices, she loved me, and so too did David, Winner's father, who was there crying like a baby holding our son, while my parents patted David as if it were his insides a child had just ripped open.

That day in that delivery room was all strange for me. I had promised that David would not be there, seeing as he had cheated. Even so, when he entered the room as my screams increased a hundred decibels more, I could do nothing but allow him to place his hand in mine, which I tried my best to crush with all my might.

It was at that moment I knew, no matter how much I would try in this lifetime, I would never fall out of love with him.

So, yes, I guess for David, birthing Winner was indeed out of love.

6

Speaking of David, my phone rang.

It was him. It was as if he was always in my mind, hiding in its cave like the philosopher, Plato, spying on what I was thinking. I did not answer, so for good measure he sent a text. I smiled. Somewhere in me, I was happy that he was still there, my pseudo-champion, the one that helped pick up the pieces when the chips were down. Still, he had hurt me, and I've always found it hard to forgive.

My mind opened the orifice where David was lodged and unfastened the vent that held the memory of our first meeting, five years ago.

* * * *

I needed a drink after my showdown with Professor Matthew Wylde a couple of hours prior at Harvard's Sanders Theatre. The rage in my body was beginning to mellow with every gulp of beer. If there was one thing a British student will do in any terrain, it is to drink beer. It was our nectar of choice regardless of financial status.

I could feel his gaze penetrating me from where he was sitting, deep in the corner. His eyes twinkled in my direction before he got up, came to me, took my hand, and placed a kiss on the back of it. "I had to slay a few dragons and knights ... but here I am, unharmed and ready to buy you all the beer in the world," he said as he motioned to the waiter to bring two more glasses of Dutch courage to my table.

"May I sit?"

I shrugged.

He sat, a soft cheeky grin on his face.

While we sat in silence waiting for our beers, my eyes drank in all of him. His face was a Picasso. With lines of brilliance and madness painted on the square canvas he dubbed a head. His lips had a slight tilt which gave them an erratic sexiness whenever he laughed. His mouth was fashioned for amorous kisses, and licks and bites. I was inexplicably confused and aroused by the odd angles of his face.

David's physicality was a concoction of idiosyncrasy in a beautifully maddening way. Love may have been blind, but attraction was not. My eyes were wide open.

The waiter brought our drinks.

"Cheers," I said, raising my glass to his.

"She speaks," he teased, the raw huskiness of his voice forcing a smile across my lips.

"You have to look in my eyes when you say it," he paused, my eyes swimming in the endless blue of his gaze, "or it's terrible sex for a very long time. We do not want that, do we?"

"We?" I laughed, his company brushing off some of the anger the professor had riled up in me.

So, I stared into his eyes and he into mine. "Cheers," I murmured. The moment, on my behalf, was brief and sweet. As I looked away, I could still feel his eyes searching me, trying to peep into my being.

"So, what is it that you do?" I interrupted his gaze which refused to leave my person.

"She does not like for mere mortals to marvel at her beauty," he whispered.

I blushed. He had a way of making me feel vulnerable. Something I was not used to. His words, his voice, his accent, were like an aphrodisiac for me.

"I am a doctor."

"So, you're...?"

"Twenty-five" he intercepted. A wicked glint in his eyes. "And you...?" he said, his eyes taking in all of my physicality "must be twenty..."

"Just twenty."

"Oh, nice. Just twenty must be one of those Roman numerals my professors forgot to mention at Imperial College."

"Indeed," I laughed, loving his sense of humour. "I'm twenty, silly."

"Ahh, I think I should be leaving," he said taking his drink and standing up. "I don't want them over there," he pointed to the bar, "knowing that I am talking to an underage drinker," he laughed.

His silly jokes and delicate sense of humour drew me in. He took back his seat, "Twenty huh? Well, good thing we're British as we are drinking on your British age."

"I like the way you think, because after what that dickhead professor said about black people, I need liquid courage..."

He smiled.

"You do not agree with me? You think he's right?" I questioned, offended.

"What I think doesn't matter. All that matters is that you were the star of the show."

Pride bubbled in me while I pushed aside the anger he had evoked in me earlier. "Thank you." My lips curled into a soft smile.

"You are welcome...?"

"Bridge."

"You are most welcome, Bridge," he said his eyes failing to peel themselves from me. I felt hot under his gaze and, at that moment, the wild thought of feeling his lips all over me flooded my mind.

He was wild and free, yet reserved. He spoke finely and the accent just added more culture to him. At times when he thought I was not looking, I could see that he was more an introvert than the extrovert he presented to me. I smiled inwardly. I was taken by him, in a way I could not explain. He was not my usual type. He was handsome and intelligent, but other than that he was not my usual type. Yet, there we were, and I was totally entranced by him at that moment.

We were drinking like fish. He called for the waiter once more in the strong and distinctive British accent that I liked. While we waited for our drinks, I took out my textbook.

It was on the romantic poets.

"Byron?" he asked

"Sorry?"

He pointed. "Your book."

Maid of Athens! I am gone:

Think of me, sweet! when alone.

Though I fly to Istanbul,

Athens holds my heart and soul:

Can I cease to love thee? No!

He stopped, just as my jaw dropped to the floor.

"Isn't that Byron?" he smiled.

"Yes ... yes, it is." I smiled. "A fan, I see."

“I can be a romantic under the right circumstances in the company of a divine creature.”

My cheeks flushed red. I blushed and I felt compelled to let him register my full name.

“Bridget Celine White,” I said.

“Angel,” he replied, reaching out his hand to mine.

Although we were surrounded by a sea of people, it felt like it was just him and me.

He told me he preferred Bridge – it was edgy and he liked it – before calling the waiter over once more. “Sorry, may I change our order please?”

He raised the glass in the air and studied the dark red contents of it. He let it linger near his nose and took in its aroma, then said the name of the wine. Which I would later come to know cost four hundred dollars a bottle.

“Lovely,” I said taking a big gulp; his smile told me I was meant to sip it, yet he loved that I gulped it.

Moving from his seat, which was across from me, he gently sat beside me.

My heart pounded. I exhaled softly.

My name is David King. And when we get back to London I will take you to the moon, Bridget Celine White,” he whispered, his lips moving ever so close to my ear.

I whimpered.

His fingers moved insouciantly across my flesh as if they had always been acquainted with it. His words caressed and placed me under his spell. Enchanted. He kissed me. Softly. On the cheek. My body ignited with desire. Our lips touched, ever so lightly. Then our eyes met as our mouths lingered precariously close to each other. He licked my lip. His lips locked on mine. Its softness, sweetness and fullness took me to the moon and back. I shared in the taste of his saliva, which tasted of mint and wine, as his tongue parted my mouth. His kiss was too much and not enough all at once. He exhaled. I pulled back. His eyes were poison. His lips moved. A smile escaped. My heart fluttered. Could it be Cupid's arrow? Lightheaded. I was falling. His hand caught me. "Angels do not fall," he smiled.

* * * *

My phone beeped again, this time it was the girls.

I entered the group chat and was bombarded with messages like *oh no... are you ok?... why would they just stop the course like that... are they bloody serious?* My girls. They always knew how to mimic the emotions I felt.

Deciding to reply when I got back into the sanctuary of my home, I locked the phone, picked up my tub of Ben and Jerry's, paid for it at the till and headed home.

The simple yet indulgent scent of Jo Malone greeted me as I took in the air. Taking off my shoes, I lifted both arms to the heavens and stretched, wishing the trouble of the day would fall off my beaten shoulders.

I pulled out two strips of antibacterial wipes and cleaned my hands. The hysteria on the news about COVID-19 had turned me into a germophobe. My father insisted that the human body needed bacteria to survive, but the news, which he called fake, told me otherwise, and since I was a millennial, it had been programmed into my DNA to listen to fake news.

The warm tones of smoky grey and smoky beige wallpaper textured the walls. It was my two-bedroom piece of heaven. How I managed to pull that off in London still blows my mind. The rent was extortionate, but I wanted Winner to have his own space, his own sanctuary for the days when Mummy was being a dragon and he needed respite. I used the art of haggling on the landlord and was forced to bring the "I have a child" ploy into play for an ounce of sympathy. It worked and he lowered the rent by £100. It may not sound like a lot, but when you are deducting it from £1,700 PCM, it was plenty. David, Winner's father helped with half of the rent, not because I asked but because he wanted to.

Money management had never been my strong point, but when Winner was born, I became an accountant. And that was how I managed to save £10,000, which in turn was able to afford me the deposit and two months' rent to secure the wonderful flat I was standing in. I walked past the mirror, but my reflection called me back. The woman in the mirror whose lips were round and full like the moon, with red nail polish and a grey tailored dress from Zara, with a black blazer on top, smiled at me. She watched me and said, "You've got this, you sexy Milf - Covid and cessation have nothing on you," which made me giggle. "Thank you for the boost of confidence," I said back to her as she winked at me and disappeared into the glass while I walked away.

The corridor was decorated with photos of Winner and my cousin Tariq. Their resemblance was so uncanny people often thought they were twins.

Winner was the rebirth of my bright star, Tariq. On the wall, next to a baby photo of Winner, was a baby picture of Tariq, which he'd fondly refer to as "me". I never corrected him because they did look almost identical as babies. Winner was not fortunate enough to meet Tariq alive, yet I felt he knew so much about his uncle through all the fond stories me and my parents would tell him.

Winner was the champion of our home, so it was only right that his image adorned the walls. He would stop and look at the photo of his ultrasound then laugh vibrantly as if he recalled having been there, inside that warm body of water. He would copy the thumbs up that the foetal him was doing in the photo as if to say, we made it bro, we are out here, and life is wonderful! Mummy is a tad crazy, but she is the best.

My phone pinged: "How are you and my Winner?" read the message. You guessed it. David. He was my guilty pleasure. We were stuck at the border between love and hate, and I found myself precariously balanced on the side of love. And it was that unequivocal feeling of irrationality that excited me with him. I did not want to be with him but being without him made me sick!

The phone pinged again. It was Alison one of my besties. Her message read: "Go get toilet roll now!" I laughed at her hysteria. The conspiracy was that toilet roll was now the most valuable commodity in the world. It had overthrown oil, gold, and gas and been proclaimed king by humans who needed to clean their dirty arses. I had not pictured the legal phenom, Alison, as one to fall for such gimmicks. It was not until my phone rang that my mind changed.

"Hi, Mum," I sang.

"Hello, Bridget, my love. I need you to go look for toilet roll for my grandson now!"

I grinned. "Mum ... you do know he wears Pampers, right?"

"It does not matter. Go get it now." She hung up before I could say anything else. I found the whole thing funny, yet I felt this crippling urge to: Get toilet rolls now!

I ran to the bathroom and guess what.

The last roll was dying off, like leaves falling from their branches.

I gasped. The irony made me laugh.

Toilet roll was indeed gold. On the news channels that championed scaremongering, images of masses gathered where they heard it was present ran rampant hourly. Like flies, humans lined up if only to take a peek at it as shoppers fought like they were in Call of Duty to get a hold of just one pack. And when they did get a hold of the world's most precious commodity, they lifted it in the air like a trophy, while crowds cheered and jeered at the winners.

Yes, it was all funny. Not funny as in ha-ha, but funny as in - is this really happening? And yes, it was really happening. We had lost our damn minds! Myself included, I am ashamed to say. And just like Gnarls Barkley, I remembered when I lost my mind.

It was 4.51 pm. The eyes of the other shopper met mine in the household aisle of Waitrose, then darted back to the last pack of rolls. A smirk etched his mouth. Perhaps his age made him feel I would apply rationale or sympathy. He did not know that on this particular day, I had zero fucks to give. So, as he wobbled with his walking stick towards the rolls, I ran after him, and I unashamedly wrestled with an old man to grab the last pack of toilet roll.

Granted, there were a few more episodes of madness to come! Nevertheless, toilet roll-gate just happened to be the first.

7

It was 6.10 in the evening: 6.30 was rolling down the hill. So, I jangled my keys and made my way to the nursery to pick up my Winner.

Winner was a bonny little thing.

I named him Winner because Tariq, while alive, had once said if you ever have a boy you should name him Winner. "Because with a mother like you, he can never lose."

Winner had dark locks which haloed his head in coiled patterns. His eyes almost blue-black like a thousand nights, yet brighter than the sun, were wide and vast like the seven seas. His legs possessed feet that scurried instead of walking and hands that clapped and created instead of resting idle. Yet with all his glorious attributes, it was the boy's smile and laughter that would make you feel as if you were in paradise.

"Come to Mummy, my precious little human," I cooed, his tiny feet pattering the floor to make ground and reach me. He flew into my arms like a Spitfire.

"Mummy!"

I smiled "Baby" then rubbed my face on his neck. Taking in that wonderful scent of innocence and his father's cologne which he forces me to spray on him every morning after I have sprayed myself. His skin, softer than silk, the colour of coffee, stayed in my embrace for a few more seconds before handing me his nursery regalia to carry. I gladly obliged. Holding them in my left hand with his tiny palm in my right.

The other toddlers would shout "Winner!" from behind us, across the road and in front. Each time we would stop, and he'd pay homage to his comrades. Their faces lighting up like moons and stars at Winner's acknowledgement.

"Aren't you a little, big star?" He giggled while I tickled his face, exposing his dimple which was a simple dent on his cheek, his left cheek. The right cheek was left untouched, and it was this dichotomy that added to the beauty of his face.

However, with all his beauty and reverence from his friends, there were some adults who wished to demonise my angel.

Such an adult happened to be the headmistress who was across the road from us cautiously waving at me.

Bitch, I muttered as my mind went to the first and last time she tried to vilify Winner.

It was a few months back. She had called me into her office. The caricature smile etched on her face before she held the door open for me told me she was going to behave like a demented clown. Nevertheless, I entered her lair in the hope that my gut feeling was just a fluke. Needless to say, it was not.

She had a lot to say and because anger was bubbling inside my blood like broth, I afforded her the grace to finish. After her slithering tongue was done, spewing venom on my son's name, she nodded her head at me, but I looked away. "Bloody bitch," I muttered. She had tried to vilify Winner for being a child, painting him as "wild" and "aggressive"; meanwhile, the blonde-haired tyrant, Billy the bully, had slapped a girl, made her cry, pulled down Jimmy's pants and committed an act of domestic terrorism by infecting the entire nursery with lice. Needless to say, he walked scot-free, the words "don't do it again, sweetie," his only reprimand. So, when she opened her biased beak to pigeonhole my angel, the devil came out. I violently flung the stereotypes she tried to pin on my child back in her face. "Listen," my finger pointed like a gun, "you should be ashamed of yourself," I hissed. "Don't you ever try to typecast my son for basking in his childhood and playing with rigour," my voice boomed. "Has he ever hit another child?" She stayed silent. "Answer me," damn it.

"No."

"Have any of the other kids or parents complained about him?

"No, but..."

"But what?" I retorted.

She became cautious. She tried to pick her words carefully, but I knew she would offend me regardless. "But I see him playing a bit rough with the other kids..."

"Ha!" I enunciated. "You see him?" I fumed. "Of course you would. It seems you're the only one with eyes in this bloody school–"

She stood up and then tried to cut me off, but my palm was swift to rebuke her defence. "You have no leg to stand on, Karen Hope." She huffed and puffed a little before sitting back down. "Do the other kids play rough with him?"

She stuttered, "Yes..."

"Have you had this same conversation with their parents?" She lost her tongue and fell mute, I shook my head, my spirit riled with displeasure. How dare she complain about my child but not the others. The irony being that she was quick to hurl microaggressions my way, but was afraid to express the same contempt towards the fair-complexioned, light-eyed gang. I wanted to say,

"Bitch, you look the same as me, you should be my ally, you coon," but instead I told her to 'go eff herself' in not so many words.

She had angered me beyond belief because in all her complaints she had failed to mention the fact that he was the only Rain Man in her nursery. A polymath who could read from A-Z, count from 1-50 and name all the colours in and out of the rainbow. She had forgotten that it was he, my assertive boy, who told Billy, "That's not nice," when he spat on her shoes and told her without prejudice, "Miss, you are too black," and that it was he who shared his food with the other kids. She had crossed out all those truths, opting instead to defame his character.

I was there once when Billy's green eyes wildly grew into a forest of red-hot rage and he slapped her. She did not paint him as a dictator or a psychopath. Instead, she called him an angel. A bloody angel!

She was denying Winner the innocence that Billy the bully was afforded. And it vexed me, it riled my blood, and made it bubble with the magma of fury. Firstly, because she was wrong and secondly, because she was black. Yes. I said it. I expected her to be my ally, to watch out for my child, but she was the first to incalculably demonise him. Insisting he was a tyrant when all he had ever been was an angel. How dare she?

So, it was for those particular reasons that when she waved at me from across the road, I cut my eyes at her and kissed my teeth, repeating the B word once more in case she didn't hear it the first time.

* * * *

As we continued our walk home from nursery, we popped into the corner shop owned by the lovely Mr Khan. "Hello, Winner," he smiled

"Hi, mister Kha," replied my baby.

"He is so adorable, isn't he?"

"He sure is." I revealed my pearly whites as I paid for an ice lolly and presented it to Winner.

His seismic brown eyes were filled with appreciation as he slurped the aqua-blue ice. "Bye, mister Kha," yelled Winner while we stepped out of the shop. *His name is Mr Khan,* I always found myself laughing in my head.

"Did you have a good day?" I asked. He smiled, exposing his deciduous teeth, which were milky in colour and short in stature. I squeezed his cheek. "Good boy ... Mummy is so glad that you had a wonderful day." I smiled, wishing my day could have been as pleasant as his. Nonetheless, the mere sight of him was enough to make me forget. Winner possessed the sort of beauty great poets wrote about. His eyes always twinkled as if stars were dancing inside, and his smile was as agile as the sun. With the luminosity in his spirit indefinable.

He was indeed my bright star.

While we carried on walking home, I pretended to take away his lolly. "No, no!" he cried as he manoeuvred it to his right hand which was behind me. I was fascinated by his tactical skills. "Smart boy," I said, trying the same joke, but this time with great consequences.

His small moon-shaped face, which reminded me too much of Mother, wobbled and his tiny full lips trembled, while his throat expelled wails that came in intervals. "Oh, I'm so sorry, my love," I whispered.

His tiny hands stretched out towards the floor. "Lolly," he blubbered, warm liquid searing down his soft face.

"I know baby, I know." I snuggled his face into my neck. He flung his head back and wailed some more, leaving residues of snot, tears, and saliva on my skin and parts of my hair.

I need to get him a replacement lolly. Fast! Because having him in my arms at that moment was like handling a grenade with the pin already taken out.

My phone rang. It was Mother. "Bridget Celine," she cooed.

My full name is Bridget Celine White. My mother's grandmother was creole, the French kind. A mulatto. Her mother, Mother's great-grandmother had been in a consenting and, as far as we knew, loving relationship with a French sailor, Jean-Pierre Etienne. Hence the middle name Celine after my grandmother and my mother's name, Cecelia after her grandmother. However, as far as I was concerned, I was British; that I knew to be true. I am also black; that I know to be even truer. But I was also 'other'; parts of me I did not know. Yet in my dreams, those parts throbbed with life and thrived in foreign lands that felt like home. Sometimes, N'Djamena, or Brazzaville, even Ouagadougou, and most nights Timbuktu, that ancient pillar of civilisation that sits on the edge of the world, an undying relic, watching as the Sphinx and the pyramids of Giza outstrip its pre-eminence in Mother Africa.

"I'll be down in a couple of hours to pick up Winner," said my mother. I knew it was a peace offering for earlier. My mother was a firm woman. Growing up, she had no room for dissent. Mother and I sometimes had an ambivalent relationship. So, whenever she turned on her conciliatory tone, it would feel like she had parted a sea and made a divide between us. And that was how I felt earlier, as if she had caused a divide. Yet, she always managed to bridge the gap.

She did not always agree with my choices, but she always stayed by me.

"I'll be over to give you hugs," she chuckled.

Moisture settled in my eyes. "I will love that," I sniffed.

"Grandma is coming over, baby," she said to Winner.

"Gra-ma," sang Winner excitedly.

"Grandma, Grandma, Grandma," we chanted until he recalled I had dropped his ice lolly. "Lolly!" he screamed, and a few faces cut their eyes at us. Oh, piss off, I wanted to shout but Winner was around, so I was forced to watch my language.

"Sorry, my love," I tried to console but to no avail, as my little human blubbered and sputtered, reminding me I had made him drop his ice lolly. Lolly pop spit drooled down his chin. "Lolly," he said, pointing at the fallen stick on the floor once more.

"I know, baby. I'm sorry, bad Mummy. Bad, bad Mummy." I jokingly smacked the back of my hand. This caused him to laugh ... a little.

Across the road, a face so handsome and sculpted smiled in my direction. "Oh, not you again for flip's sake," I moaned as I rushed home, realising it was the man from earlier, Mark.

By the time we got in, the trauma of losing his ice lolly had been erased and replaced by the gloriously boisterous antics of Tom and Jerry. "Thank God," I murmured.

After having bathed and fed Winner, the girls texted. *Girls' night tonight, be there or be dead,* it read with a winking emoji, before the bell buzzed. "Gran-ma," yelled my champion, sprinting towards the door. "Open door, open door," he insisted his hands trying to access the lock.

I opened the door.

It was not Grandma.

Before us stood Alexander the Great. My champion. My hero.

Father!

"Hello, princess." His arms widened, allowing my body to enter his warm embrace.

Suddenly my entire being felt weak, and all the tears I'd kept prisoner released themselves and flooded my face.

"Now, now," murmured Father, his embrace getting stronger, "very, very precious jewels like you do not wallow in sorrow, princess."

"What then do they do, Father?"

"They continue to shine because they are precious, and precious jewels always shine, especially during dark times."

Alexander the Great, my champion indeed.

8

Time was of the essence. It was 8.23 in the evening and Suzie's girls' night was fast approaching.

For some odd reason, I found myself longing for David, even though I knew such longing would be futile.

While I checked my hair and makeup in the corridor mirror, my thoughts went to Tariq. I wondered what he would make of my day so far if he were still alive. Would he bear the same sentiments as Mother and tell me that my course ending was a silver lining? Or would he tell me that whatever path I chose would be the right path for me? *If only you were alive, baby bro*, I thought. Although he was younger than me, he always had a discerning way about him. His picture on my wall watched me. Inside it, he was as alive as the sun. *How I wish you were here right now to help me make sense of all this*, I wanted to cry. However, Father had said jewels like me do not cry. So, I did not.

I needed to make my way to the impromptu girls' night, which had undoubtedly been planned because the girls thought my life was going to shit.

You look good, girl, winked my reflection in the mirror as I made my way to the front door.

As I opened the door my heart dropped. The urge to close the door enticed me. Nevertheless, I was incapable of moving.

A hand, strong yet gentle, grabbed me.

David.

David Art King (yes, I know it's a weird-sounding name when you say it in its entirety).

Just like his name, he resembled a work of art.

He smiled exponentially and my heart stopped.

The sweet pangs of love began contracting inside my heart.

I was decidedly and admittedly flattered by his fine looks. The sculpted jaw, the slight dichotomy of upward-slanting yet oval eyes. And the profound blueness of his eyes that illuminated like stars. His person made me feel like I was either in love or falling quickly back into it.

"Bridget White." His mouth curled into a soft smile that made my heart do somersaults. "Commiserations for the cessation of your course," he said, lips gently grazing my cheek. My skin felt hot. The nearness of his body next to mine raised the mercury a little higher.

"If it's any consolation, you look magnificent." He pulled himself back to admire me.

I laughed disjointedly. "Thank you."

"You are welcome." He held me back so he could admire the figure inside the dress some more. My figure was showcased by a short, deep V-neck, yellow silk dress with spaghetti straps, embellished with sequins and embroidery. Black strappy heels adorned my feet and canary-yellow diamond studs dressed my ears. By all accounts I must admit I looked delicious, and by the starved look in his eyes, I could tell that he wanted to eat.

My gaze took in all of David's person. A soft, gentle, almost intangible, hubris shrouded him. It was elegant.

His mien was quietly giddy. His eyes dancing like stars, witnessing the sun with shades on. I wanted to kiss him. His gaze made me moist, made the butterflies between my thighs flutter. He pulled me close, smelt my fragrance then exhaled. "You smell glorious, Bridge." I whimpered, my knees weak from the weight of his soft, raspy voice. Yet, before I could fall, he caught me and like falling stars his kisses landed on my mouth, savouring, licking, tasting, and biting till I could take no more and let out an agonised moan of deep, unadulterated pleasure.

He stopped. Please don't, I wanted to scream. Then he took a few steps back, hand on head, as though he were in serious disarray.

"What is it?" I questioned, his sexy slumberous eyes watching me like a wolf about to devour a gazelle.

"Forgive me for saying this..."

"Saying what?" I interjected, my gaze stalking him, while he prowled towards me, his eyes twinkling with mischief.

"If I could, I would strip you naked, right here..." He took a step towards me, "... right now," he took another, "... and fuck you senseless, Bridget White." He purred, stroking my bottom lip with his thumb.

My breath caught. Then my lips slowly parted allowing a soft gasp to escape.

Desperate to maintain my composure, I murmured, "Why?" my heart beating like war drums.

A sultry smile tugged at the far edge of his perfectly sculpted lips. "I believe you know why." David watched me sensuously, his gaze building a field of potent lust inside the molten lava that was slowly bubbling between my thighs.

"No I don't," I lied.

He moved behind me, his breathing rough, rugged, and carnal. Goosebumps spread across my flesh like wildfire. He chuckled, softly, then bit his bottom lip before placing a wild and decadent lick of his tongue across my exposed flesh. I whimpered, the touch of his tongue burning me with pleasure.

"Are you sure you don't know, Bridget?"

Desperate to hear his voice some more, I murmured, "No."

My skin was hot. With heart pulsating and mouth slightly parted, I whispered, "Please tell me, David."

He turned me around. Our eyes met. His gaze was ablaze with wanton decadence. His voice, deep, husky, and lowered said, "Because I think you deserve it ... to be kissed..." he kissed me, "... to be touched..." his finger gently gliding inside the wetness between my thighs, "... to be tasted..." he placed the finger in his mouth. A deep guttural moan escaped my lips. "Shh ... and to be made love to, till you come..." his eyes swam inside mine, "... over and over and over again!" he whispered.

Stricken by unimaginable arousal, I writhed in front of him before my knees weakened once more. However, before I could crumble under the erotically laden weight of his words, he caught me.

"Steady, my love."

Gently he pulled me close and murmured, "Come here, you," while his lips fiercely kissed mine. "May I seek sanctuary in the slight curves of your body, Bridge?"

"Yes."

His hot breath lingered on my perfume-veiled neck then he placed sensuous warm, wet kisses on my flesh before trailing his full warm lips over my silk-covered nipple. I couldn't help but gently scream into the moonlit, star-covered heavens.

He whispered, "Should I stop?" His hot dark gaze roamed inside mine.

"Please don't," I begged, my voice dripping with want. Keeping his eyes on me he licked the now-erect bud of my nipple.

"Oh David, please-don't-stop!" I moaned, my body shivering with pleasure while my head gently fell back.

"I won't," he groaned, then proceeded to bite the sensitive bud, an action that made my eyes roll back in delirious delight.

A hard bite of my bottom lip managed to stem the loud cries of pleasure begging to break free.

"Do you like that?"

I nodded

"No Bridget ... do-not-nod. I need you to say it." He stopped.

My eyes opened then my pupils widened in distress. "Please don't stop!"

"Look at me."

My gaze fell on his. He groaned, "Fuck, I'm enslaved by you, Bridge." He bit his lip, turned on by the dark lust on my face.

"Now..." he continued while his entire mouth covered my breast, "I want to hear you..." he urged, closing his eyes while his lips sucked and his wet tongue twirled around my nipple. "I want to hear you say you like it," he murmured. "Tell me you like what I'm doing to you. Say it to me, Bridget," he insisted, his red-hot gaze resting back inside my orgasmic, delirious one.

"I like it," I cried, my voice shaky from the tremors of pleasure he was firing into me all at once.

"I love it."

"Say it again," he demanded, his teeth biting my flesh

erratically.

"I love it, David," I found myself moaning as the flower inside my thighs bloomed and released all the sweet nectar it had kept inside for so long. Violently, I shook with unimaginable pleasure, while the orgasms came, over and over and over again.

David smiled, gently dipped a finger inside my wetness, and whispered, "I'll always be yours, Bridge."

9

Inside the black cab which oozed and dripped with the sounds of cool jazz, all I could think of was the earth-shattering orgasm David had gifted me. He most certainly was an artist when it came to pleasuring me.

Damn, I still love him, I thought, a slight smile on my face.

Even so, I had to forget him for the time being, else I go to his house and miss girls' night in. Carefully placing him at the back of my mind, my thoughts went to my friends. I wondered if I would recognise our hostess Camilla's new face. She harboured a penchant for overusing the surgeons' knives, tables, needles, and potions - come rain, shine, or sleet.

Stoke Newington was filled with its usual suspects. The orthodox ones, and the unorthodox ones. My eyes drank them all in as well as the few Caribbeans who also called this part of town home. The cab stopped in front of a lofty three-storey town house with a metal gate, glass walls, concrete pillars, and lush greenery.

"Thank you," I said to the driver, handing him a twenty-pound note. He made the superficial shuffling of someone who was looking for change. I smiled. "Keep the change."

"Thank you so much," he beamed, grateful for the nine pounds something he was to keep as a tip.

In front of Camilla's home, I sighed, then mouthed "help me" before pressing the buzzer. The chandelier in the corridor illuminated itself. "Here we go," I half laughed in anticipation of the long night ahead. Wearing a robe fashioned from silk and for someone tinier and possibly taller, in walked Camilla; slightly portly and relatively short compared to the five foot eight Amazonian Alison and myself at five foot seven.

As I suspected, the surgeon's knife had pacified Camilla's original features some more.

She was a fire flower. Her locks were big, bold, and red and filled with madness. "You look..." my eyes investigated her face, "... different"

She laughed without humour, gave me a glass then said, "Lovely to see you too, my darling friend."

"Come here you." My arms pulled her into an embrace, then pulled her back, to further ascertain the proportions of this new face.

At the very top of Camilla's frame stood a square face with seismically big, hazel eyes. However, they did not afford her the notion of conventional beauty. She edged a little to the chubby side. Endless glasses of Pinot Grigio and kosher food had helped in that regard. Once in a while she would hop into her Mercedes and travel to Harley Street, where the surgeons would chop and screw bits of her face to give her more Aryan proportions. Ironic, right?

Nevertheless, I loved her, regardless of what face she showed me.

Girls' night in was being held on the middle floor. The lift took us up. On the long sofa sat Camilla's friend, Lisa. Somewhat a friend of mine also.

She had the kind of face that said, "I am a cautionary tale for plastic surgery." Sometimes I was amazed at how many people Camilla associated herself with who preferred to be anything other than themselves. And what was more amazing was the fact that she used phrases like "beautiful", "gorgeous", and even "fabulous" to describe these people.

Camilla had some deep-rooted insecurities that she kept taking out on her face. From the nose to the lips to the nose again and then repeat. But Lisa was worse.

As me, Camilla and Lisa were exchanging niceties, Alison pressed the buzzer. Only she had the cheeky habit of pressing it more than once.

Alison glided into the living room like a supermodel from a Parisian runway. "There she is," we laughed.

"Here I am, indeed." She laughed that soft coquettish laugh of hers.

Camilla sprang from the couch excitedly. Her feet swiftly pitter-pattering across the laminated floor to reach the door. "Hi, hun," she yelled, her arms flinging themselves around Alison. I glanced at Lisa and she giggled quietly. "They're so mushy, aren't they?"

Camilla and Alison had a unique relationship, to put it mildly. The most unique in the group. One minute they were Cher and Dionne and the next they were Trump and Un, flinging missiles and pressing their big red nuclear buttons as if it were a hobby, leaving burns that healed and thankfully never turned to keloids. For now, they were jovial, relishing each other's presence. But old habits die hard. Lisa and I knew that fact all too well.

Camilla stopped in the centre of the room, her bright eyes blooming with excitement at my presence. "I am so happy to see you. Lord knows I needed a girls' night in," she squealed pulling my hand along with her into the far side of the living area.

"Me, too!" I exclaimed, grabbing the second champagne flute she offered as I had somehow finished the first.

Alison spoke. "How are you? How's this," she rolled her eyes, "school debacle going?"

"So, so."

"Hmm, so, so indeed."

"Forget about me, how are you?" I asked. Alison who loved being the centre of attention wasted no time in putting the focus back on her.

"I am great, as you can see. No man problems, no money problems, and no weight issues." She smiled, her words digging into Camilla, who deflected them by drinking some more champagne. "Ahh," she added as an afterthought, staring me dead in the eyes, "no child problems either," the knife this time digging into me. I was the only one with a child among my friends. But thankfully, I was not the only single one. That would have made me a loser, right?! And if I were a loser, so too were the other women, which consoled me a little. There was nothing I could do about my kid, so sod off, Alison.

Lisa who was Camilla's friend never spoke much. She engaged herself with alcohol and articles about the latest surgery trends, which she'd enlighten us with once in a while. And because of that, Alison did not throw any missiles in her direction ... this time.

It was mainly Camilla and me who stood in the line of fire.

My phone rang. "Excuse me, girls," I said, fleeing up to the third floor of Cam's home. In the bedroom I sat on the plush bed, patting its head as if it were a puppy.

"Hi, David," I answered, my heart palpitating fiercely. David was the love of my life. A fact I now only admitted when exclusively alone and only to my conscience, which was intangible, so I could not see it watching me or judging me, possibly saying, *you fool.*

"Hello Bridge," he breathed. I felt myself getting hot, so I got up and opened the window some more. His voice had a way of making me feel things. "Can I see you?"

I wanted to say where and when, but instead I said, "Why?" - to which he softly chuckled.

"Because I love you, silly," he said so earnestly and sincerely that I felt my position shifting on the bed as if a phantom had just nudged me. Words failed to pour forth from my mouth. "So, can I?" he implored once more.

"Sure," I answered, locking off the phone before he could say anything else.

Making my way to the dressing table, I watched myself in the mirror and smiled. "He still loves you, you sexy thing."

* * * *

I had been swimming in an ocean of unsuitable men, and there he was, King David, an island in the midst, ready to rescue me from the sharks that lurked.

Our inception was born of wildfires, since that day in Massachusetts. However, it would take three more months before we had our first date.

David was the now twenty-six-year-old doctor and I the now twenty-one-year-old prodigal child who had just returned from The Congo - Conrad's *Heart of Darkness* - which for me was more luminous than the sun herself. I returned having immoderately depleted my trust fund across the globe and nine countries of its seven continents in the name of enlightenment. Much to my father's delight - "she needs to see the world" - and my mother's indifference - "not at the expense of postponing a career". David was terribly impressed by it all. He was my perfect match.

Our first proper date was on a dull murky Thursday. The rain was incessant, and the cold painful to inhale. By the time I got close to where he was waiting, my hair had transformed from its straightened state to an afro mop. I came upon him by a hidden coffee shop in Liverpool Street. Standing in the rain without an umbrella, lying in wait for me. I immediately drowned in love for him. My very own knight without armour, which made him all the more enamouring to me.

"Princess," he murmured, a kiss from his lips resting on my rain-soaked cheek.

There was an impassioned glimpse of yearning, swimming in the deep, deep blue of his eyes. I felt myself swimming in it and, in that instant, I coveted him.

"Shall we go in," he suggested, opening the door to the coffee shop. "I know you're now twenty-one and allowed to drink in the US," he laughed, to which I giggled. "However, coffee it will be today."

"Why?" I'd asked, perplexed.

"Because I want you to be sober for love."

From that night forth, David became my champion.

He made me glow, he made me bloom, and he showcased me like the Mona Lisa. He liked my niche taste in literature, and he was in love with all my tiny little nuances.

He was an agile and continuously evolving enigma. Who liked Bach, but loved Hip Hop. He gorged on caviar but preferred Sierra Leonean jollof. He liked Caesar but admired Zulu more.

Meeting David was a serendipitous moment. And the irony was that I did not believe in serendipity.

The first kiss was like a falling star.

It fell on my flesh and exploded.

Igniting a billion particles of sweet ... sweet ... deep ... dark ... desires that he fulfilled time and time again.

That was until he did the unthinkable with my friend (although he denied it) and we became tectonic plates colliding in love and hate, then love and hate and hate, over and over again.

Our love turned into a cold, cold war. We built missiles and weapons in our heads that we never used against each other. But the tension was so thick the only way we could cut it was by breaking up.

It was only after we broke up that I realised love was an addiction. Without him, I was having withdrawals. Some so severe I thought my heart would break in two and never mend again. But day after day, it broke and as the sun swallowed the moon, it mended. Until one day it refused to break. Just like that! And I thought that was the end of it. Until now ... now that he had just told me he still loved me. Now that he had just finished giving me the fiercest orgasm before I got to Camilla's house (the friend he denies cheating on me with).

A virus was lurking, and David was the only thing I was not immune to. I had no resistance to him. But pretend I must.

David loves me. But there are certain crimes that even love cannot absolve. Yet, like a fool in love, I knew I'd be at his, one way or another, before the night ended.

* * * *

Back in the living room the girls had progressed to the dark topic of Black Lives Matter. It appeared Professor Wylde's speech five years prior had emboldened everyone to speak on race. Speaking of the professor, I sometimes wondered if he thought about me.

I wondered if the fierce sparks of rage, and possibly attraction, I felt were the same things he felt. I hated him but was yet intrigued by him simultaneously.

Although he had bludgeoned the crowd with his divisive rhetoric, there was a dark charisma about him.

Sometimes I felt like he knew. I felt like he knew who killed my cousin. The way he looked at me made me feel as if he knew something. Nonetheless, if he did know something I guess I'll never find out as we will never cross paths again. Though I sometimes wished we would, if only to pick his brain and see what types of wiring electrify his thoughts.

As I sat down, Alison was explaining that even when black women fight for BLM, they are in most cases fighting for black men's lives matter. Not blackness as a whole. She said the token black woman might be thrown in the mix for PR reasons, but that black men weren't really the allies of black women. I wanted to ask her why. We all did, but I believe deep down we all knew what she meant or where she was coming from, so we all refrained from asking.

After gulping a glass of champagne, Alison watched us as we watched her back, eager to hear more of her musings. Seeing that we were keen to take in her knowledge, she further spoke on the current trend where black men were dating white women and turning them into baby mamas like their black counterparts. "It seems we all now on an even playing field. Black men are fucking us all over," she laughed.

"Must feel good to have some company," teased Lisa, who for the most part had been silent as a rock. Alison chucked daggers her way, but Lisa did not budge as her devious smile grew wider.

As I watched my friends bewilderingly, my mind fell

on the notion that black girls are very insecure within their own skin – if the narrative the media was trying to write was anything to go by. Yet in the classroom and in the playground, it was the white girls who spoke about having surgery. Making their lips bigger, making their noses smaller, defining their cheeks with some Botox and for those who were tired of the white physique, some Brazilian butt lift. Yet it is perpetuated that it's the black girl who hates herself. However, when I watched Alison, Camilla and Lisa, I begged to differ. With all the black girl's lack of privilege, her looks are the last thing she wishes to change, I thought. Watching the natural beauty of Alison, who was a billionaire's daughter, trump that of her white companions and illuminate the room, it was made apparent she was satisfied with her black self ... physically at least.

As the girls spoke on the splintered spectrums of BLM, it became evident that tensions were rising and we were becoming immune to the effects of alcohol, so Lisa suggested, "We need something a little bit higher than alcohol, because tonight is going to be a long bloody night."

I did not know it at that moment. But a long arduous night it was to be indeed. With feelings, pride, and egos deeply wounded by the time we were to bid adieu.

10

"Fifteen quid?!" shrieked Lisa "Who is your dealer?

"My neighbour's son," replied Camilla

"What neighbour?"

That was the answer we all wanted to know, because the only neighbours she had were rich white people and all their kids went to the best schools and universities. There was no way it could be who we were thinking. Surely, she must be mistaken.

But she wasn't. "Yeah," she looked at us as though she too were surprised to be saying it. "It's strict Mary's nineteen-year-old son."

"No way!" I laughed.

"Way!"

"Little Johnny, as in Johnathan Ashby of Ashby Empire."

"Yes, that little rich shit."

"Forget who we're getting our gear from, guys. We need weed," insisted Camilla.

"Yes, we do," we all agreed.

"Let's go hunt down that rich silly little drug dealer then," teased Alison, who didn't seem too keen on our drugs mission.

When Alison said that it made me wonder if he was the little shit or if we were the big shits. Whatever the answer was, I did not care to dwell on it as I ran towards the door and after my friends. They were out in the front garden before I could make it to the door. And like a true addict, Camilla psst'd her way across to the neighbour's house. That must have been their drug code because, like a genie, Johnny appeared, a sly grin plastered on his face as he shiftily looked around. "More gear, I'm guessing," he winked, looking at all of us as if we were food for the taking. Although Camilla was a doctor and told her patients not to smoke. It did not mean she followed her own advice. *Do as I say, not as I do,* I suppose.

"I don't like the way this little boy is looking at us," I whispered to Alison, with the intent that it was a whisper.

"This little boy can rock your world, old lady."

"Did that little boy just call me old?" I hissed, giving him the middle finger. Clearly what I had previously said was not a whisper. "Twenty-five is not old," I insisted to Alison who was no longer listening to me.

He wagged his tongue at me and blew me a kiss then got to business with Camilla. Somewhere, a place where my sanity still existed told me to cover my face and run away in shame for being outside one of the richest neighbourhoods in London exchanging barbs with a nineteen-year-old drug dealer whose parents happened to be rich and white. But the part of me that was seeking a high (since I had not smoked in over a year) said YOLO – you only live once in any lifetime.

Johnny looked at me, then winked. "Because she," he said pointing at me, "is the sexiest and coolest of your old lady gang ... I will give you these four sticks for free," he concluded as the girls rushed at him squealing with happiness due to the sixty pounds Camilla had saved. "Thank you, thank you, Johnny," they chanted as though hypnotised by his illicit act of kindness.

His brown eyes smouldered at me. I kissed my teeth,

took my stick from his palm, gathered any ounce of dignity that I may have had left and stormed back into Camilla's living room where an unopened bottle of Pinot Grigio greeted me.

"You're old but you're sexy," he shouted in the distance, a slight grin forming on my face.

I could hear the girls and Johnny in the distance. They were thanking him for the good deed of pitching us free drugs and him giving Lisa and Alison his number if they ever needed gear. I was disgusted at our behaviour, but at the same time I was slightly happy. I felt lightheaded and somewhat young again, though I was still young.

"Oooh, that little cub wants to make you his cougar," said Alison as we all burst out laughing

"He's not even twenty-one yet."

"Nineteen, twenty-one, the same thing," Alison teased while igniting her weed.

Back inside the living room we danced to some drill music. The beats in our heads guided our moves which were offbeat like a toddler trying to walk. Alison could dance. But she danced like a white person who knew how to dance. Two good left feet. Instead of the rhythmic left and right feet that black people naturally had. I watched her, part bemused, part amazed, with a smile of indifference and admiration adorning my lips.

"Instead of going to Dubai or the South of France, let's go Lagos or Freetown. Let's spend our monies in the lands of our ancestors," Alison said, directly to me, while her feet continued two-stepping.

"Sure, let's do that," I replied, my own two left feet also two-stepping. "But that is not to say we shouldn't spend our monies in those other countries, right?"

"Of course not. But let's patronise our own, because

only then will others patronise us. Charity begins at home."

Feeling higher than a kite, I pulled her cheek to my lips and kissed her. "Mwah. You, my friend," I slurred, "are so bloody brilliant." I laughed, Lisa and Camilla watching us like aliens.

"Yes, I am brilliant, aren't I?"

"Indeed you are," I agreed, pulling smoke from the cannabis stick.

"We go to the Indians or Turkish for shisha and food. Now tell me, other than if they're stranded in Africa, when would you see them in our own establishments?

"Never," inputted Lisa. "Never."

"Exactly. It is only the black man who needs all the races for things. Yet it seems they need us for nothing. African food, black hair and beauty products, all sold by the Asian in the market or the corner shop."

Lisa stopped her. "So you mean to tell me black people do not own their own hair or stores?"

Spitting out my drink in laughter, I answered, "We own our own hair, but not our own stores. And when we do, we don't patronise black establishments as much as we do those who follow us around their stores like criminals."

"No," said Camilla sarcastically. Finally opening the door and entering the premise of the conversation. "You mean to tell me only the black man keeps going to a place that sees him like a criminal even with money? Why?"

"Because black people don't seem to have their own stores, Camilla," interjected Lisa, seemingly angry at Camilla's high.

Alison did not take offence at Camilla's comment. It seemed the narcotic was pacifying her reactions.

Staring back at me, Alison asked, "Have you ever seen a black person working in a Chinese restaurant?"

"No."

But we buy food there, right?"

"Right!"

"Have you even seen a black person working in the shisha shops you smoke at?"

"Yes, the security," answered Lisa

We all laughed.

"Yes, they hire you to get rid of yourself. Nothing more," added Camilla. A statement that made us all freeze like ice statues temporarily to take in its significance.

"With all the money other races make from us, you'd think they'd have the decency to at least hire us in their establishments." Alison broke the ice.

"And that is why whites are better," chimed in Camilla, a cheeky grin on her face. There was truth to her words. White establishments did hire us.

"You might be right, Cam. You might just be right," Alison mused.

Taking a seat, in an attempt to lower my high, I watched the girls and I could not believe my white friends were having black conversations.

As we lay or sat in silence, waiting for our high to make its way down, Camilla felt the urge to speak. "I do not blame black men for dating white women," she said.

The temperature in the room froze. Cold eyes shot icy arrows in her direction. Alison's hand shakily placed the chalice of Pinot Noir that was about to flow down her throat on the glass façade of Camilla's newly bought Italian-made table, before cranking her neck this way then that way in anticipation of Camilla's analysis.

A swift smile flashed across Alison's face: "Care to elaborate?"

Her demeanour unnerved Camilla. "Don't worry about it, it's too long to go into."

"No. No, no, no, no! I have all night." Her eyes flashed like daggers.

Hesitantly, Camilla said, "Sure, but it'll take too long to explain," hoping this would dissuade Alison.

It did not. "All night," she insisted, her finger tapping the house that she called a watch on her wrist.

"Well," Camilla reached over for the bottle, Alison's gaze eyeing her like prey, "I feel like black men are tortured souls."

Alison scoffed as if to say, *Is this white chick speaking on behalf of black men?* "Continue," she prodded, the malice in her voice slithering down my spine, serpent-like, leaving my back cold and restless.

I shook my head inconspicuously at Camilla, saying *don't do it, girl. It's a trap.* Luckily, she took heed and left the conversation alone, much to the relief of Lisa and me who were stuck in the middle.

Camilla did not elaborate, and though she might not admit it, I knew she wanted to say it was because she felt black men were scared of being part of the oppressed, so they felt that being with another race would alleviate that oppression. She failed to realise that a woman is a woman. She is born oppressed, black or white. She had once voiced an opinion that it is only the black woman who benefits from dating the white man. Never the other way around. One time she said the black man is trying to compete with the white man. And the way he thinks he can do this is by being with the white woman. The only problem with this kind of competition is that the black man has already lost. You cannot win with what's already a losing hand to the opposition. The white man doesn't need his woman. He will always be the alpha. But the black man does. When he's with a white woman, she's the ace. He's merely an accessory.

Which was perhaps why Camilla possessed a penchant for dating black men. Because with the men she dated, she felt like a trophy.

Sometimes when I looked at Camilla and saw how broken she too was, I wondered how David had ever kissed her passionately, as she claimed.

David denies all this. Insists she was the one who tried to kiss him when he was pouring out his heart and he outrightly refused her advance. However, I was pregnant, hormones everywhere, so I believed my friend. Nevertheless, I sometimes feel I'm believing the wrong person.

I needed to remove my mind from 'David and Camilla-gate', which might or might not have happened. "I'm dreading tomorrow," I confessed under the influence of cannabis and in an effort to break the silence that had built a fortress in the room.

Alison laughed. I knew that laugh, I had heard it before. It was the laugh black women gave when they had something more to say!

Oh boy, here we go, said the looks on all our faces.

We watched Alison, while she pondered, her face frowning and lips pressed together. "Ah, yes," she said as if a light had just switched on in her brain, "I'm sorry to say this..." she wasn't, "but aren't you," she pointed, "Camilla Silverstein the same white woman who tried to sleep with her black friend's black boyfriend while she was pregnant."

A deluge of crimson flooded Camilla's face. This was a conversation we always tried to put away like trash, due to its pungent odour which was now crawling up the walls and seeping through the air straight into our nostrils. It refused to be ignored.

"So you see, you cannot speak on what black men feel, white girl."

For some odd reason the more Camilla cowered in shame under the weight of Alison's words, the more my animus towards Camilla grew.

The hate that I had buried for her began to unearth itself all over again because it was my boyfriend, David, who Camilla had tried to sleep with. I know I believed her over David initially, but in my gut, it did not feel right. Believing her. Perhaps it was the way she had cried, begged, and vowed that she'd never do such a thing to me that compelled me to choose her truth over David's. Nonetheless, I knew David. Camilla was not his type. However, I knew that heartbreak can lead to terrible mistakes. Which was where I felt conflicted. Perhaps in a moment of weakness, David may have sought refuge in her kiss.

However, in moments of sanity, it was always Camilla who had coveted David and, in turn, harboured a quiet contempt towards me; firstly, because David loved me and so too did Josh, the guy she loved at university.

11

I met David first. But the way Camilla behaved at times around him, one would assume it was she who knew him first. At first, I thought nothing of it since it was inconspicuous flirting. Her saying things like "Bridge is so lucky to have you", to which he'd reply "I can guarantee I'm the lucky one" with a bemused look as if she were a mad woman speaking. Or the excessive attempts to touch him whenever he was in her presence.

Evidently, I thought nothing of it. She was my friend and friends do not desire each other's partners, right?

The first time I spoke about David to Camilla was the night after our second date in London. I assembled the girls, consisting of Alison and Camilla, to firstly get their approval, but most importantly to tell them of the most amazing night I had ever had.

* * * *

David called me. "There is something black and beautiful coming your way."

"Is it between your legs?" I teased. He laughed, then the doorbell rang while I ran down the stairs. A gift. Wrapped up. It was a dress. Black and beautiful as he had mentioned. I did not need to see the tag to know that it was expensive. The material spoke for itself.

"Be ready by eight. The driver will pick you up."

Where are we going?" I asked.

"To the moon," he said.

The chauffeured Rolls-Royce took me to a place

called The Moon.

I laughed.

While we were in Massachusetts, David had told me he would take me to the moon when we got back to London. And there we were, encased within the celestial body.

"You're amazing."

"And you are perfect." He smiled, taking my hand in his as he led us to our table.

He was dressed in a burgundy silk shirt with fitted dress trousers that showcased his toned legs. Everything that made me a woman wanted to strip him naked the instant my eyes fell upon him. With the way he smirked when our eyes met, I believe he knew my dark intentions.

"Hi," I murmured, our lips softly grazing each other's.

"Good evening, Bridget White."

His voice and the way he said my name did things to my sensibilities.

David had booked The Moon exclusively for us. No cheap feat, I can attest.

I did not know it yet, but his estranged grandparents from his father's side had left him a legacy of just under two million pounds.

The owner of The Moon came over.

"Dr King."

"Peter."

"Pleasure to have you and your beautiful lady here."

"Thank you," replied David as they shook hands.

Turning to me, Peter said, "My lady."

"A King, huh?" I teased. "Well, you must forgive me, Sire. I apologise profusely for not gifting you the grace and reverence you deserve," I joked, bowing my head.

He laughed, raucously, with all his heart. If he hadn't fallen in love with me already, my guess was that he did at that very moment.

A soft chuckle escaped my mouth. He laughed some more, a gentle convulsion dancing on his upper body.

"I never knew you were this witty, Ms White."

"It's the black in me." We laughed.

A waiter brought over a bottle of Chateau Mouton Rothschild 2005.

"Sir..."

"My lady first," interjected David.

"I apologise, sir, of course, the lady first, always," smiled the waiter.

"Madam, may I pour you some for tasting?"

"You may," I answered.

The wine was fine, so he poured more and left before the next waiter came to establish our food order. I allowed David to order for us.

"So," the tip of my finger touched him, "indulge me in who the King truly is."

He suddenly appeared shy. The tips of his fingers ran through his hair while an awkward smile curled around his lips.

"What do you want to know?" he finally said.

"Everything!"

"Everything?"

Clasping his hands together, he twisted his forehead into a frown. Then his eyes landed in mine. After the first five seconds, I thought they'd move or blink. But they did neither. My heart pulsated from the tension the silence solicited. Finally, he broke the ice, much to my relief.

"Well, contrary to what you see now. Life wasn't always easy. My father left when I was two." He paused, his eyes searching for a wraith in the distance. My fingers slipped between his. Electricity sparking from his touch.

"We don't have to talk about it," I assured.

"I want to, Bridge..."

That night, David told me everything. I mean everything! He told me how his father, the one he inherited the blonde hair and azure eyes from, left his mother – for reasons his mother has never divulged to him – at age two. He told me how she met his stepfather, who he calls father, aged three. He told me how life was at times hard to navigate being a half-black man with acutely Caucasian features, yet steadfastly trying to prove his blackness in a South London that always made him feel as though his blackness was leaning too far into whiteness. He told me how it was Alexander White who gave him the bug to go into medicine.

"Which Alexander White?"

"Professor, consultant Alexander White."

"That's my father."

"No way."

"Way!" we laughed, while he asked me to turn my face this way, then that way before saying, "Damn, I now see the resemblance." His head nodded as though a light had just switched on. "Well, I now have to meet your father, and you have to be my wife. It is fate."

"Fate?"

"Yes."

We may have been joking, but at the back of my mind, I wished the things he was saying would come to pass. Mrs King; it had a ring to it.

After dinner, David took me to the top of The Moon. A pianist and her piano serenaded us.

His hand reached out to mine. "Care to dance, princess?"

I gently draped my arms around his neck while he carefully curled his around my waist. He smelled glorious and I wanted to drown in his scent. As we danced, he whispered sweet nothings that made the butterflies in my heart flutter in violent euphoria.

It was perfect.

I was in love.

I had to tell the girls.

* * * *

"He is my husband, my baby daddy, he's everything!" I squealed - Alison, Camilla and I screamed in unison.

"Oh my God, tell me more," insisted Camilla, her eyes wide with interest.

"Well, he's super light..."

"Not your type," Camilla felt the need to add.

"I know, but types change, bitch," I teased.

"Preach, sis," winked Alison as I gave her a high five.

"He might be half-white, but his entire aura and big dick energy are black, black ... whew." We all squealed some more at this man who was now the love of my life.

"You must introduce us," said Camilla too eagerly.

Camilla was two years older than me and a year older than Alison. Alison and I met her at university. We bonded on the fact that we were all our parents' only children.

Camilla was studying medicine; Alison, law; and me, you guessed it, English Lit. We immediately became the three musketeers. Two Nubian princesses and their Snow White. Then, Camilla was slimmer, and her natural beauty was pronounced. Yet she still felt somewhat inferior to me and Alison in the looks department. More so me, though I felt it should've been Alison as she was the one who always looked as if she had walked straight off a Vogue magazine cover. Alison's beauty was otherworldly. Her coffee-coloured skin shone as though infused with crushed diamonds. There were no lines or hints of spots on her face. Her lips were full with eyes that smouldered instead of watched. She walked straight, head always held up high and her fashion sense was impeccable. Where we wore high-low pieces, she only wore high-end pieces ... and it worked for her.

Nevertheless, it was me, slightly introverted and casually awkward Bridge that Camilla felt at quiet odds with. I did not seek friends, yet people flocked to me, including Josh, her first crush at uni. He was a black boy to the core. He was president of the African and Caribbean Society. He preached black unity to the masses. All the girls loved him, and the undergrad boys admired him. He possessed an aura that commanded attention. He spoke with an almost inconspicuous Jamaican accent that made him that much sexier. His parents were professors at the university. He did not fit into the stereotype of a drug dealer or gangster that young disenfranchised Caribbean boys tended to fit into at the time. So, you can only imagine how much of a prize Joshua Garvey was.

Alison and Camilla fawned over him publicly.

Something I never expected from Alison. Men fell at her feet, yet she wanted to fall at Josh's feet. A thought that made me laugh whenever I saw her asking him, "Do you need any help?"

Josh was the only man I've seen Alison lose her composure over.

Camilla lost her mind over him in a more animated manner. She'd freeze if he spoke to her or paint her cheeks crimson if he complimented her "wonderful brilliance".

"Will you stop embarrassing us," Alison would tease.

This made it all the more surprising when one day Camilla came into my and Alison's apartment, squealing with glee that the boy we all fancied had asked her to his house party and invited us as her plus two.

"I love him and am going to marry him and have some good-haired babies," she whispered. And because we were so excited, we paid no mind to her good-hair comment.

Before we could finish screaming at this good fortune Josh had presented us with, Alison said, "Vintage Chanel for me, it is," as she ran into her walk-in closet.

At the party, everyone that was anyone was there. The foreign students whose fathers were billionaires, royals and tech giants were there. The influential students who didn't come from much but knew how to fake it till they made it were there. The disciples of Plato and Socrates, W. E. B Du Bois, X and King were also in attendance, speaking in intellectual jargon. The crowd was beyond eclectic, and the vibe was insanely electric.

Joshua Garvey knew how to throw a party. And, though I had not initially noticed, he had been staring at me all night.

"Why does he keep looking at you when it's me he invited?" Camilla asked, anger slithering through her voice.

"So what?" retorted Alison. "Maybe he likes what he sees." She cut her eyes at Camilla and left to go talk to Josh's friend, Calvin Smith.

"She hates me!"

"No, she doesn't tolerate bullshit like I do at times."

Huffing and puffing Camilla left.

Finally, my crazy friends had left me in peace. Before I could enjoy my own company, Josh came towards me, with two drinks in hand.

"Choose"

My finger pointed to the glass in his left hand. He smiled, bit his lip, and handed me the glass. "Cheers."

"Cheers."

For a moment we stood quietly. Me nursing my drink while he gulped his.

"Dance with me."

I nearly choked on my drink. Was *the* Joshua Garvey asking me, at the time spectacled, Bridget White to dance with him? "What, like now ... here."

He laughed, taking my hand. "Yes, here, now."

The dance floor was choked, yet he somehow managed to find space.

"I like your dress," he shouted above the blare of the music

"What?"

"Your dress, I like it," he mouthed while pointing at my body.

Lowering my head I giggled, then replied with a thank-you.

Taking my hand once more, he led me through the sea of bodies to the garden, which was scattered with old, new, and for-the-night couples, their voices hushed as they whispered sweet nothings to each other while kissing and gently touching with soft moans and gasps escaping into the air.

Josh chuckled and I giggled while we fled past them all the way to his parents' greenhouse which held a quaint yet most extravagant fountain.

"Wow, isn't this pristine."

"Do you like it?

"I love it."

Slowly I felt the warmth of his body edging closer to me. A soft kiss fell behind my neck, then his tongue trailed down my spine. A strained gasp escaped my mouth. He chuckled softly, "I suspect you like that too."

"Stop," I demanded.

He stopped. "As you wish; however, may I ask why?"

"Camilla, my best friend, that's why!"

"Who?"

"The girl you invited and told to bring me and Alison, the girl who you told had a wonderful brilliance,"

He laughed, a bemused look on his face. "Are those things supposed to mean something I'm not aware of?"

"Well, yes, it means you like her. And you can't like my best friend while kissing me."

Suddenly he bent over in laughter, yet seeing that I did not share in his humour, he stopped. "I'm sorry, but I am, in no shape or form, physically attracted to Camilla.

Granted she's a beautiful girl, but I'm inclined to women I can see myself reflected in." That's a lot of broken white hearts I thought to myself. "I only invited Camilla because I did not know how to speak to you. She was the most approachable. Alison would've taken it the wrong way and I did not want that, so Camilla was my only choice."

Boy, oh boy, this leaves me in a sticky situation, I thought. Still, he appeared so regal under those fountain lights that I could do nothing else but lean into him and allow him to ravish my mouth ...

"What the fuck!" screamed a voice. "How could you do this, Bridge? How?!" howled Camilla as she fled from the party.

That same night Josh asked me to be his girlfriend, but I had loyalties to Camilla so I refused, and until he graduated he did not date anyone else.

Camilla, however, did not appreciate this kind gesture of mine. She never admitted it, but I knew that was the day her contempt towards me sowed its seed.

I should have known she would someday seek payback.

12

THURSDAY, MARCH 19

It was 12.01 am. Toni, a mutual friend of ours, but closer to Alison, made her entrance into the living space. Behind her walked Camilla, holding the Chinese food Toni had brought for us. Alison and Lisa woke groggily from their slumber.

"Hi, girls," said Toni briskly, her gaze scanning the room filled with alcohol bottles and dead weed stubs.

"Where's the food?" asked Lisa as she dug into the prawn balls half-asleep.

Toni laughed. "Seems like you guys have had a very good night." She came towards me and hugged me.

"So it seems." I hugged her back. "Now pass me the roast duck."

Toni brought us bottles of Evian while we ate. There was a caring persona about her. Maybe it was because she was a nurse or the fact that she had five younger siblings. Whatever it was I was simply happy to have food and liquid that wasn't alcohol in my belly.

After feeding us, Toni asked what we had been up to prior to her entrance. We all laughed in unison.

"Oh, you do not want to know," Camilla insisted.

"Try me," she replied.

"Well, I was talking about the time Camilla tried to have sex with David while Bridge was pregnant and he rejected her," said Alison, seemingly still drunk.

A cold chill spread through the room. Toni smiled sympathetically at Cam.

"Oh, please, do not give me white-women tears, Cam," said Alison, starting to sober up. Now the room was uneven, two Nubians and three Anglo Saxons. Yet Alison had no chill.

"When you were trying to sleep with my best friend's man you weren't crying, so why cry now? Do you know how profane it is to force yourself on a man whose pregnant girlfriend is also your best friend, all because a guy you loved at uni preferred her? Sickening," spat Alison.

"You know what," Cam finally summoned the courage to stand up for herself, "I have apologised a thousand times and I'll do so no fucking more, so you either accept it or get the hell out of my house."

As an afterthought, Camilla reminded Alison it was David who had initiated the kiss; however, no one was listening, possibly because no one believed that part of her story.

Alison got up to leave, and so too did I. After all, it was me she'd been defending.

"No, Bridge, stay. This night is for you, I want you to stay, but I cannot sit here and allow white tears to solicit a guilt that isn't warranted from me."

Softly, she kissed my cheek, told me she loved me and waved goodbye to Toni and Lisa.

"Bye, girl," they said in unison.

My heart was a little broken. Alison was my ride-or-die. Yes, we may tease each other, but no one outside my family and David stayed steadfastly on my side the way she did. She loved me righteously, like a real sister would, so watching her leave hurt me.

I might not have told her before, but she reminded me of my bright star Tariq. They both possessed a quality whereby you could not help but love them, and if they loved you back, you felt like the most special person in the world.

I recall when Tariq died. She bought a first-class ticket, flew from Heathrow and was in America seven hours after I had told her the news. It was such a selfless act and that was when my love for her was cemented. The first time she met Tariq, she said if I ever had a boy, he'd look like my cousin. Her words came to fruition – Winner is a copy of Tariq.

Alison was not known for being maternal, yet when I proclaimed her godmother to Winner, she excelled in her duties in a manner that surpassed all my expectations. She calls him "my son"; this was coming from a woman who borderline hated kids.

She was my Tariq in female form, and the more this fact presented itself to me, the more my animus for Camilla seemed to grow.

Inside the room, no one spoke. In the corner, Camilla sniffled and tried to wipe phantom tears from her eyes. I smiled. It was faultless how she played the victim card in times of distress.

"Why do you do that?" I asked

"What?" she said, squinting her eyes to produce the tiniest hint of tears.

"That fake shit people like you tend to do to make the other, and by other, I mean us black women, appear villainous?"

"Oh please," she tried to laugh haphazardly, "you sound just like Al ... crazy."

"And you sound just like you ... delusional ...

delusional about Josh, delusional about David and certainly delusional about my sister Alison and me being crazy when you're the only mad woman in the room."

The other ladies in the room contorted their faces in either bemusement or indifference. No one spoke or defended Camilla and, for the first time, it seemed she was feeling what it felt to be a black woman in a room that tries to portray you as crazy when you are fully sane.

After minutes of silence had passed, Alison decided to come back, much to my delight.

Camilla watched her. We watched Camilla.

"I am sorry, Alison. I should not have asked you to leave simply because our opinions differed."

Alison looked at me. I gave her a smile that said accept her apology. So she did.

Lisa finally decided to speak. Offering an answer to Toni's initial question which had caused chaos among the group.

"Well Toni, before you came, we were speaking on the dark matters of race."

Toni laughed. "You mean to tell me that you are speaking on race during a pandemic."

"The best time to, if you ask me," replied Lisa.

She nodded her head in agreement. "So, what race was in the spotlight?"

"Al's and Bridge's," answered Lisa who had now properly found her feet in the conversation.

"Oh, someone's alive," I teased, to which she chucked a cushion my way, which was swiftly intercepted and thrown back at her.

Camilla, who had finished gulping the final droplets

of water in the bottle, without warning said, "I think there is an unconscious bias amongst black people."

My head propped up from its slouched position. "Really ... what is that?"

Camilla smiled, a little too insidiously for my liking. "They unconsciously believe that white people are better."

I smirked. Either that or it would've been a scowl. "Hmm. Care to elaborate? As I do not find myself among the paradigm you so speak of."

"You are an anomaly, Bridge. You do not think that because, fortunately, you are the minority." She placed an arm around me. I swiftly peeled it off. "The majority of melanated folks aren't of the same conviction as you."

"And how do you know that?" Alison sneered, visibly agitated by Camilla's remark, her nostrils flaring like a bull seeing red.

Camilla raised her hands in surrender.

"Don't backtrack now, Cam. Say it with your chest," she said in a tone that made me very afraid for Camilla.

"Ladies, ladies," chimed in Toni.

"No, I want to know what she meant," shouted Alison as she stood up and hovered over the now pseudo-scared Camilla. I found it ever so uncanny how people like her could be the aggressor one minute, then victim the next. "Go on, explain your statement," demanded Alison, her body edging closer to Camilla's whose own frame appeared to pull back.

"Well, look at you, for example..." Alison staggered back a little. "You are one of the most sought-after criminal lawyers in the city."

"That I am," nodded Al, proud of this achievement.

"But you do not feel that is enough."

"What?"

"Well you could've hired a majority black team, since you're part founder of the firm. But you consciously chose to hire the white lawyers you interviewed instead of the black ones. Even going as far as to say, 'I can't believe she would come in for an interview with a nappy-headed afro,' about one of your interviewees." Struck with embarrassment and shame, Alison tried to find a foot on which she could defend herself; however, Camilla quickly unbalanced her by saying, "I'm not yet done Alison," so sternly that for the first time it was Alison whom I was scared for. Camilla was on a roll and was not yet done with prosecuting Alison. Even though I felt conflicted for my sister, I'd be lying if I said I did not find it entertaining – for lack of a better word – to see Camilla revealing harsh truths to her. Lisa sat sipping water with a clear smirk on her face. Toni did not know whether to smile or grimace, so her face was stuck between the two. I could not hold in my bewilderment, so I laughed out loud in a very uncomfortable tone.

Camilla continued: "You even admitted that she was more qualified than Kate, yet her hair somehow rubbed you the wrong way. Now tell me if that's not an inferiority complex!"

Her words crashed on us like a tonne of rocks.

Embarrassment blotted itself all over Al's face. "So you see, whether you admit it or not, you chose those white people because you felt they were better than that black lady, even though you yourself said she had the better grades from St Andrew's."

"Wow, that's fucked up," said Toni.

"Very," I added, disappointed in Alison as she had never told me this story before, and I am her best friend. Maybe she felt comfortable telling Camilla because she hoped she wouldn't understand the connotations of bias her action had.

Boy was she wrong!

Alison, unable to counter Camilla's prosecution, laid her defence to rest.

"Well, that was tense," I chuckled for lack of a suitable response.

"Here let's take some shots," offered Toni, who'd just come from the bar, as a peace offering. "We can move to another facet of race relations after these." She smiled – a smile that hoped her words wouldn't come to fruition.

13

It was 2.30 in the morning. I was making my way to David's. My finger pressed the security system, then waited, while my heart palpitated violently. In the distance, the corridor light switched on and illuminated the figure walking up to me. I took in a deep breath and then exhaled.

Was I mad, what was I thinking? I need to go back! But as I decided to flee, his image appeared.

A smile ever so small and soft appeared on his face, glistening like diamonds. I did not know if my heart was breaking or healing at the sight of him. All I knew was that the pain was intensely sweet like swallowing thorns covered in caramel.

Though my animus towards him and Camilla remained, I could not help but be drawn to him.

"Carpe diem," he murmured, pulling me into his arms.

Take the moment, my heart pleaded, ecstatic and giddy that the man I loved was standing, magnificent, in front of me saying that he will take his moment.

"Good morning, Bridge," he whispered in that voice that did things to my femininity.

There was a special almost electrifying type of gravitas to David. He did not mean to exude it, but he simply did. He possessed an internal nobility that showcased itself outwardly to the masses.

"Come in, please," he invited, his hand reaching the

lower part of my back and leading me in. "It's a pleasure to have you here," he said.

"I'm sorry I couldn't answer your calls. Women's palaver," I laughed.

"Not a problem," he said, as he led me to the living area. The light was dim and, in the background, a low but effervescent medley surrounded us through speakers hidden inside the walls.

He watched me intently and I wondered what he was thinking. Perhaps he thought, *what is this crazy woman doing in my home at such an ungodly time*? seeing as I had texted earlier to say I would no longer be coming. Or perhaps he was thinking, *I want to make love to her, right here, right now*. But he looked so calm and collected that it was hard to tell. Regardless, he had all the nuances of a gentleman ... who wanted to make sweet love to me.

"May I offer you something to drink?"

And because I did not want to sound like an alcoholic, I said, "water please." He came back with a glass of still water. I knew he wanted to ask but did not know how, so I answered for him. "I am here because my girlfriends are arseholes and I needed company of the male persuasion." He chuckled, and it was a beautiful chuckle, like music.

"Whatever the reason, I am simply glad you're here, Bridge."

David's kitchen was the antithesis of traditional. Marble countertops and sleek stainless-steel hardware designs embellished the entire space.

He was sitting on a bar stool under the pendant light and I, at the dining table, under a small softly lit chandelier. He drank cognac while I drank a glass of water to wash down some alcohol before consuming more.

Slowly, he rubbed his hand horizontally on the polished concrete work surface, his eyes the entire time fixed on me.

As soon as I was sitting opposite him, my eyes fighting to avoid his gaze, he said, "you are my safe place, my haven, my light, my love, Bridge," his index finger softly grazing the back of my hand. Electricity sparked from the slight touch his finger rendered to my flesh.

He was King David. And through him I could remove all the armour I was not even aware my body was wearing.

He made me feel as if my vulnerability was not a weakness. He touched it and treated it as sacred. I wanted to tell him that I still loved him and that every night before I fell asleep, his was the last name left lingering in my mind.

Yet all I could say was, "Thanks."

He chuckled, I suspected from embarrassment; he wanted me to say more. He needed me to say more.

He deserved more. But I refused to give him more.

Camilla-gate still felt like a fresh wound.

14

Humans are more inclined towards panic and anxiety than rationale. So, I was not surprised when they placed their faith in the scaremongering press, who sensationalised the virus. Hysterical caricatures occupied news channels and articles. They were relentless in trying to convert non-believers. "This virus is the devil," proclaimed the UK's leader - his hair groomed in the maddening style of the English eccentric. He stood, aloof and fortuitous inside the TV screen. I chuckled. His critics believed he tactfully employed the dishevelled and scruffy look to appear approachable.

I, for one, did not care. I was busy stuffing my face with the delights of Ben and Jerry's ice cream.

Whatever he was, he was relatively entertaining. He was a corpulent man with yellowing veneers, who engaged in a questionable relationship with the truth. One who volunteered seductively plain responses to complex inquiries. A populist. And to some a dangerous bloke with incorruptible Eurosceptic beliefs. There was something ludicrously charming and charismatic about the unclean-looking public school boy.

My gaze rushed back to the TV screen when he mentioned education. Could an offspring of Eton and Oxbridge utterly understand the quandary I was in? Would he perceive the load of failure that had offloaded inside me, as a sign of weakness, or would he discern that the draconian measures employed by him and his caucus had shackled the hands and feet of my education and that of my students?

Was he to offer me some sort of salvation? I wondered as my ears and eyes were glued to the TV. He spoke in an accent salivating with poshness and privilege, with all traces of multi-cultural Britain scrubbed off, his slight lisp not going unnoticed to my trained ear. "We arrive today at the crucial issue of education," he said, his hands folded: "As you are all aware, these are unprecedented times," then unfolded, his right hand reaching behind his back to either scratch an itch or pull up his trousers. He briefly spoke of the brilliantly counterintuitive notion of keeping all schools open, but his advisors must have warned him against it because he quickly discarded the idea and proposed that only a handful of private schools stay open. "Hitherto, these institutions are the only ones accounting for a zero per cent infection rate. This attests to the undying truth that they are the ones capable of continuing without any interference from the government and the DfE." His two comrades on either side of him nodded their heads in agreement. And in one sweeping statement, Norris had made sure that the milk and honey of learning for wealthy students would continue flowing.

I snorted, "You've got to be kidding me," while he continued speaking, his hands gesturing wildly.

I had hoped for him to overrule the initial decision of the DfE and re-open all schools, allowing for students who tested negative for the virus to attend, which meant that I could be there and gather further classroom experience, but all he did was to hammer the nail in the coffin.

The three schools that he had mentioned did not even allow newly qualified teachers within their perimeters, let alone an unqualified student teacher who looked like me. "Thank you very much," I sighed.

* * * *

My life had been violently uprooted and left unmoored. But I was still privileged with the choices available to me. My BA at UCL still afforded me a place in society. The same was not to be said of my students. The socio-economic inequity between the state and private schools had once again reared its ugly head. The UK's leader had not offered any solutions to mitigate the barriers that the poorer children whom I taught were to face. Barriers such as the digital divide that distance learning would cause. Some would not be able to access reading materials or class work because there was no computer at home. Some of the students I taught needed infrastructure to bridge the education gap. The classroom provided a safe haven from all the demons at home and in the streets. The banishment to home-schooling left most at even more of a disadvantage without any accessible alternatives for maintaining their studies when school doors closed. Some of their homes lacked the hardware and tools for distance learning to thrive.

However, I guessed that wasn't our leader's problem.

It was a shame, and it made me feel ashamed for beating myself up when I still had the world as my oyster. It was those kids I should be pitying, not myself.

And the more I thought about it, the more it dawned on me that perhaps teaching was not for me, after all.

* * * *

I woke up to the news of a peculiar kind of Armageddon. The end of the world was nigh, and the powers that be called it "lockdown". An authoritarian model effective from 1 pm on March 26. The unruly sounds of cars zoomed outside my window, and the pitter-patter of feet stampeded outside. Everyone was in a rush to take in the final days of freedom. Looking out my window, I saw a man inhale the fresh air as if it were his last supper. It made me smile. My first real smile of the day.

Humanity's jugular was exposed and COVID-19 was out for blood. The draconian measures that were to be put in place included no travelling, closure of all schools except three, and total annihilation of shops, restaurants, and public spaces. It sounded like the recipe for a dystopian novel. But it was to be our reality. I wondered how it would pan out. Because humans do not like to be oppressed. Even for their own good.

The weird truth about the lockdown was that it was truly the first time that the wealthy were allowed to reign free in beautiful London without the eyesore of the poor and the emerging middle class. They were forced to remain indoors.

It was also before and during that lockdown, for some odd reason, I was invited to a series of get-togethers with friends, family, and strangers. It was through these get-togethers that I found that the virus was not the only conversation worth having. Conversations about humans were more pressing: in their black, white, and Asian shades.

I was to partake in white conversations about black. Most importantly however, I was to partake in a conversation about my bright star Tariq, with my living foe, professor Matthew Wylde.

15

FRIDAY, MARCH 20

With all the talks about blackness occurring in every conversation I'd been having, it felt like a disservice to blackness to continue wearing my weave. So, I opted instead to get braids done that day.

I was on my way to Illustrious Coils Hairdressers in West Green Road, Tottenham.

Inside Illustrious Coils, the floor was littered with the useless remains of hair: red, black, blonde, blue, and even green. The aroma of drying hair choked the air and the voices and accents of highly tanned people filled the air. It was like home for me. The home I never grew up in but loved visiting once in a while. The hairdressers who mainly took ages to finish one's hair because they were busy engaging in conversations among themselves and other customers - as if they were doing your hair for free - said "hi" to me. I said "hi" back, because though they at times angered me with their tardiness, there was a sense of comfort whenever I was in the salon.

The vibrant beats of Awilo Longomba danced through the speakers. My dancing is partly horrendous, but the beat was too good for me not to shake my hips in my head. The owner, dressed as if he had just stepped out of a GQ magazine, danced for us. Shaking his hips like liquid. He was Didier Jean-Pierre, sapeur extraordinaire of the infinitely wealthy Congo. Didier was the owner of the shop. His charisma was unmatched and his smile glowed like diamonds. I frequented the salon for three reasons – to braid my hair, see my hairdresser, and to see what Didier, a prominent sapeur, was wearing. I always admired how he dressed in the finest designer threads just to sit in a tiny room behind the shop and keep tabs on us.

One day I asked him, "Didier, why do you dress so well for this area?"

"C'est de bonnes manières!"

Fortunately, private school had made me semi-fluent in French, so I understood what he said. "Indeed it is," I replied, impressed with his resolve.

Didier was his employees' boss, friend, and even bodyguard. There was a time one of his stylists Alisha's Yardie baby father came in to "box her" because she had cussed out his other baby mother in Tesco, and Didier would not allow him to lay a finger on her. He said, "over my dead body you will hit a woman in my shop. If you touch her. I—" he beat his chest, "Didier will give you the beating of your life. Try me if you think I'm lying." Maybe it was the strong African vexation in his tone or the conviction in his eyes. Whatever it was, it placed the fear of God in the Yardie and he went about his jolly way. Since that day, my heart has held a special place in it for Didier Jean-Pierre.

To put it mildly, he was a hero. And it did not hurt that for a man of forty, he was easy on the eye, yet never inappropriate with the ladies.

Though I was happy to see him, it was Aunty, my hairdresser, I was eager to see.

Aunty was overtly politically incorrect without any degree of malice. It was Aunty who first said the word 'fat' in a neutral tone.

It was offensive as well as refreshing. The ignorance or rather enlightenment of being oneself. I loved her. To a degree, I lived vicariously through her. She said things hidden in my thoughts that my mouth could never expel.

She uttered the word 'Paki' without hesitation. At first it prickled my ears and I was forced to gaze upon her face and then peek into her eyes. But there was no malice, no hate, or preconceived notions about the word. It was simply a woman talking about a people in the way in which they too referred to themselves. Like the word 'nigga'.

She said things like: "Asian men are supposedly the least-desired in the bedroom. Even their heightened education limits them to Asian women only." With this, I had to laugh quietly because she said it as if she had sampled an Asian man before. "Naughty woman, Aunty," I had replied, to which she laughed cheekily, and that answered my burning question.

Aunty was a wide and burly woman who said "Ah-ah!" instead of "Oh my God." She said "fan-tas-tic" instead of "wow" and most importantly, she called me "my daughter" instead of "Bridget" even though we shared no family relations. She was the family member I never knew I needed.

Her name was Aunty. Evidently, it was a stand-in for her actual name, but somehow everyone sang it as if it were the name bestowed to her upon birth. And for one incredible reason or another, her real name never felt the urge or need to expose itself to me for the four years I had known her. It was by chance, a freak accident upon which her name, like dark magic, was unhooded and laid bare before me.

It was a gloomy day in November 2018. Rain was falling as if sharp objects were being thrown at Mother Earth. Inside, the salon was stuffy and the glass walls were caked with steam. In a corner, the son of one of the hairdressers was busy conjuring shapes out of the steam on the wall. Aunty was braiding my hair. Her hairdressing skills were infinite. But she was, above all, the braiding champion. There was none other like her. The thicker texture and longer length that my hair acquired during her services were a testament to that.

As she placed the colour 1b extension to elongate my tresses, her phone rang so violently the room went still. She gently patted my head and answered.

"What, modafocker?!" Her voice boomed with a severe bass. I was shocked, yet bemused. Never had she uttered anything profane to anyone. Even she confessed that profanities were abhorrent. So, I knew the motherfucker she was addressing must have truly been one.

"... Me!" She huffed. Her chest heaving up and down ridiculously. "Me! Eniola Bisola Adebayo?" And that was the first and last time I heard her name.

As I got closer to her chair, she turned around and saw me. "Ah, my daughter," Aunty motioned, excitement building in her voice and demeanour. I was as excited to accompany her presence as she was mine. We met halfway through the room and hugged excitedly. She grabbed my shoulders, shook me left, shook me right, then backwards, and pulled me into her warm embrace once more. "I'm excited to see you, ooh!"

"Me too," I smiled, wrapping what little I could of my arms around her.

She laughed. "Your hand is still too small to fit around me, abi?!"

Her jeans held on nicely to her voluptuous shape. A glimpse of love handles poured out at the waistband, but "my boyfriend loves it" she was always proud to say. Her confidence was a treasure. The world could not bring her down. She was on top of it.

Her accent was thick, mild, and in parts non-existent. It was a skill she carried in her tongue, which I admired.

"See as you're fine like this," she smiled, my own mouth emulating her delight. "If my son was a big oga he would have married you sha..." she paused imperceptibly, "but even I have to cut my coat according to my size" - a wrinkle of sadness occurred across her forehead. I could not at that moment entirely grasp what she meant. All I knew was that poverty to any degree made one choiceless.

"Here sit," she used the palm of her hand to wipe whatever hair or grease may have been on the chair.

I sat. Aunty's reflection in the mirror watched me. "What?"

"Nothing."

"No. Something. Say it."

"It's nothing, my daughter."

"Okay," I said.

Aunty fidgeted with her fingers, huffed and puffed a little, then began to speak. I laughed quietly.

"I just think weave looks better on you." The words she had been fighting to contain finally spilled forth.

"Why?"

"Because you look very posh with oyibo people hair."

"What does that mean?"

She pretended she did not hear me as she wrapped the cape around my neck.

My eyes watched her in the mirror as hers diligently tried to evade mine. Her hair was a rainbow and all the other colours outside it.

The first time I made Aunty's acquaintance, I almost tasted the candy floss in her pink locks.

Then, she was slimmer, her face a tad weary but her voice was still big and large like the ocean. "Any hairstyle you desire I am your supplier," she had said. I almost burst out laughing at the silly wittiness of her words. And while the other ladies stalked me with their eyes as if to say, "leave this crazy woman alone and come to us," I went with Aunty. She was not forceful or brash. She did not tug at my hand or even try to persuade me otherwise. She simply wanted me. It was as if to say, "if you're destined to be my client, you will be my client." It was as if she believed in fate and the notion that what was hers will be hers. And it was that, that quiet belief she carried in her that drew me to her, all the way to her chair where she braided my hair and, for good measure, added a candy floss pink for being her first customer of the day at 4.20 pm.

"So why shouldn't I do braids when you are my braider, Eniola?"

She stopped, looked me dead in the eye inside the mirror, then laughed, a bold, loud and heavy laugh. She was happily shocked to hear her real name.

"I think you should do weave because of what your mentor at your first school said," she answered. Her words were a reminder falling on me like a tonne of bricks.

Aunty, the plump Nigerian hairdresser with luscious thick lips she always painted red, and straight eyebrows she always drew black, did not busy herself much with petty words. So, when I told her about the argument, I had with my mentor about the way she chastised me for my 'messy hair' because I'd left it as an afro, she had said, "My daughter, you must conceal your blackness small, small. You know oyibo..." the word she called white people. "... Oyibo do not like too much black, black. You have to lessen your blackness for their comfort,"

After she said this, the only words that would come out of my mouth were: "I do not care. If their comfort is based on diminishing my blackness, then the oyibos can piss off."

She had sighed. She did not want to offend me, so she said, "Okay, ooo."

So, as I now sat in her chair acknowledging the words she had uttered were in good faith, I took her hand, looked at her in the mirror and said, "Fuck my mentor. I am doing braids."

Growing up in the household that I did, I was never afraid of offending others, with the exception of my mother. The irony was that it was she who made me confident in my blackness. Sometimes I knew I offended people. At times with my beauty, which some believed a black girl should not possess in such infinite amounts; at times it was with my intelligence; other times with my privileged upbringing that some people called posh, which offended me to no end, but mainly I offended others with my blackness. Because I was never ashamed of it. Quite the opposite. My undying pride for it offended those who could not fathom why. This was why when my mentor said my afro was messy, I had told her she smelled of wet dog and it made me feel like throwing up every time she came near me. Needless to say, she had never said anything about my hair since. And if not for Aunty reminding me, I would have forgotten she had said that.

"Aunty, I want braids and that's that."

"Ah-ah!" she cried. I laughed. "You this girl you're stubborn, ehn," she too laughed. "I like you, sha."

"I like you too, Aunty," I said, her hand gently caressing my shoulder.

Aunty had all boys. I had a feeling she fulfilled her aspirations for a daughter through me.

While I sat in the hairdressers, a white girl who seemed to have lost her way entered the premises. The other hairdressers watched her like a pot of gold. A most awkward thin-lipped smile crawled like a snail around her mouth. “Erm, I want to do corn rows,” she mumbled. And as if her words were a switch, the hairdressers lit up and began speaking one over the other to get her as a customer. The hairdressers haggled among themselves and she, smart enough, went with the cheapest. Cheapest for a white person, that is: £140 cheap for cornrows.

While she shampooed my hair, Aunty laughed at the amount the other hairdresser had extorted from the girl. “Poor girl,” I said.

Aunty bent down and in a low tone whispered, “That Jamaican girl is so greedy. It’s pure wickedness what she just charged that girl.”

I agreed because the Jamaican hairdresser could not really do braids. “Should I say something?” I asked.

“No, because she will say I sent you, then begin to cuss bumbaclot dis and bumbaclot that.” She chuckled.

“Aunty, you are a very funny woman.”

“Thank you.”

“So, what do you think about the virus?”

“You mean the chinko virus?” exclaimed Aunty.

“There’s no conclusive data to suggest what you’re saying is true,” I said, perhaps a little offended at her ignorance.

“You can pepper me with proper English all you want, Bridget, but we both know the truth,” she said, this time using my name. However, I did not know the truth, nor did I agree with what she was saying, because I did not know it to be true. We agreed to disagree as I went back to the chair.

Aunty was the secret love of my life. She said the most outrageously politically incorrect things that I could not say but was always delighted when she said them. Maybe it was the fact that she said things without the sinister undertones of racism. Race was never a factor even when she mentioned it.

On the TV, there was a Caucasian rapper acting so black it compelled Aunty to stop my braids and shout, "Ah-ah, who's this black boy?" to which the salon, including the white girl, erupted in laughter. "No now, is he albino?" she questioned, positively unsure as to where the young man lay in the race spectrum.

"He is oyibo, Aunty."

"Na lie..." she half laughed, "this gangsta boy."

"Yes, Aunty."

"Na wa, ooo, my eyes have seen everything in this London."

Looking around, Aunty realised she did not have enough hair to braid mine. "Ahh, there is no more hair," she said looking at me with those puppy-dog eyes.

"Fine, I'll go."

She laughed slyly. "Thank you."

* * * *

In the hair shop I felt eyes behind me. I looked back and this immigrant who barely pronounced English words correctly, and whose breath was laced with curry and alcohol, was audacious enough to follow me as though I were a criminal. How dare he, my blood boiled. I had seen his country and its million slums. I wanted to scream something racial at him, but I knew it would not come out the way Aunty said it. Mine would be filled with contempt and rage. And though the words tried to break open my lips and fly out, I managed to keep them contained. Anger was a fleeting emotion and Father always advised me against fleeting emotions. My only choice was to say, "Stop following me, you dick," before shame shrouded the man and he slithered away.

Left alone to look for the correct hair, shame enveloped me. Why did I feel the urge to say something racial first as opposed to dickhead, which was all he was? His race did not define his dickheadedness. It was his action that defined it. I was so angry with myself that I almost went to say sorry to him. But then I thought, what if he was indeed following me because I was black? Would that justify me thinking of him with a negative racial connotation the same way he thought of me in his head? If it was a white guy, I would not think to say 'you white piece of shit'. I would simply say 'you piece of shit'. So, there I was applying the same negative connotations to another oppressed group as if I was the master. Nevertheless, what made me even angrier at myself was the fact that had I used a negative racial connotation, I would be invalidating my uncle, Father's best friend: a brilliant physicist, a man of impeccable intellect, and also Asian. I could not limit him to a derogatory term, just because someone who looked like him made me feel uneasy.

Back in the salon Aunty was on the phone. "Sit" she motioned. I sat. Ten minutes later I was still sitting.

I made a move to leave, which was when she sensed my annoyance. "My daughter, my daughter," she mused, my face contorted with annoyance. "I'm sorry, please, sit."

I watched her, my face trying its best to remain serious, but the cheeky grin on her face would not allow me.

"You know I don't like waiting," I hissed.

"I know, I know," she teased sticking her tongue out at me in the mirror.

"I saw that."

"I was talking to my niece in nija," a shortened version of Nigeria.

"How is she?"

"Very unwell if you ask me.

"Why, what's wrong?"

"Her mind is what's wrong," fumed Eniola, the playfulness that was once bubbling in her voice and face disintegrating.

I gave her a slice of hair from the Expressions packet in my hand, and she began braiding a stick of my hair.

"She wants to follow these yahoo boys instead of focusing on a serious man like Donald.

"Who is Donald?"

"Did you hear me? I said yahoo boys."

"Yes, I heard you, Aunty."

Yahoo boys, the term she used for fraudsters, always made me laugh.

Aunty did not like Nigerian boys for her nieces. She claimed they were all 'fraud stars' and that one had corrupted one of her nieces to travel with drugs without her knowing the full extent of what she was doing. The only Nigerian boys she vouched for were her two sons who were still stuck in Lagos with her mother. "Those boys are good boys. They will never be 'fraud stars', God forbid," she would say while clicking her fingers over her head to ward off evil spirits.

"So who's Donald?" I teased, her face softening a little.

"You this girl," she jokingly tapped my head. "Donald is an oyibo man who wants to marry her, but she says he's too old. He's only fifty-five."

"Fifty-five is ancient. How old is your niece?"

"Twenty-four. She's no spring chicken."

I laughed out loud for two reasons. First being that Aunty always said, "You're too young, Bridget, the world is your oyster." Meanwhile, I am older than this niece of hers who happens to not be a spring chicken. Secondly, I laughed because she always insisted that I find myself a good black man. Even David wasn't black enough for her, though she found him irresistibly handsome, and literally blushed the first day he came to the salon with me and called her beautiful. She was adamant that I should participate in undiluted black love. Yet here she was forcing her niece to marry a white man.

"Aunty, I don't mean to sound rude–"

"But you're going to be rude nonetheless."

"I'm afraid so."

She tugged at my hair. She wanted a reaction, but I diligently ignored the slight pain in my scalp.

In the corner beside me, the white girl was oohing and ouching as the hairdresser attempted to braid her sensitive scalp.

"You speak about the importance of black love, but you're being a hypocrite by imposing the opposite of that same love on your niece."

Aunty sighed as if I were meant to know why she wished this for her niece.

"Bridget, you don't get it, do you?"

"Get what?"

"Not everyone is afforded the privileges you had and still have. You are rich. You did not grow up amongst immigrants. You had a choice to say I do not like caviar. People like us do not even know what it means. Let alone have the opportunity to refuse it."

I was trying to understand, I wanted to understand, but I was still unsure.

"Ronke doesn't have the means nor the right to refuse Donald. Ronke is a poor girl, from a poor family. Donald, believe it or not, is her saviour. He can bring her overseas to a land of milk and honey. He can support her and her family. Those yahoo boys will just foolish her and abuse her beauty for a temporary period. Donald is British, born and raised. He is single and deliriously in love with her. He can give her papers."

Aunty did not have her papers. Ten years and she was still waiting for her indefinite leave to remain. But she did not lament. Her spirit was enviable, filled with positivity and hope. I admired her for it. She was unconquerable. Yet she did not feel her niece, Ronke, would have the same resolve she possessed, thus why she wished for her to marry Donald.

"Now do you understand what I am saying, Bridget?"

I lowered my head. "Yes, I do, Aunty."

Aunty stood motionless, eyes downcast, and for the first time, I knew what it meant to be black. Her kind of black. The black that existed only in grey spaces. The black that was removed from colour. The black that refused to lie down and die because society rebuked it. The black that, though impoverished, suffering, and chastised, still found the will to be a hero.

"Aunty did I ever tell you this...?"

"Tell me what?"

"That I love you, and you are my hero." My hand gently touched hers.

Her palm ever so calmly shivered in mine. She smiled softly and then placed her other hand on mine.

"Thank you, my child," she whispered, her voice dripping with emotion. "I wish you were my daughter because I love you more than words can express ... even with all your stubbornness." She kissed my head.

I felt choked, and for the briefest of moments, I too wished she were my mother.

16

As I left the salon, I saw a kid literally driving his mum up the wall. She yanked him so hard I thought his arms had ripped from his shoulders. "Stop pissing me off, you little shit," she yelled and he said, "Piss off." Mother never spanked me but my face would have been a mosh pit if that were me and my mum. Instead of smacking him, the woman burst into tears and the boy hugged her. *Stay at home with your kids*, they said. Clearly, they were not thinking about this lady and her kid.

Further down the road next to Seven Sisters station, I met a homeless man. I did not have any coins, so I apologised. "I'm so sorry I don't have money on me."

He then proceeded to say the unthinkable: "I have contactless..." he smiled pulling out the card reader. My eyes bulged in his direction. Shock tickled my being, then pity as his desperate eyes pleaded with me to apply empathy to his plight. As I tried to ponder whether or not to tap my card on his device, he interrupted my thoughts. "Even a pound is enough, lady," he added, trying his hardest to enthuse me to give charity.

I asked him why he was begging. His reply moved me to pity. "Alright, type in £20."

His whole body lit up like fireworks. "Thank you, Miss." He got up from his stoop, all the while pressing in the numbers of my charity into the card reader. "Thank you so much, Miss. God will bless you."

"Amen," I received, tapping my card on his device. "You have a good day now."

"And you." He reached out his hand before realising it was dirty and I might be put off. He retracted his hand, then lowered his head, and he wiped his hand on his brown-green jacket. "Sorry," he mumbled.

I watched him. His stature sank under me though he was at least six feet. It was not a sight that made me happy. To see a man who could possibly be exceptionally handsome under his unkept beard recoil in shame in my presence because he was homeless and a pariah of society.

I opened my arms and hugged him. I had not meant to. I only meant to reach out my hand, shake his and find the nearest public toilet to wash it.

He hugged me back. The look in his eyes when I offered him actual humanity made me see him for who he was: a human being just like me.

"Erm..." I stuttered. "I'm going to grab a bite in that coffee shop." I pointed in the distance, his eyes following my finger. "Would you like to join me?"

"Yes please."

17

SATURDAY, MARCH 21

It was 7.38 pm. David had invited me over for dinner.

Although that night at his - a couple of days ago now - had been extremely tense, I could not help but accept his offer to see him again.

While we drove to our destination. David's voice mutilated the song coming from the speakers. My gaze lingered on him a little too long, my heart contracting with lust each time his voice rose and fell when the singer hit the falsetto. I wanted to kiss him. His mouth, the shape, texture, and colour of it made me feel such a way. They were full and fluffy, as if my lips would land on clouds if they met his.

At the restaurant he looked my way and winked. My heart dropped and somersaulted with delight. His light azure eyes had a way of hypnotising me. He went around the table, wrapped his arms around me and laid a soft kiss on the nape of my neck. "If there are a million lifetimes, I will be in a million and one with you, Bridge," he whispered. It felt like I might disintegrate from the touch of his words.

In case you're wondering, David is the good man I always push off the cliff. Because he is the good man who once pushed me to the edge of that cliff, then off it for good measure.

Yes, perhaps it was Camilla who had initiated kissing with him, but it was he who allowed the kiss to happen. She had leaned in and he had not recoiled or told her to stop. He had allowed it! And for that, my contempt for him grew, till it became a forest which overpowered my love for him.

"You should've stopped her!" I screamed, seven months pregnant.

"I'm sorry, Bridge, I was not in my right state; before I could stop her, her lips had landed on mine."

"I hate you, I hate you ... leave!"

That was how the cold war between David and me had begun.

I loved him. But the past had me conjuring up ways to bury my love for him every time it exposed itself to me. I hated the fact that I was still stuck and unable to withdraw myself from the quicksand of lies, deceit, and pain he had caused. I hated that he had forgotten it. I hated that I hated myself for being unable to speak on it.

Vulnerability was not my strong point.

We had sought therapy, but I had been unable to speak. The words had barricaded themselves inside the walls of my throat. We had sat with my parents and his. He had prostrated himself before me, man, and God. His voice chanting, "Forgive me, Bridge, forgive me." But I was no ethereal being, so I did not.

Finally, we had sat, just him and me, man and woman, lovers. "Tell me what I can do to make it better," he had offered, emotion glistening in his arctic gaze. "I love you with all that makes me human." His hands shivered feverishly inside mine. "I will do anything and everything to make this right. Let me make this right, Bridget. Please," he had pleaded, hot tears burning his face red. I know such expressions should have pulled at my heartstrings. They should have made me feel pity for his plight. But what about my plight? I was the one constantly in the fire, not him, and that realisation raised the hell that I'd been tip-toeing over; scorching him inside out.

"I hate you!" The bass in my voice rose a thousand decibels.

"I know," he had agreed, his head in my lap, while he sniffled and convulsed. But I did not want him to *know*, I wanted him to *feel* my hate. His agreement was superficial.

"I never want to see you again" my scream had pierced the air.

* * * *

That was then.

Now we were having dinner in a private room in one of Park Lane's finest restaurants. Lockdown was almost upon us, but as we were to discover with Partygate in 2022, the rich, beautiful, and influential had ways of breaking the law without consequence. David's colleague a prominent professor and consultant at Royal Free had invited him and other friends for dinner. I was his plus-one much to everyone's delight at the table.

"She's so beautiful, David ... wow, aren't you a lucky ... she's everything I would wish my woman to be," they said, thoroughly impressed not just by my outward appearance but also by my intellect.

David and I brought the aesthetics to the room. We were art. Two star-crossed lovers, stuck between love and hate, yet always leaning towards love.

"She is the most beautiful angel on earth, is she not?" he mused, his lips gently touching my cheek. It felt hot, his touch. Our eyes met and I smiled shyly, biting my lip as I did so. He exhaled softly.

The entire table seated in the private room watched

us.

“If only I had such chemistry with my wife,” the director of the hospital’s husband teased his spouse who sat beside him.

“Why aren’t you both married?” questioned the director with a cheeky grin.

“Because she will not have me right now. But I promise I will marry her soon,” David said, his eyes revealing his sincerity.

Though I did not say anything, I wished with all my heart he would.

* * * *

We were amid black excellence. The two most important people in the room were black. David’s colleague the consultant was a Caribbean man, and the director of the hospital they all worked at was a woman of Congolese descent. The rest were white. To say I felt pride at being black in that room was an understatement.

“So, what is it you do, Bridget?” asked the director.

I chuckled, then took a sip of champagne, unsure if I should confess I was the only underachiever in the room and admit I was studying to be a teacher.

“She’s studying to be the best English teacher in the world,” David spoke on my behalf, his palm gently rubbing my hand, while my eyes watched him with gratitude.

The director, who was probably privy to the news and my predicament, made no attempts to diminish the words of David.

“To the best English teacher in the world,” she smiled, a genuinely beautiful smile, while raising her champagne flute in the air to toast me.

It was an act of kindness. A simple yet profound one that almost made me cry.

"Thank you," I murmured, my voice a little shaky. She may never know it, but the confidence booster her words jolted into me could've lasted a lifetime. It was not often another black woman placed me on a pedestal and allowed others to celebrate me on that pedestal alongside her. Consciously or subconsciously, we had been programmed to see each other as competition. She could have scoffed at the myriad of things wrong with what David said. And due to her position in life, she would have had the right to. Yet, with all the faults, she chose to celebrate me.

Later that night I would pull her aside and thank her, to which she would reply, "If we cannot uplift each other, who will?"

She was my hero.

****

"La liberté n'est pas gratuite," said the director

"So, the black man's punishment for being free is that he is not truly free and that he should be the pariah of society?" I asked.

"In essence ... yes."

A wounded chuckle bubbled in my chest.

"You did not think you'd be given freedom for free, did you? There is always a cost that goes with it. And only when you are the oppressor do you know that you won't give it out for free... But the oppressed are always foolish to that fact, especially your kind..." A junior doctor, a prodigy of the consultant, stopped abruptly.

The room fell silent.

In the distance, I heard the gentle, yet distinct, voice

of the Michelin-starred chef ordering his sous chefs about.

The words of the junior doctor loomed over the room like a lofty tower.

The consultant watched him like a father would a child about to step into flames, yet hoping he would see the fire before it burnt him.

I laughed, cackled even. All eyes, including those of the junior doctor, were on me. His face was painted with a smirk that rubbed me up the wrong way.

"Sorry, I did not get your name."

"William."

"Ahh, Billy."

"No, I said William."

"Okay, Bill," I retorted, turning his face red with fury. I had him where I wanted him. I had unsettled him, ripped him off whatever fucking pedestal he felt he was sat on because he was a doctor and I a trainee teacher at twenty-five.

Smiles were painted on the faces in the room, even the white ones.

"Now, Billy," I giggled - he was watching me through eyes etched with both terror and humour - "why would you say such an unfounded thing?"

There was doubt roaming in his eyes. Doubt as to whether he should answer me, and truthfully at that.

We gauged each other. I could feel the excitement beating like a heart inside the room. A part of me hoped he would back down, but he was a man and I - a woman.

He was ready to go to war.

"Unfounded, how so?" he returned, the earlier doubt fleeing from his gaze. "Do you disagree that the black man is in no hurry to be truly free?"

The question poked holes in me. Yet, David, the director, and the consultant were unscathed, unmoved by the words of this white boy. Could it be that they felt removed from the paradigm Billy spoke of, and if so, a rebuttal would have meant they somewhat associated themselves with what he said? I did not know what it was, but I wasn't going to sit around and let him get away with such a broad statement.

"If the black man isn't truly free, it is not his fault."

"It's not ours either," he snapped. "Take the Jews for example..."

"Bullshit, spare me the Jewish comparisons. With billions from reparations, anyone can buy freedom."

"Then tell the black man to make money and spend it amongst themselves rather than spending it everywhere except at home. I'm sure you're familiar with the term charity begins at home."

"Are you dumb or stupid Billy? Without money you cannot make money. The Jews received financial aid and more for their suffering. We got nothing." You dumb fuck!

The director nodded her head in agreement, and soon a sea of heads bobbing in unison followed.

"Alright. Fair enough, I agree that the billions received in reparations helped. However, the Jews are also free because they are united, and you cannot tear a united front apart. From the look of things, it seems some black men hate self-unity. They prefer to be united with and validated by everyone other than themselves."

I hated Billy's words, but I could not find a way to totally disagree. With the looks on their faces, I knew that David, the director, and the consultant were in complete disagreement and knew exactly how to dispel Billy's remark. However, they were enjoying the debate between the two youngest in the room.

Out of ammunition, since his rebuttal had annihilated my arsenal, I tried to fire back with: "I blame the media for their portrayal of us."

"Well if that's the case then you must blame yourself also," he remarked, eyeing my black flesh.

"How?"

"I hate to say it..." he paused - a soft smirk on his face.

"I'm sure you do," I retorted.

"Nonetheless, it needs to be said. Your people don't exactly present themselves in the best of lights, do they? The hoodness..." he spoke, his fingers mimicking inverted commas, "... of some black folks is just too much."

"Interesting, because I happen to know more non-black, sorry I mean white, hood rats than I do blacks."

"Oh, stop lying," he laughed as if I were. For the sake of diplomacy, I decided not to engage with his comment. As Mother said, ignorance was bliss, and it appeared he revelled in that fact and was living blissfully inside it.

Even so, it appeared the director did not like ignorance or the bliss of it. "Billy," she smiled, "correct me if I'm wrong but I'm sure you told me you know a white boy whose DBS check contains a record of petty theft and public disorder ... I might be mistaken, but that must surely count as hood-rat behaviour."

Blood rushed to Billy's face, staining his cheeks crimson. The room watched him indifferently. His throat expelled a wheezing laugh. He coughed, then grunted as though sick. Sick by the sight of apathy towards his shame.

“Excuse me, I need to use the gents,” he murmured, fleeing the room as if he were escaping a leper colony.

Grinning, I added, “I guess Billy thought he had big balls because he went to Oxford and can conjure up coherent sentences and pepper us with quotations in Latin ... or French in this case.” The room smiled. “Evidently, he hadn’t seen the size of the director’s.” The room erupted in laughter.

When Billy came back from putting his fragmented pieces together, he made sure he did not speak on race relations the entire night.

Boy, did I love the director.

18

Park Lane was as quiet as a grave outside, except for a Ferrari zooming past, followed by a Bentley, its roof missing, cocooning a Russian oligarch and his mistress who was busy taking selfies, for her Insta, I assumed.

David weaved his fingers in mine, the rekindling of our flesh feeling somewhat spiritual.

For a minute or so we walked silently, before turning right into South Street. A pair of police officers walked toward us.

"Good day, sir and madam," they said, their heads bowed as they walked past.

It did not escape me that we were indeed close to lockdown. Only the rich and beautiful had rights and freedom of passage in these parts of the city, and the latter could only get access if they were accompanied by the former.

There were traffic cameras that ascertained who you were based on your number plate. If your income did not reflect the approved threshold, the boys in blue would chase after you like a criminal and escort you back to your 'you-are-not-rich-enough' area of London.

With fewer people venturing out, one could feel the aura of the green expanse of Hyde Park, a short distance away. The air felt fresh. The subtly lit interiors of English townhouses and period buildings lined the streets, their owners either asleep or watching TV. Inside one particular period building a porter watched us, his ubiquitous face either from the Mediterranean or the

Middle East caged inside the gates of a home he could only afford to protect, never to live in.

Sadness struck me, the same sadness that sat inside his gaze.

“Hi,” I said, much to his surprise.

“Good evening, madam,” he smiled, breaking apart the sadness that once was. It was as if I was the first person to acknowledge him in this part of town. And he appreciated that kindness. The kindness of being noticed.

* * * *

I felt like a trophy as David lifted and spun me around. We were two teens in love all over again.

I was giddy with him; playful, as we mimicked karate moves from the Matrix. If there were CCTV cameras around, all they would have seen were two bodies moving their arms and feet with huge smiles on their faces.

For the time being at least, it seemed I had forgotten our past. He had been my champion at dinner with his contemporaries. He had shown me off like a diamond and had made love to me without even touching me.

“Thank you for tonight.” I pulled him close, kissing the back of his palm. He smiled, and I was dazzled.

“You are everything I need in this life, Bridget. I know school cessation and this lockdown may not be favourable for you. But it gives me a chance to win you back ... properly, and to see you and be with you the way I know I deserve.”

He kissed me. The kiss started off tepid. Then became boiling hot.

“I covet not just your body,” he gently whispered, soft kisses falling like feathers on my neck. “I covet all of you, Bridget. All that makes you a woman ... a human ... mine!”

A tiny moan escaped my mouth. His words were orgasmic. If not for the fact that his lips retreated from my flesh, a downpour of elation would have exploded inside me. The nether region of me, that is.

"Let's go home. I've got moves I want to show you, bad boy." My tongue licked his lips. He groaned.

"Do not tempt me, Bridget White, lest I fuck you senseless right here, right now," he said, pinning me against the glass wall of the Berkeley Square Bentley showroom where he had bought his vehicle.

"Oh please, I would love that, kind sir," I laughed.

"Well, the damsel must wait ... the night isn't over yet, baby girl," he said, kissing me. Sulking, I took his hand as we made our way to his friend Tunde's house in Dover Street.

The façade as well as the interior of the building was opulent. Outside, a metal wall concealed the property, which shone like a star from the distance. Inside the compound, steep walls of greenery greeted you as though they were titans. The lit runway gave directions to the towering main door, which opened and revealed the immaculately dressed Tunde.

"David, my dear friend," his arms opened to embrace his university buddy.

"This must be Bridge," he said, extending the hug he had offered David to me.

"You have a wonderful home, Tunde."

"Thank you," he said.

Inside, chandeliers illuminated marbled floors so radiantly, you could see your own reflection. Money had evidently not been an issue when Tunde chose to build his home.

* * * *

"There is no vitality in the interpretation of our ancestors by the white man. We are simply stones. Picked up, without a fight, and shipped to foreign lands with educated barbarians and savages. Where men who sell the gospel like a viper would its poison to a babe reside. And we lap up their words ... like, like..."

"Gospel" I mused.

"Exactly," Tunde smiled.

"How ironic, even when we are the fastest of humankind, our history is slow and sad and pathetic, almost like a white man in a 100m race."

The table could not help but erupt into raucous laughter. For all his faults and flaws, Tunde held a robust imagination for his continent. Something that I found profoundly admirable. A man, despite the true picture, seeing a better picture. He envisioned mercurial changes for Africa which one was unsure to be positive or negative about. His covert or perhaps even overt idealism could either be viewed with admiration or humour depending on whether you thought Africa was a shithole or not. He proposed an array of discomfiting ideas that somehow proved profound in his mind.

He was a black man who solicited even darker forces to help him at times. Forces not of our world or even a world we know. But only of a world we assume. A world which straddles the opaque latitudes between grey and black, white and grey, but never black and white. He was not ashamed to speak of this world, openly, freely as if a man were speaking of religion. In religion, they are called spirits - in science, energy ...

"And in Star Wars, the force," teased Calvin - his sense of humour finally making an appearance, much to the table's delight. Calvin was also David's friend from university. He held an aura about him similar to David's. There was a quiet brilliance about every facet of him. He, alongside David, brought a brilliant male aesthetic to the room.

Tunde was dangerously flawed, sinister, yet as brilliant as the sun itself. There was an ugly beauty about him. He saw the necessity for evil to thrive alongside good. For madmen to have sane men carry out atrocities that they couldn't physically engage in - men like Henry's Cromwell or Stalin's Beria.

Tunde so far was being an amazing host with all his somewhat philosophical anecdotes. However, I noticed that when it came to his wife, Margaret, he was a mindless automaton. Obeying her orders like a slave. It was relatively interesting that a man as big and black as he, was turned into putty by the fair and fragile Maggie. Maggie's beauty was softly exquisite, with small lips that were finely shaped and upward-slanting eyes that had ominous fires brewing inside. She carried a ravenous spirit about her, and it was for that reason that I felt the urge to ask her, "As a white woman who's with a black man, what do you think about black women?"

As an afterthought, I realised that my question may have come across as confrontational.

Everyone at the table stared at me as if my question was obscene, except her. My query did not rattle her. Staring me bang in my eyes, she replied, "The presumption is that black women are bitter when rich black men date outside their race." The faces in the room lit up with befuddlement and amazement at her blunt answer. I was impressed by her.

"Are they?" I questioned sarcastically.

"Yes. Some are. And rightfully so. Would white women be angry if Ronaldo or Beckham - if he weren't married – dated or married a black woman? You bet they would! Without a doubt, they would. And then it would be black women saying white women are so bitter. They should just accept the fact that we are prettier, and their men like us more..."

"Exactly." I agreed.

"The truth is there aren't that many uneducated black men doing well for themselves. So, when they do, I believe it is right and proper that the black woman expects them to be with a black lady..." Some on the table watched her, as though shocked that this was her prognosis. "... It isn't bitterness it's more an annoyance at the inferiority complex of certain black men, I believe."

It shocked me, as I had not expected to agree with her, but agree I did as she continued to elaborate on her answer to my initial question.

"As a white woman, I am not oblivious to the fact that certain black men pursue the gratification of white women. Not that I mind," she smiled at her black husband.

Tunde was gobsmacked, much to the table's befuddlement. David hid a chuckle under his breath, while I could not help but laugh out loud as Tunde left the room briefly.

Maggie, if she did acknowledge it, did not show that she was privy to her husband's embarrassment. Matter of fact she proceeded to add more fuel to his fire by stating, "I know this isn't palatable for me to say. But white women do not have a saviour complex, and a lot of times us white women are with your men because they make us feel like we can save them ... from what exactly I'm not sure, but they make us feel like saviours, so we pretend to be so."

Her last words were reminiscent of those of Professor Matthew Wylde. In the crevices of my mind, I could hear him repeating almost verbatim the same sentence.

"Perhaps I should go check on him," said Maggie, finally coming to her senses.

"Yes," replied the entire table, as her heels clicked and clacked on the marble floor away from the table.

In the distance, she shouted, "To answer your initial question, I think black women are great."

"She's quite a character, isn't she?" said Calvin.

I replied, "So far ... I like her."

Calvin teased, "Give it time." Then he winked at his lady who swooned at the sight of him. David slid his fingers into mine and kissed me.

"To black love," mused Calvin, his glass raised in the air.

"To black love," we all returned, glasses raised.

19

Calvin who was a jester, though he did not know it, was a sight to behold. His complexion was a mixture of coffee and caramel. Whenever he smiled or laughed, the dimple on his chin appeared. The confidence he carried with him was reminiscent of David's: quiet yet overpowering, the perfect combination. His girlfriend who proudly sat beside him was Adut, a supermodel from Sudan. An actual supermodel. Needless to say, her beauty was impeccable.

Calvin in comparison to Tunde was comfortable in his blackness. He was not a rare breed of black man, but the fact that he adored the black female form, and was rich, tall, and handsome could've been shocking to some. Calvin's parents and all those he knew in high positions looked like him. He did not feel that whiteness would elevate him in life, which meant he never felt the urge to indulge in it. He stood on the shoulders of black men and women who actually made the world go round, and according to him: "No number of white bodies can elevate me further." If it wasn't for the fact that the work of art, David, was the love of my life, I'd be swooning over Calvin the same way his girlfriend was.

His uncle was the attorney general and his other uncle, who was his mother's cousin, was the president of his country. His idea of power was black. His idea of love was black and his idea of wealth was black. So, it was impossible for him to be impressed or seduced by anything else. Everyone at the table was seduced by his resolve, including my kind and wonderful David, who raised his glass and made a toast: "To Calvin and black supremacy!"

"To Calvin and black supremacy," we all returned.

Calvin, pleased with his audience's reaction to him began to tell us about the dark forces holding his continent back.

By now he was standing majestically where the bottles of red wine were. His eyes scanned the bottles before pulling out a 2017 Chateau Lafleur Pomerol.

As he examined the wine bottle, he said of Tunde, "He may not have great taste in certain things, but his taste in wine I must say is quite impressive." We laughed. He opened the bottle, poured a glass for his girlfriend and me, then for David and himself. He tasted the wine, waited a second, then feeling satisfied began to speak. "The problem with Africans sometimes is that they like to perpetuate the romanticism of poverty."

"Care to elaborate?" I cut in, eager to know why he felt this.

"Because 'woe is me' is their motto. You'll try to help someone, yet they are always poor..."

"Someone like who?" queried David.

"The poor people. Take my drivers, cooks, gardeners and every other handyman in the continent. I give them more money in tips than I do their actual pay, yet they'll never tell me they are doing better, because they want handouts. Failing to realise that self-sustainability is better than what I can give them." His words were quietly bloated with contempt for their avarice.

"So, would I be correct in asserting that your belief is, if the continent and its people become self-sufficient, and in a wider context stop waiting for a saviour who doesn't look like them, then they'll start progressing rather than regressing?"

"Exactly, Bridget. We are our own saviour, whether singularly or collectively, only we, as black people, can save ourselves."

None of us disagreed with Calvin.

"Ahh, another thing," he raised a finger while taking a sip of wine, "another thing we Africans in the diaspora need to stop doing is believing that our motherlands are dumping grounds for second, third, and fourth-hand goods."

"Why is that a problem?"

"Because it perpetuates the idea that nothing good or new should be afforded for those back home. It means we in a sense see our fatherlands the same way the Westerners see them."

He had a point, I thought. A very valid one. Nonetheless, David was not one for words, he was a man of action, which is why he said, "You say all these things but how do you reconcile them or rather how would you if you could?"

Walking over to where we were sitting, Calvin rested his right hand on David's shoulder. David shuffled a little causing me and Adut to softly chuckle.

"David, my fair-skinned brother..."

Even David had to laugh at this as he placed his hand on Calvin's and said, "Yes brother, please enlighten me."

"... You're far too gracious brother, and enlighten I shall."

"Hear, hear," I mused, winking at David, who blew a kiss I caught in return.

"Well, to resolve self-sufficiency, I opened businesses and paid for school fees for my workers. I do not want them to work for me perpetually. It will gladden me more when I go back if I see that they have moved on to bigger and better things, which is what young Jacob is doing. He is in his final year at the technology college in the capital. Daily he blesses my name to God…" he paused, spinning the wine in the glass.

"Bro, that is admirable," insisted David.

Calvin gave the white-people smile, which made us all, including him, burst into bouts of laughter.

"I love your sense of humour, baby," Adut finally spoke in a soft Sudanese accent that sounded sultry.

"Thank you, my love," he said, kissing her crimson-painted lips. "Finally, King David, I am reconciling Africa being a dumping ground by owning multiple factories that produce quality food, furniture, and clothing at affordable prices. Made in Africa for Africans."

"My man," cheered David as he got up and hugged his university buddy. "An African champion, bro."

"In this lifetime and the next, bro. I want the apotheosis of my life to be 'A great African man who fulfilled greater ideals for the glory of the continent'." His words were almost poetic brimming with resistance against Western ideals and we all loved him for that.

While Tunde and Maggie remained upstairs, Calvin continued to illuminate us with Africa and some of her magic. He spoke of the Kamajors from the Mende tribe of Sierra Leone. Men of war and violence, if and when needed, but also men of the earth of the people and ultimately of love. In some ways reminiscent of the Norse warriors of old within Scandinavian terrain. Men who believed in the gods, in magic and every other matter here or there. The difference he said between the former and the latter was that those gods of the blonde-haired, blue-eyed men had long died while those of the Kamajors were still alive, stopping rains or causing deluges depending on which was required. I was deeply fascinated with this Africa that the history books never revealed to me.

Some time had passed. Tunde and Maggie had still not made their way back. As I was about to suggest we go up to meet them, angry footsteps stampeded downstairs.

Making his fingers in the shape of a gun, Calvin placed it to his head, then mouthed 'shoot me now' as he winked at the group with a cheeky grin on his face.

Calvin's sense of humour was witty; everyone revelled in his company.

Tunde got closer to us. He had rage and hate in his eyes. However, upon close inspection I realised it was something far more sinister; revenge, a dish I was not yet aware he wanted to serve me, because I had laughed loudly at the embarrassment his wife had caused him. Also, I assumed he had concluded that if not for my initial question to his wife, he would not have felt humiliated in his own home by her in front of us. So, as payback, he too wanted to embarrass me.

Ripping the bottle of red wine from Calvin's hand, Tunde gulped an immoderate amount, before walking over to his seat. Exaggerated drawings of shock or humour painted on all our faces.

"A bit dramatic, isn't he?" I teased

"Just a little," sniggered Calvin, pinching his thumb and index finger together for emphasis.

"I do not fancy black women," he spoke with an affected and orotund undertone, before smiling directly at me. The opacity of his smile was odious, and though it was meant to rile me, it did the opposite, which triggered his being and made the table, including his white wife, happy. It was now my turn to return an odious smile. His nostrils flared like a bull.

“Would you like me to be your champion, my love?” asked David.

“Me too, Bridge” offered Calvin.

“Thank you, gentlemen, but this black girl, Bridget White’s got this!”

David and Calvin beamed at me with pride.

Tunde exhibited a capricious nature. Hot and cold. Cold and hot. And nothing in-between. Earlier he had straddled within greyish spaces. Now he was firmly placed in my black space, and I was about to show him that blackness was capable of illumination.

I hadn’t noticed before but now that we were at great odds, it was essential that I took in all of the enemy. Tunde was fair in complexion. Yet there was a dark almost frightening strangeness that lurked in the sharp curves of his knife-edge smile or the darkness of his eyes that weren’t only laid in his eyeballs but outside their circumference. His head was not large but big enough to give him a formidable almost primitive appearance. There was a gap, one so slight it was near imperceptible. But I noticed it and whenever he spoke of things that made my flesh crawl, I wished to pry the gap open, rip the words from his throat, and fling their torment back in his face.

I later also noticed that he, Tunde, embodied all the dull and mordant markings of an upstart. The pretentiousness, the over-emphasis on how much money he had, the desperate desire to be admired. He was new money trying to dress his world in all the fine silks and histories of old money. But I saw the poor runt he once was and all I could do was snigger in silence at his own blindness in refusing to acknowledge that none of us were impressed by him or the millions he had acquired plundering his continent the same way the white man did.

“Do you smell that?” I asked.

"What?"

"That rancid need for attention seeping through your pores!"

A crooked smile cut across his face. He looked at his wife for assistance but all she could do was give him a look of pity, turn away, and drink her wine.

"It's going to be a long night. Drinks anyone?" an excited Calvin inserted. Everyone said yes, except Tunde and me. Despite this, Calvin filled my glass, winked at me and took a seat at the far end of the room.

Getting up, I moved towards Tunde's chair. He shifted uneasily, an action that made me smile. There was a sturdy wooden table behind his seat. I sat on it. My eyes gauging the circumference of his head. I could tell he wanted to relieve himself of his seat, but such a move would have made him appear weaker, so he had no choice but to stay put. I had cornered him.

"You strike me as an individual who wants to be the best among equals."

"What...?" He tried to turn and face me but to no avail.

"You think you are unassailable but everything about you is pregnable. You are shrouded with the cloak of inferiority, my dear Tunde, and you wish to conceal it by being inarticulate and plain foolish. I thought, perhaps, this mysterious brain David initially professed you had would materialise. I was wrong! You are the philistine Professor Wylde speaks of," I admitted, though I did not want to use the professor's words, that he was correct about some of our men. "You not fancying black women has no impact positive or negative on my life. If you compare the black men that me or Adut are with, you could never compare, and I mean that on the most basic level, which is looks..." I deliberated, standing right behind.

"... Oh, and before I forget, were you not liking sexy black model pics on Instagram? Or was that another Tunde?" I asked, recalling a time David had said Tunde's white wife would not be too pleased with his choice of likes on Instagram.

David cut in as Maggie's gaze tried to split Tunde into two. "Guys, guys," he said, trying to change the complexion of the conversation from severe red to a little orange. But no one was paying him any mind. We were all still red hot with anger, especially Maggie as she had just found out her husband did, after all, like some black booty.

In an effort to redeem himself, Tunde tried to crack one or two jokes, but they were pain-inducing, and no one laughed, not even him. When that did not work, he demanded praise and adulation by speaking about his financial exploits. But no one had any reverence to offer in his name. All he could do with our indifference was muster a wry smile that flushed his face red. I felt the tremors of his rage, but it did not shake me. I stood unmovable, our eyes cutting each other down until he fled. I'm not sure if it's me. But it appeared his kind did not like it when someone like me held their ground. He had appeared as the aggressor. But had been left the victim. His ego severely bruised. His plunge into madness was intoxicating. It was odd what a sane mind was capable of under extreme stress.

At least he now knew that my saviour was not white. It was me, myself, this black girl named Bridget White.

20

Thirty minutes or so after cooling down, Tunde decided to annoy us with his presence once more. This time, however, there was an erratic look of excitement on his face. Something that piqued my interest.

What could he be excited about? I thought.

"Ladies and gentlemen," he announced, his hands clasped together. "I have the best surprise for you all..." he almost skipped with giddiness "... care to follow me to the drawing room."

His excitement, which was somehow contagious, made us rush upstairs behind him.

"A special guest is about to grace us with his presence..." We watched each other in excitement. "Who can it be?" asked Adut and Calvin simultaneously.

"His fame eclipses even the Queen of England. He is the most famous deportee the world has ever known. He is, for lack of a better word, the most enigmatic man on the planet..."

David raised his brows at me, then shrugged. I nudged him playfully while he wrapped his arm around me, a boyish grin printed on his face.

* * * *

The door to the drawing room slowly opened. I could hear all our hearts beating in anticipation. Tunde's smile widened like a Cheshire cat as the door fully opened and illuminated the special guest.

Gasps of adulation left everyone's mouth. Calvin

looked around the room as if to say, do you see who I'm seeing?

His cool blue gaze turned and met mine.

I was a deer caught in headlights.

I wanted to look away, but his eyes hypnotised me. They drew me in like a moth to a flame. And just like that, he lit a fire in me.

I exhaled.

He smiled.

My heart boomed with the ferocity of a thousand war drums.

Oh my! I thought, blood gushing to my face. I raised my hand to my face, an attempt to cover the crimson patches that had formed on my cheeks.

I was mortified!

He paid no mind as he walked majestically towards me. I wanted to melt into oblivion, but my feet were glued in position. The only thing I could do was muster a pained smile as he finally reached me. His cologne, rare, exotic, and distinctive.

I felt my face getting redder. Something I did not know until that point was possible.

Please walk past me, please walk past me, I found myself pleading in my head.

He stood right in front of me.

Damn! I screamed internally.

"Good evening," he said. His voice was smooth, deep, and ... *Stop*, my mind shouted.

I closed my eyes and smiled awkwardly. He was torturing my soul and he knew it.

I opened my eyes and nodded my head in acknowledgement at his greeting.

"My name is Matthew. Professor Matthew Wylde..." he grinned, reaching out his hand. I did not take it. Softly, he chuckled. "A beauty as illuminating as yours should not be so dull."

I cleared my throat. "Bridge," I muttered

"Sorry, I..."

"Bridget," I shouted, interrupting him.

He smiled. "I heard you the first time, Nubian. I just wanted to hear your voice again," he said softly biting the inside of his bottom lip.

Please, deliver me from temptation, said my body to my mind.

"Okay, nice meeting you," I said, quickly shuffling away from him.

I could not believe it. My sworn nemesis was in London, in the same room as me. His looks had not regressed, not that I had expected them to. Oddly enough they had evolved to a much more handsome state. Something I had not deemed possible. His arctic azure eyes brimmed with warmth and his full cotton-candy-coloured lips bloomed like roses. And his hair, the darkest of a deep blonde, which was once full like a bucket in the ocean, was cut ever so low, exposing the sultry nakedness of his face. I was weirdly aroused, and I think he felt it. Embarrassment struck me like lightning. But fortunately, the wholeness of my melanin encased what would have been severe crimson patches all over my face.

21

Five Years Earlier

From outside the café, Matthew watched Bridget from an angle which was neither straight nor crooked. Her face was tense with torment. He wanted to touch it and draw a smile on it.

But the thick wall of glass created a barrier. She sat, sunken, in her chair. Her head slightly bowed with fingers aimlessly scratching at the table. Her lips moved every now and then. He did not hear the words, but he saw them. They were a repetition of "fuck, fuck, fuck".

She looked up and their eyes met. He wanted to run, to hide, but she had seen him. Her lips curled into a scowl. A lopsided smile forced itself upon his lips.

There was madness in her beauty. It was quiet from a distance, but the closer he got, the more he saw it loud and clear, like a disease, a plague, which could consume any man if he weren't strong enough.

However, he was a titan!

He took a seat in the chair opposite her. He sensed fire raging mercilessly inside her, and it caressed his soul.

Bridget raised her gaze, their eyes met again, it felt like an eternity, he exhaled, and she bit her lips.

Her beauty is truly maddening, he thought, a slight curl forming on his lips.

He watched as her eyes darted all over him. Her erratic gaze struck up several fires within him. She was tortured, her soul was dark and her heart empty.

She was a broken beauty, yet somehow, he felt the urge to fix her and put back her fragmented pieces.

Her fist clenched, he smiled and motioned for the waitress.

"What can I get you, sir?" asked the waitress, taking out her pad and pen. He motioned to Bridget. "Madam, what can I get you?" the waitress asked smiling.

Bridget lifted her cup of coffee with agitation. "I'm good."

"Oh-kay," sighed the waitress, her eyes rolling.

The waitress's frustration and Bridget's indignation humoured him.

"Two espressos," he said, as the waitress scurried away.

Bridget pushed back from the table, grabbed her bag, slung it over her shoulder and tried for the exit. His cold blue eyes followed her.

She was haughty in her expression. His lack of communication riled her skin, he felt it in his bones. Her agitation excited him.

Her body shoved his shoulder as she sped past him. He did not look back. Instead, his fingers tapped the table.

In the distance, her steps ebbed away.

A moment later, he heard those same steps rushing back towards him ... "Alright, dickhead, what the fuck do you want?" she fumed through gritted teeth, as her hands slammed the table, spilling the contents of her unfinished drink on him.

The hot liquid seared sweet pain into his flesh.

"Welcome back." He smiled.

"You've got some bloody nerve, Matthew!" Bridget yelled, compelling the people in the coffee shop to turn around to look at them.

"Why? Because I spoke the truth?" he huffed as his cold eyes burned into her.

She scoffed, then sat back down. "Your words couldn't be further from the truth, white boy."

Holding his hands to his chest, he chuckled, "Ouch, that hurts."

"Piss off."

As she began to gather her things to leave once more, he stopped her. "Stay, please. I'm sorry if I offended you just now, but I am not sorry about earlier."

"Why are you here, what do you want? Wasn't our earlier interaction at Harvard enough for you?" she asked, taking back her seat.

The professor leaned forward. Bridget flinched. He smiled. "Good, you feel fear," he said, staring into the depths of her soul. He knew she felt naked. He saw her shiver. She looked away. His stare must have been too intense. "I'm not the one you should fear," he said, "the enemy looks nothing like you and me."

Her gaze snapped back in his direction. "What does he look like then?!"

"A thief," he replied.

"A thief?"

"Yes."

"I'm not sure what thrills you get from speaking in riddles, but you need to stop," she demanded.

"Your beauty is far too transcendent for such trivial things like my riddles to aggravate your soul," he teased.

She smiled, but to him it was more a cry for help.

"The enemy looks like a thief..." he paused. Bridget's eyes waited impatiently as they darted left, right, up, down, imploring him to finish what he was saying. "He is a thief because he stole your cousin."

Her lips quivered, her eyes blinked, and her throat let out an agonised groan. But she did not cry.

He was proud of her.

"I know that Tariq White, the last of those three boys killed by the police, was your cousin. Which is why you're here to protest by shouting 'hands up, don't shoot'."

"Who are you?" she asked yet again. This time he heard the sincerity and need in her voice. It soothed his own fragmented pieces.

"I am simply a man. A man who knows a truth that he may someday reveal to you."

Perplexed, yet somehow satisfied by his answer, she gently laid a hand on top of his.

"Thank you. I do not agree with you, but thank you for bringing some of the truth to light yesterday at Harvard. Your rhetoric will embolden some to be more overt in their racism. But what it can also do is have the opposite effect." Her hand softly rubbed his.

His lust for her shamed him. He looked away while his heart pulsated. He knew that she did not have the slightest idea, but she was a force to be reckoned with. In front of her, he was mortal, he was a man, he was in love, he was hers, for the taking, for lifetimes, forever ... if she wished it.

Her brown gaze sparked at him, building fire in his heart. He wondered if she felt the same things he felt. Matthew wondered if Bridget's heart exploded into a million pieces every time their gaze met. Did butterflies gather and flutter their wings inside her heart each time he smiled? He wondered all those things.

For the rest of the evening, they spoke about everything under the sun. She told him how the death of her cousin had compelled her to realise that black lives mattered. Prior to that she had been cocooned in privilege and did not pay much mind or care for those who weren't in that same bubble as her. Realisation only slaps one in the face when it is close to home, she had said. She was brilliant; academically, she was a tour de force and she was only twenty. He was enamoured by all of her. She had a right to hate him, yet she was sitting here in conversation with him, treating him like a human being. Although not forgiving him for what he had said, she somewhat appreciated his own genius.

He found Bridget to be enigmatic. Something the negro shouldn't necessarily possess from the point of view of his biases. So, he took her on like a project to find out if the words Hume had spoken were true. But on every occasion, those words had proved unfounded, untruthful. Bridget was a tour de force. Smarter than he was at the same age. A brilliance so achingly potent he sometimes felt she held the sun inside her. And to top it off, he was falling in love with her. He was a star, and she was the universe.

His thoughts for her were sacred yet profane. He wanted to touch her, even though he saw her as an ethereal being. Being in her presence made him feel otherworldly. Even if some of her words were sharp like blades and would sometimes, just sometimes, cut him into tiny pieces.

22

Inside the drawing room, the professor shone like a bright star. Tunde, his wife Maggie, Calvin and Adut had already taken a million selfies with him. David and I, however, carried on as though we weren't as impressed by him as the others were. This appeared to rile him a little, especially when he asked David, "Are you familiar with my work?" to which David replied, "I don't think so."

We were all familiar with Matthew's work. Most especially his speech at Harvard. We all knew the undertones and overtones it carried then and more so now. We all knew that although he was wrong about most of his views about blackness, he was at the same time correct about plenty of them.

Black people were still shouting "hands up, don't shoot". They had still not mobilised and sought out a proper plan of action. We were still divided, and black lives were yet to matter. As Matthew said - hundreds of years later and we still did not know how to play the game our oppressors had created, we still did not know how to save ourselves. Perhaps, it was this realisation that made us welcome him like a pin-up rather than the pariah he had been at Sanders Theatre.

It had been five years since I last saw Matthew. I had long forgotten that he and I had sat opposite each other inside that café a day after his speech. I had promised myself on Tariq's behalf that I would only remember him in an inhuman state rather than the somewhat human one he had shown me in the café. I had forgotten that we had shared a moment. What that moment was - I cannot say. However, it was evident we had both felt something.

Now here he was once more, making me feel something I could not necessarily place. I wanted to ask him a myriad of questions. None more pressing than the truth he would someday reveal to me. What was it that he wanted to tell me? Was it something to do with Tariq's death? There was so much I wanted to ask and know. However, I held my tongue because I believed that the answers I sought would somehow find their way to me, now that he was in London.

By some odd coincidence, David and Matthew sat next to one another. Their resemblance, for two complete strangers, was eerily uncanny; the only difference being one was black and the other white.

Needing to start a viable conversation, Matthew addressed the room. "What was the topic of conversation before my arrival?"

The room went quiet. Tunde watched us with pleading eyes.

"Black women," replied David, I assume with the hopes of shutting up the professor. It had not escaped me that David was privy to that brief moment Matthew and I had shared upon his arrival. I could feel David's agitation at this fact. Regardless, I had no choice but to ignore it for now.

"And what was it about black women that was so encapsulating...?"

"David, my name's David," he snapped.

"Tunde's dislike for them..." inserted Calvin before the professor could return David's animus.

The professor's stare cut through Tunde, who cowered in shame under the penetrating gaze of the white man. I was weirdly pleased by this. I was not keen on the professor but less so on Tunde. Matthew was not in the least impressed by this revelation about Tunde. Nursing a glass of the newly opened Rémy Martin Louis XIII, the professor laughed disconcertedly. “A black man who doesn’t like black women ... what a weird dichotomy, don’t you agree, Maggie?”

Jolted by the question, Maggie gave a wry smile and agreed, presuming it to be the ideal answer for the professor.

Matthew watched us. We watched him back. He downed his drink and, like a servant, Tunde sprang from his seat, sprinted to the bottle of cognac, and poured him some more alcohol.

“Thank you, Tunde.”

“You are welcome, Professor.”

“Margaret?”

“Yes, Professor.”

“Do you consider your husband to have a mental illness?”

“I beg your pardon...”

“My apologies, please, allow me to elaborate,” he said as we all watched, eager to hear his prognosis. “If a mother has a child and decides she now hates him, the world would say she’s a monster, and if they were being kind, she’d be labelled mentally ill, right?”

“Most certainly!”

“Then you must surely be of the same conviction if applied to black men who now hate or dislike the black woman through their own volition...” He stopped, his eyes taking in how uneasy his words now sat with her. “Do you or do you not agree, Maggie?”

She half laughed, half frowned. “You are a brilliant man, Professor,” she paused. “That’s all I can say.” He nodded his head in acknowledgement, with a cheeky grin on his face. Needless to say, Tunde was burning inside out and we all loved the flames.

Some of us may not have liked the professor, but we could not deny that we felt privileged to be inside his labyrinthine mind.

"It is the natural order of life to gravitate towards what resembles us. Even the animals know this, except some black men who carry no influence in life unless it comes to breaking down the black woman." Matthew pondered, his eyes focused on me. "It is a shame that the only time certain black men are noticed and heralded as champions is when they are publicly denouncing the importance of their women who have birthed, fed, bathed clothed and comforted them ... Surely you must notice your own psychosis, Tunde," he said taking a sip of cognac. Even if David did not wish to admit it, I could tell he was impressed. Impressed by a man who did not speak ill of the black woman. It was odd that it took a white man to tame the big black Tunde and make him realise the errors of his ways.

If not for today I might never have known that Tunde harboured such contempt towards women like myself. And as far as I could tell, nor too did David. I wondered how their friendship would pan out after tonight. Would David hold him in the same high regard he once did? Evidently, there was nothing wrong with a black man loving a white woman. It is a human condition to find things other than ourselves desirable. Nevertheless, there was something profoundly wrong in disliking reflections of one self in order to appease others.

David had not confronted Tunde that night regarding his aggression towards me, as I had asked him not to. However, I would later come to know that a melee had ensued between David and Tunde downstairs while I was upstairs with the ladies, which led to Tunde getting punched in the mouth by David for offending me.

I was shocked by the apology Tunde offered me at the end of the night. Now I know why. Needless to say, David and Tunde's friendship was never the same again after that evening.

As I was looking around the room taking in the awe on all our faces towards the Professor, my eyes fell inside his. Time, ever so briefly, stopped.

In the brief silence that covered the room after Matthew had lectured Tunde, I could feel his gaze vying to engage with mine. But I refused to let that happen as I forced my hand to grip David's and kiss him on the lips for good measure.

The professor almost inconspicuously looked away. Even in his cool rage, there was a profound handsomeness about him that I did not wish to admit.

There was also a discerning interiority about him that I wanted to take a hammer to and break into smithereens.

Out of nowhere, David began whispering sweet nothings in my ear. As I had been drinking a strong cocktail, my senses were a little altered, so I wasn't aware that I was giggling quite loudly. Whatever was making me laugh, the professor did not like it, especially as David was the cause of the amusement.

"Bridget," Matthew called, causing me to snort from the shock of my name in his mouth. His hands, which he had clasped, unlaced themselves. "What is the dumbest thing you wished for as a child?

"To be an adult."

He laughed softly, and suddenly whatever feeling of dislike I held for him began to untangle itself.

A crescendo of heads bobbed up and down in

agreement at my answer.

Placing himself inside the conversation, David spoke, "I agree, because adulthood lays bare the ugly truth our parents try to hide from us; truths like the black woman being the most disrespected, even by her men." He shot a fierce look at Tunde.

Maybe it was the drink, but suddenly the professor and David began morphing into one, with the professor starting to become more and more palatable every time he and David agreed.

Matthew, not wishing to be outspoken by David, cut in, "You know what I hate most that society does to black women?" Whenever he spoke I realised that there was a protean quality about his voice - at once low, high, humming, whispering and silent in equal measures. Something that enticed me.

"What?" I returned.

David, refusing to allow Matthew to grab my full attention, spoke before the professor could answer. "I hate that it's always 'quantify your pain or trauma black woman' vs 'I am here for you now, this instant. We can talk later ... if you want, but I am here for you, right here, right now...' I will never make you quantify your pain or trauma ... Bridge." His gaze settled on me. I felt lightheaded almost as if I were falling ... falling in love with David all over again. Without a doubt, he was my hero. And heroes deserved public displays of affection, which I gave him

The professor, severely agitated asked to be excused.

"Do you want me to come with you?" Tunde queried.

"No, stay. I just need some fresh air." He exited.

The professor was a complicated man. But

complication breeds fascination and if you go deep into the belly of such fascination, you might just birth admiration. He was sinister, singular, an oddity that kept you spinning in his web. Releasing you only when he desired. Calling him 'an enigma' was an understatement.

23

The professor was not knocking on the door of the pantheon of the greats in academia. He was already inside and possibly its brightest star.

He knew that and so too did everyone in the room, including David King and, most importantly, Bridget White.

The professor might have said the black man is a fool. Yet, for all that made him a man, at that moment, eyes fixated on Bridget, he could not deny that the black woman was indeed an ethereal being.

Her gaze made him feel acutely vulnerable and for some odd reason he loved it, the way she made him feel. She provided him not only with physical desire but intellectual intimacy. Two things no other woman had offered him simultaneously.

There was a copious mythology about the professor. Sitting in front of his audience consisting of Bridget, David, Kevin, Tunde, Adut and Margaret, it was evident why he was who they said he was, a man larger than life.

Matthew considered himself a man of culture. For someone who had been terribly pained by his deportation from US soil, he liked all things British. He hated going to the stores or restaurants filled with white European immigrants. In his mind, they cheapened the aesthetic of prime Central London with their varied European accents, which he claimed were brimming with ignorance and illiteracy. He preferred quintessential British restaurants and stores. Places which may have been overpriced but possessed an exquisite aura of Britishness about them. He liked being served by British people as he felt they had an element of class about them. They knew how to be welcoming; the foreigners, in his mind, were too brash, too uncouth, and sometimes too eager – too eager when you were wealthy like him. He hated the inauthenticity of it all, though he knew that was how the world worked.

He possessed a subtle yet overt arrogance when among his so-called less-than-white counterparts. Though it may have been covert, he made it known that he felt he was superior. Mainly because he was white British and because his pedigree was different to theirs. His father was a judge and his mother a prominent member of the Conservative Party.

Although he harboured a dislike for the lesser kind of his people, he felt right at home with Tunde and his friends. Perhaps it was the fact that Tunde and his friends had money and came from a very good pedigree. Also, the fact remained that regardless of his predispositions, Tunde was an exceptionally industrious man. Everything he touched turned to gold. The man knew how to turn coal into diamonds.

Tunde was fascinating and multi-faceted. However, with all his achievements and wealth, Matthew was not impressed by some of his statements. Matthew considered himself an alpha male, even if Tunde was the more muscular of the two. He did not believe in the notion that a woman could elevate a man, especially if that man has power and wealth.

"In life it is always the man who makes the woman look great," he said, cognac in hand, eyes staring directly at Tunde.

"It seems only the black man and other non-whites need the white woman to look great." He raised his finger in objection to Tunde's attempt to interrupt. "This in actual fact means such a man is a failure. Because to need a woman to elevate you in any aspect of life means you are a failure." Tunde went quiet. He could not defend himself. Despite all Tunde's millions, the professor had lessened him to a white woman's bitch. Everyone felt Tunde's agony. However, it was not enough to petition their sympathy. For some, it even produced a great deal of pleasure. Matthew went on to further elaborate on how he felt that black women were indeed the champions of the black race, insisting that some of their black men were the great failures and reasons why the race, rather than progressing astronomically, appeared to be regressing steadily.

The room was filled with some of the brightest minds who weren't in stark disagreement, but due to the professor's colour could not explicitly agree with him either.

The audience's emotion was the professor's currency. With each word, his wealth spread like an iron curtain. He was strip-searching the crowd with his words. Their naked emotions were laid bare for him to play with, especially Tunde's.

Matthew found it strange how black men like Tunde looked up to men like himself. When he spoke, Tunde listened. To some degree Tunde revered his words. It was as if he wanted to be him. Something the women in the room did not feel towards Margaret, he noticed.

Matthew assessed the room. He was neither unaware of his genius nor his presence. They were both things he was acutely aware of. Everyone was fascinated by him, even those who tried to hide it, like David.

The only person who did not appear captivated by him was Bridget. She tried to pay him no mind. Nevertheless, he noticed her surreptitious glances. He noticed when she smiled quietly and coquettishly at his unconventional jokes. He noticed how she would softly exhale when his gaze met hers and lingered inside hers a little too long.

He craved her beyond rationale. When she spoke, all eyes fell on her. She possessed a prolific beauty. It was the kind of beauty that accepted love as a tribute.

It was uncanny, but the more he tried to clandestinely look at her, the more he saw how much she favoured her cousin Tariq. It was their eyes. Their eyes were the same. Bright, bold, brown, and filled with all the possibilities in the world. They had something in their eyes that said 'I can do and be anything I want'. It was a confidence that was at once subtle yet raging in equal degrees.

She had his heart, if not for anything but for the fact that she believed the world could be hers. Perhaps, even, that it should be hers.

He wanted to speak to her, alone. But everyone desired her attention. Even Tunde. No one else might have noticed. But he did. He noticed that whenever she spoke, Tunde would gaze at her, his eyes never leaving her even when others might. He noticed how his chest would heave a little faster whenever the room's attention was on her. He noticed how Tunde quietly but greatly admired Bridget's intellect. He noticed the longing in his eyes whenever they were on Bridget and the apathy in them whenever his wife - who was beautiful and clever but nowhere near the altitude of Bridget - spoke.

Matthew noticed everything.

He noticed how at times his audience wanted to break free from the topic at hand and delve into his speech at Harvard, yet did not know how since he had a way of stepping over the topic whenever they tried to bring it up, mainly because he did not wish to open the wounds he knew Bridget was healing.

He noticed how Bridget was the brightest among equals.

He wanted to touch her. When she made a joke, he found himself competing with David and perhaps even Tunde to be the one she decided had found her the funniest. He noticed he nodded vigorously in agreement with her statements, something that made him laugh inwardly.

In her presence he felt merely a part of the crowd, while she was everything.

He wanted to please her, to make her notice him. And he knew nothing would make him more noticeable to her than if he brought up Tariq.

As Matthew wooed and angered the room in equal measure with his brilliance, it did not for a moment escape him that he and Bridget kept bypassing the elephant in the room: Tariq. Matthew wanted to say his name. He may have been wrong, but he felt that she too wanted to say Tariq's name. He felt as if she wanted to ask if he brought any good news for her. In the café he had said he would reveal a truth to her someday. In Massachusetts, he had said it was an officer who had killed her cousin. But the police had said they would investigate. Which was like being the judge and jury at one's own trial. Of course, one would vindicate oneself.

Matthew so desperately wanted to bring up Tariq. However, the general subject matter of conversations that night did not allow him room to directly bring up Bridget's cousin. Bridget may have been a force of nature, but he knew her heart was still too fragile when it came to her cousin. He did not want to break her heart further. Not on that day, in that room, when she physically looked like she had just fallen from heaven.

Tunde, seeking to somewhat redeem himself said,

"There needs to be a study of conscious bias in African schools." As an African, the progression of the continent was something he cared for. The professor watched him, unsure of what to reply. "There needs to be a mantra, a ritual if you will, that says our fairer-skinned counterparts are not better than us."

"Care to elaborate?" the professor seeking enlightenment queried with a strong sip of his cognac.

"Well, take for example the Lebanese or the Asians. In their homelands they are virtually nobodies. Yet they travel to the continent, and they are regarded as people of esteem and credibility. They are offered loans that I may not be offered even though the benefactor is the same colour as me."

"Is that why you said you don't feel bad when they leave without having paid their loans, fleeing with the money to better their home countries?" asserted David.

"Exactly, charity begins at home," replied Tunde.

"What if charity doesn't deserve to be given a home?" the professor questioned. "The laws of capitalism do not factor in charity. They only factor in profit. Are your own people as industrious as the Lebanese or the Asians, or do they consider politics before business?"

Tunde and the rest of the room watched Matthew. How did he know so much about the African dilemma? That chronic dilemma wherein the countries were run by the Africans but the businesses were owned by a multitude of foreigners.

"The truth is, we are just as industrious if not more so than the others. However, that self-belief is lacking. For some odd reason it seems we find it easier to help out others rather than ourselves; hence the reason that those who loan the bulk from African banks aren't Africans."

"So you're saying if it's not naturally in us, we must teach it to ourselves?" questioned David who alongside Matthew and Maggie was the least African in the room.

"Exactly. The same way the Europeans indoctrinate their students in school to perceive whiteness as superior and deserving of all the good their countries have to offer is the same way we too need to mould our educational curriculums to preach, believe, and practise such. If the next generation of three to four-year-olds grow up believing in the ideology of black supremacy, I guarantee you the black man and his continent will believe in its superiority. And belief my friend..." Tunde's hand patted Matthew's shoulder, "is the only thing that has taken us to the moon, the only thing that makes us reign over the lion, that makes us build machines that conquer the seas and the skies."

"Let me get this right..."

"Please..." urged Tunde.

"Are you saying the African must believe in himself the same way the rest of the world believes in themselves?"

"Yes, exactly that."

"Why, I would have thought that was a prerequisite of any race."

"Welcome to the nuances of Africanness, my brother. A continent filled with titans who are yet to ascertain the cardinal truth that they could indeed be giants not just of their continent but of the world if they applied such belief."

The room marvelled at Tunde. For all his idiosyncrasies, one could be forgiven for saying he was indeed a great African with greater ideals for his continent.

Matthew was quietly beguiled by Tunde. It was peculiar how he managed to possess redeeming qualities through all his maddening views.

* * * *

Her body, tall, slender, with slight curves in the right places made Matthew swallow. Bridget oozed sexiness without even trying. In the distance she danced to the piano beat David was playing. The professor's eyes and those of everyone in the room were glued to her as her chocolate skin twisted with soft yet impassioned sensuality. Her long braids moved in unison with her. She was indeed otherworldly. And Matthew was indeed falling.

While all eyes still looked at her in awe, David switched the tempo of the keys. The beat got louder and his fingers moved faster. As if new batteries had been inserted in her, Bridget quickened her pace. She flung her neck back while her braids moved with intended delirium. Adut wooed. Even Margaret appeared to be in awe judging by the way her mouth was slightly agape and by how her body tried to inconspicuously mimic the moves Bridget's body was generating. David, clearly smitten, could not wipe the smile and look of adulation off his face. The strings in the professor's heart pulled a little as he saw how she returned his admiration.

They were all watching her, and though there were five other people in the room, it was clear that Bridget was dancing for David and him alone.

The professor did not know if it was jealousy or anger that was rapidly moving in him. All he knew was that he needed a refill of cognac to calm his nerves.

On his way to the bar, he was about to walk past her, but his desperate need for even the slightest touch from her would not allow him to pass by. Their eyes caught each other. She stopped, he exhaled, and her lips ever so gently parted.

His heart drummed with everything a man who

wanted a woman might drum with. Gently, he took her hand and softly placed it inside his palm. Maybe it was in his mind, but he thought he heard the quietest of moans escape her mouth.

In the background, the music stopped. David was raging with something that could only be described as jealousy.

"The heavens must be dim tonight."

"Why?" Bridget implored Matthew.

"Because the brightest star is stood before me." He leaned forward, placing the gentlest kiss on her burning cheek before walking away. He did not look back but he knew with all his heart that she was feeling some of the things he was feeling at that moment.

Stepping into the finely manicured garden with his refilled glass, the professor closed his eyes.

Behind him, someone approached. It was Tunde.

"Black women like her aren't interested in mere mortals like us, Professor," smiled Tunde cynically.

"Oh, but I'm not simply a mere mortal, my dear friend Tunde." His arctic gaze blazed. "I am..." he smiled with equal cynicism, "Matthew Wylde. A phenom!"

24

Standing in one of Tunde's palatial bathrooms, I watched David from the mirror. He was angry. The professor's subtle yet explosive advances at me had enraged him.

Yet all I could think of was how sexy he was in his rage.

"How dare he come to my friend's house and try to woo my lady? Bloody twat!" he swore. "And you, Bridge," he fidgeted, pacing back and forth, "it's almost as if you're not averse to his advances ... don't let that white boy spin your head." I wanted to laugh, and he knew it as soon as I clasped my hand to my mouth. However, unable to hold in the deluge of my amusement, I began to laugh.

"Let me get this straight; is the king jealous of a mere mortal like the professor?" An annoyed smile curled his mouth as he crossed his hands and looked sulkily into the mirror.

"Oh, don't be like that, baby. You know it's only you that I desire, only you that I want." I bit my lip while pressing my body against him. Roughly, he grabbed my waist then lifted my dress exposing the roundness of my booty before pressing it onto his clothed erection. I groaned as he stood back and watched me with sweet wickedness in his eyes.

David was majestic: tall, dark in his own way, and handsome beyond rationale.

The first three buttons on his shirt were undone and on his face was painted a look of dark, carnal decadence.

Our eyes met in the mirror, and I could see my

reflection swimming in his fierce blue gaze, which made the nest of pleasure between my thighs throb.

Turning around, I whispered, "Let's make love right here, right now."

David exhaled, his hand reaching lightly across my neck, igniting shocks of desire in me. His strong yet gentle hands gently slammed me against the glass. A rugged groan escaped my mouth while the hotness of his gaze and breath scorched my flesh.

His tongue teased my mouth before wildly parting my lips, allowing vicious and savage kisses to consume me. I laughed deliriously from the severe pleasure.

"Take it off..." he commanded, his breathing rough and desperate.

"As you wish, Sire..."

A glint of wickedness smouldered in his azure gaze while he watched me undress.

Standing back, a mischievous grin cut across his full-bodied lips as he removed his silver cufflinks then proceeded to fold his shirt.

Our eyes met, I bit my lip, he smiled, my heart fluttered.

"Do you need some help?" He sank to his knees before I could answer. Gently he unwrapped the straps of my heels, all the while placing soft kisses on my feet.

I thought I might die with pleasure.

"Turn around," his husky voice demanded. "I need to see your love faces," he said as slow and scorching licks of his tongue slithered up my spine.

At first, he stroked me gently. But I needed more, so I begged him, "Harder, please."

"Are you sure?" He pulled back my braids, causing sweet pain. Arching my back, he placed a hand around my neck and lightly choked me, "Like that?" he growled, biting my ear.

"Yes ... like that," I gasped, palms clasping the mirror.

The first thrust intensified my breathing. The second was fierce and raw and carnal, stifling my moans. The third was animalistic, followed by the fourth and fifth ... "Shh," he growled, his thumb wildly parting my lips while I licked and sucked on it.

"Take it, take all of it, Bridget," he breathed, teeth gritted as the thrusts kept coming and coming and coming, while I panted madly till my legs and my will could bear no more. "Oh God," I half screamed, half gasped before the tremors of his manhood violently shook my world with ecstasy.

25

SUNDAY, MARCH 22

I woke up at 5.32 in the morning.

It was Mother's Day, and I was in David's bed. Finding my phone by the bedside table, I texted Mother and wished her a Happy Mother's Day. Later in the day, she would bring Winner to mine so we could all spend Mother's Day together while enjoying her glorious food.

Lying in David's bed, my mind went to Matthew Wylde who had been somewhere, lurking inside my dreams, his image at times morphing into David or Tariq.

As I pulled back the curtain, I saw a sky stuck between grey and black and white. Celestial objects such as the dying moon and a billion stars stared back at me while the sun fought its way through the underbelly of the clouds. It was a beautiful sight. All of God's heavenly creations looking at me as if to say, today is a good day to be a black girl.

David was fast asleep. I wanted to kiss him, but he looked so at peace I refrained from doing so. Quietly I whispered, "I love you too, David King. I always have and I always will."

I loved David. In all his caramel glory, I loved him. But he had doubts. I think he felt I would prefer a darker-hued man. I do not think I've ever made him feel that way. With the exception of me one day telling him: "Mother seems surprised at me dating someone of your complexion." I had not meant it to come across the way it did, but that was exactly how it came out. And since then,

David has been trying to prove his blackness to me.

To a degree, David was similar to Father. There was a quiet arrogance and a spoonful of self-assuredness about him. They both had a way of making you feel tall when acknowledging you. Their eyes did not glaze over you, nor did their mouths frown when saying "hello". They held your gaze, their beautiful eyes saying "I see you". And perhaps that was why a fleet of beautiful beings bowed at their whim. Mother and I included.

But David was not pure like Dad. No, his blackness was diluted and to some extent in his mind flawed. We seldom discussed it, but it was there. The elephant in the room.

Sometimes I wondered if he overcompensated for not being a full-bodied black human. "My father is so black..." he'd say, forgetting to add that this father he so spoke of was his stepfather and that his biological father was white as snow. Perhaps it was the way I sang praises about my black father that turned him against himself, publicly claiming, "I am black," though he was grey, a mixture of black and white. Perhaps he wanted to emulate the old man and be my champion. He would mention his own father being in the riots of '81. But he always forgot to mention that he was merely an observer. Never getting his hands dirty, a branded diplomat. Unlike my father who was a rascal and championed the frustrations of a people. The irony being it was his father who was a Brixton native while mine came down from Hampstead Heath. He was quick to state: "I'm a doctor" when I said Father was a consultant. And when he too became a consultant, he asserted, "I'm following the path of Alexander." Growing up, he was neither proud of his blackness nor his whiteness. Apathy and indifference were applied when it came to both. But my dad espoused and stoked the flames of black supremacy in him. And when I said, "I prefer my men one hundred per cent black," it made him more eager to hide himself. But what he did not know was that I loved all of him in all its binary elements. He did not need to split himself in two for me. I preferred him as two whole halves. I told him: "I love you as you are." He would say "thank you", then smile as if my words lacked sincerity.

I recalled the first and only time I said to him without malice during a heated conversation: "You are not black enough, David King."

He looked at me as if I had cursed his name. And I looked away as though I had. My words were a sharpened blade and I knew they had cut him ... deep. His cheeks flushed crimson. He tried to smile off the redness of the beating that my words had inflicted on him. But the half-white side of him would not allow him to. He rubbed his cheek. Perhaps an attempt to remove the colour from it, but the blood-stained mark stayed steadfast and defiant as if to say *You cannot disown me, David. Not today. Today you must claim me the same way you claim the black part of you.*

He sighed heavily. I felt bad. I had not meant to offend him. Who was I to say if he was black or not? If he felt he was black because his stepfather was black, then so be it. It was not as if he was completely adopting an identity that he was not already.

I had said something sacred yet profane.

His pride was broken. He was a black man and I had shamelessly come and reminded him of his whiteness. The ostracised part of him. The part he had exiled. The part he did not want to relate to.

I had opened a can of worms and they were crawling all over everything, including my conscience.

He appeared mortally wounded and in need of a coup de grâce. "I'm sorry I did not mean it like that, David," I reached out my hand to his. He slithered away.

"Don't touch me, Bridge," he sighed, then looked me in the eye. "Please don't."

Needless to say, I had never questioned his blackness since then. My son's father, though mixed, was as black as they came.

26

MONDAY, MARCH 23

It was 6.05 in the evening. I had fallen asleep with images of my bright star Tariq floating in my subconscious. I only believed in our realm, yet his incessant appearances in my dream world begged me to ask myself why? Since I had seen the professor the night before, it was as if my cousin was restless inside the realm he occupied in my dreams.

When I woke up, my body was drenched in sweat.

After taking a brief shower, I opened my emails whose annoying pings had found their way into my dream.

There was an email from the DfE and one from my university. Neither bore any good news. My course was still terminated. I had made a conscious decision after Wednesday to try to not think about the conundrum I was in. I was willing to occupy myself with everything and anything as long as it did not include discussing my predicament. I needed to keep myself from falling into a pit of self-pity. White conversations about black may have been a dark topic. But at least they kept my mind removed from the fact that my studies and career prospects were non-existent at the time.

Underneath the emails from the DfE and my university was an email from the principal.

I was not sure how I found myself in the stately home of Principal Greaves. I assume he pressed the letter W, my last name appeared and before he could press the recall button, the email invite he had intended for others had been sent to my inbox.

Initially, I did not want to go. However, I felt obliged since he was the boss but, even more so, a part of me wanted to enter the crypt he called home.

The pale dimly lit faces of Principal Greaves, Caroline, Peter, and a fleet of beige-faced academics ushered me in. There was no one there of my kind, even though Raheem was to arrive later on. An ominous feeling drew a rugged croak from my throat.

"Good evening," I mustered. Some said "evening" back and the principal grunted as he watched me - hawk-eyed.

I was enticed by the urge to cower beneath his gaze, but my will refused.

He was called the vampire. Supposedly, it had been started as a joke by one of the macho male teachers in the school a while back, long before I had even digested the idea of being an educator. Needless to say, that teacher's macho-ness was crushed to smithereens by the time the principal got wind of his new alias, and he was swiftly relieved of his Head of Physical Education position and permanently exiled from the school.

He had gone, but he had left a stain, one that had an odour, a smell that the principal could not get rid of.

Vampire!

The word possessed a scent to it. One which could not be conclusively ascertained. Regardless, it smelled thick, fiery, and suffocating.

He did indeed resemble a vampire if the depictions of them are true; pale and bloodless, with green and purple veins writhing and slithering beneath his skin. I remember he once cracked a smile and I thought his face might break into a thousand pieces. Hearing him laugh was a rare occurrence - like seeing a blood moon. I had never heard it before, except once, and it sounded like a hyena eating a warthog alive. It was blood-curdling. Nonetheless, there was music and poeticism to it. Odd, I thought, yet intriguing to the extent that I was forced to laugh along with him.

"Banishing studies and pupils from the classroom is an egregious violation of human rights," moaned the principal to no one in particular.

In an attempt to gain the principal's attention and approval, my mentor added, "Actionable policies which disproportionately affect the majority are not just diagnoses."

He, Greaves did not respond, much to her disappointment. Standing up, this time to address the room, the principal said, "We need less rhetoric and more action. Since the government is incapable of the latter and unwilling to break the impasse, I, Thomas Greaves will champion it. I will not kick the ball into the long grass. I will score a goal. Which is why my school, Lady Liberty High, will remain open." A hint of craziness trickled through his voice. He spoke like a mad professor, hands flailing, spit flying and eyes bulging as if venom had built up inside.

The entire room stared at him. A little perplexed perhaps.

I wondered what Tariq would think of Greaves if he were still alive. I always wondered what he'd think of the people I have encountered in my life since his passing, especially Professor Wylde. What would he think of the mad professor?

"And how will you do that, sir?" asked Peter who was not pervy that day, head low and eyes lower to offer reverence to the principal.

Greaves gave a snort, bored his eyes into Peter as if

he were a peasant in his home and, slightly above a whisper, said, "Watch and see," while Peter recoiled into the sofa as if a serpent were slithering towards him.

I giggled quietly. Raheem the only other body of my shade who was now present cut his eyes at me, as if to say, "Stop embarrassing us." I threw him a dirty look and he shook his head in disgust and turned away from me.

"Prick," I muttered.

With the principal, there was an eagerness for people to out-laugh each other at his dry sardonic humour or to say "yes, you're absolutely right," louder than the other person. I was the only one who mustered a wry smile and neither agreed nor disagreed with him.

The preamble of his speech was that the virus was not to conquer our educational liberty. The only idea of his I steadfastly agreed with.

Everyone in the room was either pale beige, rose-tinted ivory, or fair olive, with the exception of Raheem who was golden umber and me, black, since I hate the term brown skin.

The TV was on, but it was muted, and rightfully so.

I was sitting among an elite fleet of academics. High-achieving members of society with Masters and PHDs among the extensive list of accolades they carried alongside their names. They unravelled the most profound puzzles as if it were child's play and spoke about the Socratic dialogues in Plato's Republic as if it were a book about the ABC. I sat, admiring them, listening, and taking in knowledge, my eyes still glued to the TV which was showing a riot about race relations in the United States. As per usual.

The principal and cohorts of Liberty High educators continued to speak ... That was when the thought weighed down on me like an albatross. *Do not say it,* the sane or perhaps insane part of me begged. But I was always the type to go against my mind and follow my heart. I could not hear the TV but the anger coming from the protesters was deafening. They were protesting injustices faced by black bodies even in the face of a pandemic and looming lockdown.

"Being black in some countries, most especially America, should be listed on *A Million Ways to Die in the West*! Don't you think?" I said my eyes removing themselves from the TV and landing on everyone in the room.

The principal dropped his cigar, starting a slow fire which quietly cackled as the plush rug began to burn. Caroline dropped her glass, bloodying the white carpet with red wine and almost extinguishing the cigar. Melanie slowly bowed her head to escape my glare, and Peter the perv scoffed, at a loss for words. Raheem was indifferent.

I suddenly felt like a lone lioness surrounded by a pack of hyenas. In that room with all those blue and green and hazel eyes watching me, I felt like the only black girl in the world. I gently swallowed with trepidation and excitement, the way a moth would before the flames consumed it.

The principal bent and picked the cigar off the rug, stamping out the fire as if in an exorcism.

He sighed deeply, "I think I need more whisky." The liquid splattered inside the short glass as he poured it irrepressibly and irresponsibly. Everyone in the room watched him. I knew I had asked a question that plunged them into uncharted territory.

White people knew about racism, but they did not like talking about it, especially with black people.

The principal cleared his throat and his Adam's

apple snaked as he swallowed saliva down his throat.

I'm sure he now wished Caroline had never implored him to invite me.

His eyes darted to the TV and stayed there for a while. "America is a shithole country," he scoffed, his index finger pushing his spectacles firmly on his nose, "but some of these," he looked around as if he were literally trying to grasp the word.

"Black people," I offered.

He sighed, "Yes. Some of these black people do not make it easy on themselves."

"Bullshit," chimed in Peter, beating me to it.

"Peter this has nothing to do with you," the principal hissed like Voldemort.

"Why? Because I am not black?" snapped Peter. "I may not be black, but I am human, and I agree that black lives matter." He spoke, fist in the air while he stared at the muted TV that roared with angry faces of all shades calling for the heads of the officers who killed an innocent black man in broad daylight. "Look at that," he jeered, "just look at it." The principal was forced to look at the video of the white police officer kneeling on the neck of the black civilian as the subtitles: "Please let me stand, I cannot breathe" appeared on the screen - an eerie echo of Eric Garner's last declaration before he too was murdered by a white officer of the law.

"Do you think they would do the same as they did to that black man to a 37-year-old white man in downtown Manhattan? Should value on life be placed on one's geographical location and race? No! because being black is an external as well as internal warfare."

Peter was right. This was not the first or second or third, nor would it be the last time you'd see a black body being executed in the name of *I was afraid for my life,* or *I thought he had a weapon.* "Tell me how that is fair? It is an all-out assault from all sides, and it is ripping us of valuable lives."

I decided to temporarily remove the perv from Peter's name. "Continue," I coaxed as his white contemporaries alongside Raheem watched him with suppressed rage.

"There is systemic racism in institutions. For example, I get a free Uber to school, matter of fact we all do. Guess who doesn't?"

I looked around as if there was another black person in the room. But there wasn't. Only me, since Raheem was evidently a coconut.

"You," Peter pointed, "it's you, Bridget White. You're the only one who takes the train to school." I laughed nervously. I wasn't sure if I was deeply hurt or offended.

"Why would you do that?" I murmured, eyes settling on the principal.

"Because you are young and vibrant and full of life. Uber is for us old lazy folks."

"But I have a kid and I wake up extra early to get the train ... you bloody don't!" I screamed. My breathing became frantic.

I was fuming.

How dare he?

"How dare you?" I hissed through gritted teeth. "I bust my arse each day to make it on time, and be there for you even though no one wants to send their kids to this godforsaken school of yours." I got up, and I did not care if I was the poster girl for 'angry black female'. That piece of shit principal was going to hear what I had to say. "So, you leave me more disadvantaged than people who are already more advantaged than I am because black people are health freaks, right?"

The principal stood up to argue his point, but he had no leg to stand on, so he sat back down.

The principal went red. Shame consumed him. "I am sorry," he whispered, "I was wrong." The apology was a foreign sound to my ears. Was he, Greaves, apologising to me?

He was, and this act of acknowledgement on his part pacified me and made me see him in a different light. A man capable of admitting his wrongs. Something I did not expect, but still cherished.

"Thank you, sir," I said. And for a brief period, we shared a moment. I did not know what it was, but it felt good.

Before I could forget, I added, "One last thing. I would be just as impassioned and raging if it were black police killing white men like flies ... So, if you're my white friend or colleague and stay quiet during my oppression, do not say 'hi' to me in the corridor at school..."

Everyone started. "It's gravely wrong ... disgusting ... inhumane."

I guess they did like saying "hi" to me in the corridor after all. Even Greaves, who never spoke to me in the corridor, agreed.

Tired out from the talk of black and white, I decided to take a lone tour through the Greaves estate. There were no kids adorning the walls. No grandkids. Just photos of the dead and dying. I wondered if that's how my life would have turned out if I'd never had Winner.

The principal's home oozed wealth. The paintings alone were a gold mine. I felt as if I was stepping into a different world. The kind of world where money did not shout. It simply said "hi". The principal's house demanded that you respect the owner. There was no obnoxious pretentiousness. The house reeked of old money, of the British upper class. I felt as if I was back in time among the aristocracy. There was a top level where we weren't allowed to go, and I knew for a fact that's where his catacomb was. The crypt where he neatly laid in his coffin to sleep at night.

As conversations sprang up intermittently throughout the night, I realised that for the most part, I wouldn't say Greaves was wrong. But he wasn't totally right either. Could that be possible?

I did not find all of his views reprehensible. He was, as we all were, entitled to an opinion. The principal was not well-informed when it came to the colour black. His representation of black people was greyish.

When I returned to the vast drawing room, the conversation was still flowing on the spectrum of race. It was funny, but for the briefest of moments, the principal came across as blacker than I was. He was impassioned, filled with conviction, and unafraid to speak his mind. All of a sudden, I felt enlightened by him.

Smiling at the principal, and without an ounce of malice, I unwittingly said,

"You are a black woman!"

The entire room stopped. The principal's face splintered into sixty shades of crimson. For a moment, my words pacified his tongue, blunting its blade and cancelling its sharpness. The occupants in the room, including myself, were temporarily dumbfounded. For the weight of my words had not struck me. I had been thinking them in my head, yet somehow, they had been said out loud.

I was not sure if it was the word 'black' or 'woman' that triggered the principal to go silent or whether it was both. But a part of me secretly enjoyed the repulsiveness he felt at my remark. The room drummed with silence, so I felt it my duty to elaborate on my supposed offensive statement. Surely a man with the calibre of intelligence that the principal possessed knew what I meant. Right? However, you can never be sure with his kind, or people for that matter.

Elaborating on my statement, I said, "You never back down. You stand for what you believe. Even when we hurl missiles your way, you are unmovable, like the object that's in the way of an unstoppable force..." I paused. A soft smile touched his lips. "All traits of the black woman." I felt the need to insert. "The black woman would rather be seen as the villain than the victim. And that is a great attribute in life, regardless of what popular belief would have you believe." His head nodded with approval as I edged closer to him, my hand almost taking his in mine, yet resisting at the final moment. "You are not an aggressor who then plays victim, changing your tone when the heat starts to choke you. You stay in the kitchen and either you or the fire will burn," I concluded.

His jaw tightened. His eyes hardened and my heart withered as if an active wind was slamming against it. He smiled. Almost softly, but not quite, and slowly whispered, "I guess I am a black woman." His ponderous eyes fell on the room with inconspicuous acceptance.

It was at that moment that I knew I fancied the principal. Not in the romantic sense but in a sense of admiration. He was who he was. A man of virtue and principles and views that I did not agree with but could grow to respect.

An opaque silence dragged itself around the room, heavy with darkness. My face cracked ... a smile appeared

... then a laugh. And before I knew it, the room was translucent with laughter. "In that regard, I guess I too am a black woman," added Catherine and one or two other white bodies.

For the first time, I felt some sort of kinship with the principal and his kinfolk.

He was, after all, human!

27

I had been away from the group for over half an hour. My departure was due to David's call, in which we spoke about our son, the professor, and ultimately Tariq. I told him I had dreamt of Tariq incessantly. He had told me not to worry. Perhaps there was something I was to find out about my bright star soon.

Upon my return, Catherine my mentor was in a heated conversation with the group about Arabs and North Africans.

Mr Suleman the religious education teacher and ever-quiet and gracious North African from Algeria, who must have arrived while I was on the phone, tried to chime in. Nonetheless, Catherine like rain blotting out the sunshine on a summer's day piped up, "Forgive my interruption," she snorted sarcastically, "I'm pretty sure you're not even a real African." She stopped, the gravity in the room disintegrating as we all felt suspended by her bold and sweeping statement. "Your people don't even like the real Africans, they consider themselves Arabs at best and North Africans at worst."

Mr Suleman was speechless as if what Catherine had said was true. I looked at him with disdain in my eyes while he lowered his head in what I could only describe as indifference.

After some minutes, with the conversation having flown left, right, and centre, Mr Suleman located a rebuttal in his head. Anger had been brewing within him about Catherine's remark. "As a matter of fact, I am African, Kate," he said, refusing to say her full name. There was so much conviction in his voice, one would have assumed he had been waiting all his life to make such a statement.

We all looked at him, perplexed. "Who are you to tell me what I am?" He pointed, his finger landing on her like an accusation. "On my job application I ticked the box that said African." He felt the need to enlighten her. "When my students ask 'are you from the Mediterranean', I proudly correct them by saying I am African. So don't you dare tell me that I am not African."

For the briefest of moments, I was proud of his bravado. However, Catherine was a lioness and she was not about to rest until she got her kill.

Her canines were out. She was ready for blood.

"Would you marry a black African woman?" Catherine cut in, her question taking the entire room by surprise. Hassan Suleman coughed then laughed. An obvious deflection, I thought.

I took a long sip of my wine then sighed. *Boy, oh boy,* said the voice in my head.

"Why would you ask me such a thing?"

"Why won't you answer?" We all waited.

Seemingly at a loss for an answer, Hassan snapped: "I am not going to sit here and be disrespected by a woman."

"The only person with their knickers in a twist is you." And there we had it. Catherine was also a black woman and I liked her even more.

However, she was not yet done, the kill was too sweet and she'd be damned if she offered Hassan a coup de grâce. "Even now Libya is practising slavery. And guess who they're enslaving,"

"The true Africans?" I offered.

"Yes."

Feeling the incessant urge to defend his people or perhaps himself, Hassan interjected, "Did you know we supported our brothers in the 70s and even had parties celebrating our continent?"

"Stop talking about past pseudo-glories," snapped Catherine.

"Why? I don't hear white people refrain from talking about past glories. You people are even proud of your colonial past. So let me be happy about African unity. Even if it is in the past."

"Well it appears you did not, or could not, comprehend my statement."

"Which was?" His eyes shot poisoned arrows in her direction.

"Are black Africans enslaved or not in Arab countries?"

Hassan Suleman refused to answer.

Catherine and the entire room had our answer.

That night, the more time I spent with the principal, the more my admiration for him planted its seed. The principal wasn't necessarily formidable in his physicality - he was as bony as a twig - though his face might give the devil a fright on a cold dark Monday night. It was his intellect that made him frightening. The same intellect men like Heidegger and Hume possessed. Nevertheless, unlike the latter, he was not an overt nor closeted racist. Just a white man misinformed about the black man. I know, a contradiction since he was a well-informed man academically. But you read academics. You do not read black history. Especially not the one written by white men.

* * * *

Raheem, whom I had rejected when he asked me out on a date after I first started at Liberty High, kept flinging dirty looks my way whenever our eyes met by chance. *What a fool,* I thought. Perhaps he was lingering in the crevices of my mind because he seemed to have heard me think him a fool.

He wanted to say something. He was going to say something. I felt it.

He closed his eyes for a moment. Perhaps contemplating, deliberating on what his words were to be. Lips pressed into thin brown lines; he sniffed like a bloodhound. There was madness in him. A green vein popped from within his skull and lay, slithering inside the skin of his forehead vying to break through and spit poison at me. Fortunately, he managed to keep it contained, even if just for a moment.

Suddenly the tone in the room changed. The pale bodies in the room watched us with feverish excitement. I guess black-on-black violence was, after all, entertaining.

There was fiery contempt in his bludgeoning gaze. He smiled, a sneer. And though I did not wish to admit it, I was slightly fearful. I was in no mood to engage in warfare with my skin folk. But as the saying goes, not all skin folk are kin folk.

His head was cocked like a gun, and when he began to speak, I felt the bullets hit me in the chest. Bang, bang, bang, they sang.

Why are most black women single mothers..." his eyes paced up and down my face, "like you Bridget?"

His words were an eyesore like the tower of Grenfell, before and after.

The principal, for lack of a better reaction to Raheem's assault on me, grunted. Caroline and Peter sighed ... heavily. Hassan applied ennui.

He was toying with me, dangling a bone in front of me. I should have bit off the hand that dangled the bone. His words, though not bearing personal significance to me as David was actively involved in Winner's life, stung on behalf of all the single black mothers. However, the pain felt acute, more so because of the fact that Raheem looked like me.

For a moment my hand toyed with my braids, then managing a smirk, I replied, "Firstly, my dear Raheem, I am not a single mother, my son's black father is diligently active in his life. Something I cannot say for your father or your mother who raised you in that piss-smelling one-bedroom council flat ... Does she still live there?" I asked to add some pizzazz.

I know that it's said when they go low you go high. But fuck that, I was ready to get down and bloody dirty with this son of a bitch. Yes, I wanted all the smoke. Perhaps he was not aware but if it came to it, I was about that life!

Shuffling in his seat, it was clear I had unsettled him. He did not know that one of the other teachers had told me about his upbringing. Evidently, this was not something he wanted to be announced for all to hear.

He laughed wildly, this time unsettling me and, by the looks of it, everyone in the room.

"Why are you so aggressive? All I asked was a simple question, but your answer was so hostile and unwarranted. Don't be that angry black woman, Bridget." He said it with a wicked glint in his eyes. All eyes fell on me. I tried to soften my face, because at that moment I was truly angry. I wanted to speak but if I did all that would come out would be rage which was what Raheem wanted.

It was a disarming tactic. Telling a black woman, they

were aggressive. It forced them to begin shrinking themselves or lowering their voices for fear that they were perpetuating the negative black stereotype, especially in a room full of white people.

The principal, who I did not believe possessed an understanding of the nuances of what Raheem had just said, expelled a dry laugh. He was old, rich, male, and white. The most privileged group in the world. He did not know what the oppressed felt like. To some degree he was blinkered by privilege. Surely, he couldn't fathom the raging wildfires Raheem was violently igniting within me.

"Raheem..."

"Yes, sir," his head jumped to attention, excited to finally have his name uttered by the principal.

"In this room, as we are currently, what would you say the black man's magnum opus is?"

"Sorry, sir, I do not follow," he laughed sceptically, sensing the direction of the principal's sudden interest in him

"What you did just now ... tearing down the black woman, breaking her into such minute pieces she loses her confidence and voice; it's like a work of art ... don't you agree?"

Raheem exhaled shakily, scratched his head then lowered it. "That is not my magnum opus, sir..."

"Oh, but in this room, it is..." his voice boomed with ice-cold scorn. "Don't you agree?" he addressed the other occupants in the room, who all nodded their heads in unison. "Surely you must be ashamed. I would be if I were in a room of black people, and I began to tear down a white woman who wasn't even in the wrong."

"Of course, sir, but that's not my intention. My mother is black..." he stopped, realising how close it sounded to a non-black person saying *but I have black friends.*

Suddenly it struck Raheem that the white bodies in the room that he was trying to blend in with were not as anti-black as he was.

It was an odd pattern, but I had noticed that certain men like Tunde and Raheem only engaged with the notion that the black woman deserves reverence because the white man says so. Did the white man have such influence on certain black men?

"I am sorry Bridget. Please forgive me," he pleaded, all the white faces watching him in disdain.

"No, I do not!" I said, and happy faces in the room beamed at me. It was not my duty as a black woman to ease the ego of the black man to my own detriment. The two great black men in my life, David and Father, told me that a long time ago.

Needing a breather, I left for the garden. The breeze was cool; closing my eyes I took in its coolness.

"Are you alright," sounded a voice behind me.

"I am fine."

Standing beside me, the principal smiled - a genuine smile. Suddenly, all the hard, bigoted, and arrogant edges softened. His wrinkles had ironed out and even a little colour had painted itself on his face. And right there before my eyes, he transformed into a human. The dead grey of his eyes lit up like silver and his fangs retreated into his gums, revealing a bright clean set of veneers. "I like you, kiddo ... I must admit. It's refreshing to see a young girl..." my eyes glared at him, and he cleared his throat "... young woman stand up for what she believes in. You are by all accounts a tour de force, Bridget White. You are without a doubt the most impressive student teacher the school has ever had." I nodded my head and returned his smile. It was nice to see him come out of his crypt and bask in the light.

He was an impressive man himself. And for the next fifteen or so minutes we spoke about a plethora of things. The dexterity and virtuosity of how he turned black into white and good into bad was mind-bending. And every once in a while, he entertained me with his dry sardonic British humour which dripped off his tongue like stale beer.

With the principal there was an eagerness for everyone to impress him. I think he appreciated the fact that I wasn't so eager to do so.

The principal was a good man to his students and even me it seemed. I hadn't known who at the time, but on Wednesday, my last day of school, someone had left a bouquet of flowers and a handwritten card with a signature. It had read:

Bridget White, you are doing an impeccable job. Your path will surely be illuminated because you are a bright star!

The gesture had warmed my heart. And it was only now, in his home as his guest, that I knew it was the principal who had left me the gift.

He tackled period poverty by providing free tampons and pads for every girl in each toilet. On some days when his tight schedule permitted, he personally tutored the gifted and talented Years 10 and 11. He made personal calls to their home when he felt something might be wrong with a certain pupil, and because everyone feared him, if indeed there was something wrong, the parents or carers made sure they immediately rectified the problem.

By the end of the night, as I was about to leave, he pulled me in, hugged me then proceeded to kiss the back of my hand. Our eyes met. He smiled and for the first time I realised that the dark greyness of his eyes was more nuanced than I had ever cared to notice.

"Goodnight, Bridget."

"Goodnight, Principal Greaves."

He laughed.

"What?"

"It's just that–" he laughed heartily this time. "It's just that your Uber is outside."

My lips made contact with cheeks, the wrinkles on his flesh feeling like waves. "Thank you."

I did not know if I would see the principal again, since lockdown was to continue until after June, which was when my course ended. But if this was the last time, it was a perfect last time, I thought as I sat in the Uber heading home.

28

The Professor Returns

It had been five years since Matthew Wylde last stepped foot in England.

America had been playing cat and mouse with him. They had wanted to remove him from her bosom that same day at Harvard. However, the laws of the land and hundreds of thousands of dollars delayed his deportation. Five years later, however, Matthew had willingly offered himself up to be deported.

There were more important things to fight for, he had concluded. Things like Bridget White.

Since he had seen her at Tunde's, he could not remove her, consciously or subconsciously, from his being. He was a man who obsessed over things that piqued his interest. Bridget did more than that.

Matthew could not sleep. Dark images moved inside his head.

Those images belonged to Tariq White but mainly to Bridget White, and they refused to leave him, especially images of the latter. His body was soaked in sweat as though he had been chasing her in his dream.

He could not forget her beauty or her pain. Both haunted him, and he felt the inexplicable urge to see her.

He was not supposed to want her like he did. But yet, no matter how hard he tried, he could not erase her memory; those lips that were full like the moon, or eyes that seduced him the moment they fixed on him. He could not forget any of it.

He needed a cold shower. Perhaps the cold might wash away the warmth she brought to his being. Sluggishly, he removed himself from the bed and made his way to the bathroom. He turned the water to its coldest setting, but still it was not icy enough. However, it had to suffice. The cooling liquid crashed down his body, gently beating him. The water was meant to calm his lust, but it did the opposite. His manhood stood, erect like a pole. Unable to control his desire, his mind wandered to how it would feel if she were there, next to him, her nakedness accompanying his as the water flowed down their bodies. He wondered what it would mean to kiss her, touch, and hold her. He wanted to know what she'd feel like inside. Matthew imagined she'd feel soft, warm, and wet. He would slide every bit of desire inside her. His fingers, his tongue, and his manhood. He could hear her moans. Her pleas for mercy, for more, for him to never stop. He could hear it all. He wanted to feel it, just as much as he heard it, but reality would not allow him. So, he gave himself a few seconds as his manhood finally turned limp, admitting defeat, and going back to its natural state.

He would call her in the morning. He needed to tell her something.

He knew who had killed her cousin, Tariq White.

* * * *

Matthew had arrived in England two months before lockdown began. During that time, he had acquired a new job, a new car and a new house.

America thought that by banishing Professor Wylde, they would taint and ruin his reputation. They were wrong.

The professor only gained more notoriety upon his disgraced return to England. The English, always fancying the underdog, loved him. He was their hero. He did what their politicians could not do, and gave America the middle finger, and for that, the people warmed to him. Some, in very high places, however, were on the fence, angry at him, but couldn't publicly voice it.

The British took their political correctness very seriously. America did not give a fuck.

Prominent universities clamoured to hire him. Oxford, Cambridge, UCL, LSE, King's College, and the rest of the top ten wanted him. His presence at their already prestigious institutions would add even more credibility. Matthew Wylde had inadvertently become the most sought-after academic in the world, with the exception of America, that is.

Upon his return, at Heathrow the media clamoured to give the public a glimpse of the *Brilliantly Mad Professor* as quoted by *The Sun*. Dressed in stone-washed jeans with a red T-shirt and opaque shades covering his sleep-deprived eyes, he was given the reception of a rock star, as opposed to that of a national disgrace. He saw and heard the fanfare, but it had no effect on his soul. He might never admit it to himself, but he was slightly broken, not because the world had broken him, but because the invincibility that he'd always depended on had proven fallible.

* * * *

Entering a room inside Oxford University for a job interview, academics with eager faces stood up to greet him. "Such a pleasure to observe your presence, Professor," quipped the gathering of distinguished persons.

"The pleasure is all mine." he insisted as he took a seat on a sturdy oak chair. The room of distinguished men and a single woman watched him with excitement inked on their faces. They almost made him feel their glee.

"How are you?" asked the chancellor.

Matthew knew what he meant by that question. And the chancellor knew Matthew knew what he meant. Nonetheless, they were both aware that Matthew would not be answering that particular question that day. Instead, Matthew smiled and awaited the ensuing inquisition.

Those in the room watched him, a little bewildered perhaps. A wry smile appeared on the chancellor's face. "Pardon my insensitivity, Professor..."

"Nothing to be pardoned, sir," he cut in.

"Thank you," he added while Matthew nodded in acknowledgement. "What I meant to say is we," he gestured at the room, "are elated to have an academic of your stature, vigour, and unquestionable passion at our institution ... there is none comparable to you based on talent and achievements." His portly face beamed with appreciation.

"Your words are far too kind, Chancellor," Matthew joked as the entire room softly erupted in conservative laughter.

A few seconds later the chancellor added, "Nevertheless..." he paused, "we cannot bypass the recent inconsistencies that have marred your illustrious name."

Matthew knew this was coming. He did not think it would affect him. However, coming from the chancellor he felt a tad uneasy. He was not sure why, but he did.

The chancellor sensed his uneasiness, like a father would his child.

"We are not here to judge you, Professor, nor will we ever ... your father was a dear friend of mine, and it would be a grave folly if I were to judge his son."

His kind words eased the tension. Matthew smiled at him with gratitude.

"We want you here. As a matter of fact, it is imperative that we have you here at Oxford. All our alumni who preceded you were not individuals who necessarily followed convention. Which is why we know of them. Life remembers the radicals, the rebels, the innovators, the bad guys. Seldom do we remember the good guys." He smiled, his words like music to Matthew's ears. He continued, "We do not remember them because they were the best type of people. We remember them because they were the brave ones, and as we all know, fortune has always favoured the brave. And you are brave, Matthew. Just like Harold your father." His grey eyes grew giddy as if Matthew were Harold, the chancellor's old friend, sitting in front of him. "I cannot express without bias how delighted I was to see you say things that no one else was brave or wise enough to say. You refused to stand on any fence. You take the kill, and that's the exact reason why we need you here!"

For a brief moment, the chancellor reminded Matthew of his father. The pride on his face, his kind words, were all akin to how his own father would speak to him.

All was going swimmingly until a grey-haired dragon-eyed man spoke. "All is well with what you've expressed, Chancellor. Professor Wylde is indeed one great singularity," he managed to smile without appreciation, "but we here at Oxford are much more reserved than our American counterpart, Harvard. Inflamed outbursts of personal or political insights aren't always a good thing," he sighed, clearly apprehensive of Matthew's impending or perhaps imposing presence at the university.

Silence filled the room. The man's words were not necessarily met with universal approval, yet one could not definitively state otherwise.

Seeking a way to diffuse the ominous energy in the

room, Matthew smirked. "I suppose you hated my speech then..."

The room croaked in uncertain and reserved laughter. "... Even so, I will not apologise for what I said, and what needed to be heard by all, not just some. America was regressing, and the world along with it by allowing such barbarism to occur. I needed to say something. It was imperative I did so," uttered Matthew indignantly, the elder gentleman lowering his head in either shame, indifference, or annoyance.

"In the Oval Office, they remain tight-lipped. The ones leading the race for the White House are beyond incompetent, and yet still no one found it necessary to intervene ... they should thank me," fumed Matthew. "I made America great again. I made them look inside themselves. I made them question not just others but themselves, and that was something they needed to do," he insisted, slamming the table.

"They don't see my passion nor understand what I'm trying to say..."

Interrupting, the chancellor raised his voice, "But we do, Professor. We at Oxford embrace your idiosyncrasy. Bursts of madness give rise to ingenuity, and you just so happen to be the inculcation of both." The chancellor smiled.

Gathering his decorum, Matthew asked, "What are you saying?"

"We are saying that you are the exact type of scholar and academic that this institution needs. You push the boundaries. You elevate our thinking. You reach our inner consciousness no matter how hard it tries to hide from us. We need you here, Professor." The league of gentlemen and the single female all agreed. The only dissident was the ancient blob of greyish flesh with dragon eyes.

"It is settled then?" asked the professor.

"It is," replied the chancellor.

29

TUESDAY, MARCH 24

I had not had a good night's sleep since Wednesday the 18th. It was now Tuesday the 24th. Six days since doomsday.

Either way, there was no rest for the wicked, or good, as I'd like to think in my case.

The words "angry black woman" by Raheem zoomed inside my head, while the principal's kindness jolted me from the seat of apathy I had been sitting in.

Last night had indeed been an odd night in every way possible, I thought, removing my person from inside the duvet. Body aching from lack of sleep, I fell back down on the bed, my hand searching for the TV remote.

Found it. The morning news came on. I muted it. It was literally the same thing every day.

Virus, virus! Plague, plague. Lockdown, lockdown!

An hour or so later I woke up from a sleep I wasn't aware I had fallen into.

My phone was ringing. The number was not withheld; however, it was unknown.

Cautiously I answered, "Hello"

"Good morning, Bridget."

The professor.

My assumption was that it was Tunde who had given him my number, since David made sure all his friends had my number in case something ever happened to him.

"Hi."

"Hey," he laughed. "Can I see you, please? There is something I need to tell you."

Could it be the truth he had promised? I wondered.

30

The past few days had been so hectic I had completely forgotten it was my best friend Alison's birthday.

It wasn't until Uncle, her father, messaged me:

Surprise birthday party for Alison Yemi Johnson.

Starts at 12.

See you there, Bridget. X.

The day before, on the 23rd, the Prime Minister and his cohorts at 8.30 pm had imposed a stay-at-home order effective immediately (which most of us did not follow until it was legally enforced on Thursday the 26th).

Oh, shit, I had thought, wondering how I could get a last-minute present now that non-essential stores were closed. No Chanel, Hermes, or Louis Vuitton for me to pop into and buy her a gift.

Voila! a bottle of vintage Dom Perignon that Father had gifted me when I began my initial teacher training sat in my kitchen. The bottle was still in its finely curated box, so I took it, placed it on the table and took out one of the spare birthday cards I always have and wrote a sentimental note for my bestie.

Calling my dad, I thanked him for saving me from the wrath of going giftless to an Alison party.

"Anything for you, princess," laughed Father.

The weather outside was glorious so a baby-blue short suit with trainers it was. I would put on my heels when I arrived.

In the taxi, I thought about the many stages of life that Alison and I had gone through.

* * * *

I loved Alison like I loved my mum. Granted if both were drowning, I would save my mum without hesitation. But I loved Alison, nonetheless.

She and I had first met at school. I was seven, she was eight. Standing in the vast corridor of the school's first floor flanked by light-beige bodies, I noticed her beautiful blackness. Her soft curly afro was wild yet tamed. She looked like art, like someone Michelangelo would have painted. Her skin was deep copper accentuated with gold highlights.

The sides of her lips curled almost imperceptibly as she walked towards me. I looked around to see if she could've been looking at someone else. She wasn't.

"Follow me." She took my hand as we ran giggling through the corridors.

Standing before a painting, she pointed. "Do you know who that is?" I shook my head. "That's my father," she said with great pride.

"Wow," I murmured.

"Yes, wow indeed," she replied. "He basically owns this school, which means I basically own the school also, and now that you're my best friend, you can kind of own the school too."

"Thanks."

"You're welcome. My name is Alison," she said, hugging me.

"I'm Bridget, but you can call me Bridge."

"Bridge and Alison, besties for life."

* * * *

Although Alison was black, she had privilege. It was the kind of privilege that surpassed white privilege. Wealth, plus an obscene amount of it at that, was what made Alison, most of the time, oblivious to the fact that she was still black. She believed in the concept that money buys respect, and for what it's worth, it did. She did not like certain white people, especially some white women. Yet she liked white men. She was able to compartmentalise her emotions the same way white women who loved black men yet despised black women did.

According to Alison, however, unlike black men who date white women because of their inferiority complex, Alison only dated white men because they were mainly the ones on her level.

Alison was an oddball. She liked white men, but she loved blackness. So much so that if you weren't me or her family or her friends, you might label her a pseudo-racist ... sometimes.

Alison was indeed multi-faceted and multi-talented.

She ran a charity in Nigeria with her father's money and sent money to help improve the lives of some orphans by paying for school, home, and entertainment. Some might assume she did it due to an excess of money. However, the way she spoke of those kids I knew she did it out of love and because they were after all "my people" as she'd say.

Growing up and even now, it was Alison who made modern-day Africa come alive for me. Granted, Mother and Father spoke of the greatness of African kings and queens and their vast heritage. But our greatness always seemed dead and buried. Alison dug up the artefacts, polished them, and presented them in blinding proportions to not only me but everyone she came across. Lagos and Abuja were a metropolis for the filthy rich. The prices of real estate and cost of living were on a par with Mayfair or Knightsbridge. Money rained down on its inhabitants and the pictures she showed, which the media would never publish, were even better than her explanations of all the beautiful places she had encountered within the continent. It was she who painted inside the blank and black canvas of the Africa that my formal education had drawn in my head.

She told me about the men who had been ordained by our ancestors and given the spirit of fortification. Men whose flesh neither bullets nor knives could penetrate. Men who called upon rain like their infant children and it ran from the heavens with giddiness down to them. She told me about the Kamajors in the Mende provinces of Sierra Leone, who appeared and disappeared and reappeared like premonitions as a means of evading and taunting their enemies.

At first, I did not believe her. Then as the years grew and I went from a teen to an adult, my beliefs began to come into their own. If I could believe the spirits in the white man's books, then why couldn't I believe in my ancestors' spirituality? Was divinity only exclusive to the Caucasian or Arab? Surely not. After all, it was only an African monarch, Osei Tutu, whose throne fell like manna from the heavens to him. Neither Alfred, Alexander, David, Herod, Genghis, Catherine of Russia, Constantine, Elizabeth II nor any of their contemporaries were offered such grace. Osei Tutu was the only one the heavenly bodies deemed sovereign enough to offer a tangible gift made of that all-important commodity, gold. If kings were indeed ordained by God, then surely God favoured a black king the most. This fact, according to Alison, meant that African spirituality could not be all bad. It must be mainly good. She made me see African spirituality as sacred never profane as we have been taught to see by our own kind, who were taught by those opposite to them.

* * * *

"We're here!"

The driver's exclamation removed me from memory lane.

"Thank you," I smiled, touching the contactless card reader as we were no longer allowed to pay with cash for fear of spreading the virus.

The private lift made of glass, so you could see all of Canary Wharf, zoomed me skyward to the penthouse floor.

As the doors opened, I was greeted by a handsome young waiter in a tuxedo, "Champagne?" he asked with a smile.

"Don't mind if I do." He placed a champagne flute in my hand, before leading me to the main doors which opened to reveal the interior of the ultimate floor of this 39-storey skyscraper.

"Ah, my daughter." Alison's father swaggered towards me.

"Uncle," we hugged.

"You grow beautiful more and more each day," he smiled, holding me back to assess my face, then pulling me back in for an extra hug. "Has that boy David asked for your hand in marriage yet?"

"Uncle," I hissed, his words causing both embarrassment and happiness.

"Well, has he?"

"Not yet."

"Tell him to hurry.

"I'll be sure to next time we meet," I laughed

"Good girl..."

Uncle was short in stature. Just tall enough to escape the four-foot brigade and land on five foot one. Nonetheless, he commanded so much respect and attention, the fact that he was so diminutive was an afterthought. Uncle, as he liked me to call him was almost as wide as he was tall. His eyes were quick and sharp like a samurai's sword; his nose broad and flat like the plains of the Sahara. There was an inconspicuous handsomeness about him, so much so that if you searched only for shallow beauty conventions you would completely miss it. His teeth which had been replaced by veneers were white with hints of ivory for the illusion of reality.

As we were talking about my "sister" as he refers to Alison, his wife Lola graced us with her presence. "Bridget, the beauty," she said, gently kissing my cheek.

"Aunty, you look magnificent, as usual." I returned her kiss.

Alison's mother was the polar opposite of her spouse. She was a mountain of a woman. One would assume, if there were talk of domestic violence, she would be the aggressor. Yet something told me Uncle was not a man to be tested. So, I was happy that such talk never existed. For the sake of Lola that is. Though she appeared physically formidable, she always seemed to shrink herself for the glory of Uncle. It was a magnificent ruse, the way she enshrouded herself in a cloak of mediocrity, when, in fact, she was beyond genius. Yet because of the confident nature of her husband, she presented herself otherwise.

The things we do for love, eh?

This was a peculiar fact but all four of our parents

have only been in the same room at the same time four or five times since Alison and I met eighteen years ago. Nevertheless, our parents loved us both as if they too were best friends with each other.

While Alison's parents and I engaged in small talk, the birthday girl finally made her entrance. All eyes fell on her. With a cheeky yet excited smile on her face, she walked up to us and softly cast her eyes down before her parents.

"Mummy, Daddy," she hugged and kissed them.

While I greeted my parents with a simple hello or a hug or a kiss, Alison had to bow down before them. An act of reverence that made me respect the humility of it all. Alison was different from her usual self when it came to her parents. Her accent changed from proper English to a hint of a fake Nigerian accent. She was like a chameleon taking on both African and European quirks.

"Come, let's go say hello to my other friends," said Alison to me after kissing her parents goodbye.

Everyone in the room was beautiful. Even those that were aesthetically challenged. Money did indeed possess the magic to transform and polish dull things.

Africa's elite were on display, and I was thoroughly impressed. People assume it is those who have never had anything who like to boast. But the filthy rich also like to show off.

"My father just bought me a new Ferrari as if he forgot that the new Lamborghini just came out," complained one girl. "I had to fly first class instead of the PJ because my pilot was sick, can you believe it?" questioned a bald young man. It all made me laugh. First-world problems for the offspring of third-world citizens. What a life!

In one of the corners of the panoramic glass walls that surrounded the penthouse, Alison pointed out a thin, long-necked lady who was talking to a bulkier woman. The way Alison spoke about the long-necked lady, I felt like MI6, the FBI, Interpol, or the CIA might burst in at any moment. She was a fugitive. Her father was the exiled ex-president of one African country known for its diamonds.

"Hello, Amina."

"Hi, Alison." They hugged. "Happy birthday, you look so beautiful."

"Thank you. This is my friend, Bridge."

Amina nodded at me, then said, "You're not African, are you?"

I did not know how to answer such a question. I had always considered myself British. So, this was a fiendishly hard question that Amina posed. "I'm British..." I paused, nodding my head at no one in particular - I continued "However, I am very certain that my roots are planted deeply somewhere in Africa, Amina."

Neither pleased nor displeased with my answer, she replied, "Well good. So, I guess you agree that..." she stopped to accept a new glass of champagne from the waiter.

"Agree to what?" I asked, perhaps too eagerly, as I thought it was to do with my ancestry.

With one eyebrow raised, Amina drank a sip of champagne and said, "Do you agree that we should not take their vaccines? Let white bodies try them first. Let them try their own antibodies before us Africans, right?"

"Yes, right," I was eager to reply. For the first time I was seen as African by an African and it felt nice, warm, and comfortable to be classified as us rather than you.

"It's a pleasure to meet you, Amina" We quickly

hugged as I was led away by Alison to meet more of her friends. We walked past one of her friends who had a chihuahua. That rat-like dog that the rich somehow preferred. The friend was big and stocky, a physicality that made the dog look more like a rodent. "Happy birthday, beautiful," he said, kissing Alison before getting back into conversation with his girlfriend.

"Interesting friends you have," I teased, to which we both chuckled.

In the far corner to my right, the grand piano's keys were being succinctly played by a world-renowned pianist. The music was so crisp and clear, it sounded like a recording. "Wow, she's amazing," I said as we continued around the room.

In the distance stood a group of four. They were speaking so passionately, I could hear them from where I was. Two of them were Indians who claimed Kenyan and Ugandan heritage. Then a young white man who said he was African - as if he was African. But he was Dutch or at least his ancestors were. Then finally a Chinese man who said he was Nigerian. A Chinese Nigerian. *What an odd dichotomy,* I thought. Nonetheless, his nuanced accent possessed all the musings of a Nigerian studying at Oxford University.

These four were talking about the continent and its new rulers.

"... It seems you guys are our new masters," said one of the Indians to the Chinese guy who squinted his eyes a little at the statement.

He laughed without humour. "Does that mean the old masters like the Dutch right here are dead then?" he said, softly slapping the back of the white guy, who wasn't too happy about it.

"Bro, I am African; what are you talking about?"

“I guess he is the only African among us,” the Asian laughed at the Caucasian. “Anyway, Jan, if my people are the new colonialists, surely you must accept that yours are the old.”

The white guy pretended he hadn’t heard and allowed the statement to go over his head. Nonetheless, he did have this to say, “Aarush is correct. The Chinese are the new colonisers. They go to the motherland to do one thing and one thing only, pillage. They have ruined the sub-Saharan part of the continent and continue doing so. Believe it or not, China is America’s big brother when it comes to racism. Look at how they’re treating black people for a virus that’s called the chi...” he coughed, “I meant the coronavirus.” All four including the Chinese guy laughed. But he had a point. Blacks were being treated horribly for something they never started. Although the Chinese African tried to claim the kinfolk of his father as our allies, it was evident that during the pandemic they weren’t really our allies. Even so, I could not solely blame them, because the truth was, no one was our ally, sometimes not even ourselves.

Alison, intrigued by their conversation and feeling the urge to insert herself into it, went over. They all hugged and kissed her, showering her with compliments, which she deserved and gladly accepted.

“Talking politics are we boys?” she slid in impressively. “Good,” she said before they could answer. “Well let’s move from the continent to England ... You all voted Conservative, right?”

Heads nodded in agreement.

“Now, you proclaim yourselves Africans right, so is no one the slightest bit offended that there are no senior black MPs inside the party?”

“They have brown folks,” said one of the Indians.

"They're not black."

She was right. They were not. Not a single one. The Attorney General, Secretary of State, Chancellor of the Exchequer, all not black. It was as if they said we can go dark but not black.

"Listen," said the other Indian from Uganda who hadn't yet spoken, "I am aware that the Conservatives apply implicit bias to blacks. They prefer the Indians or the Pakistanis because they blindly see themselves closer to the white man than they actually are. Anyone in power will appoint those who suck up to him the most. In this case the black man doesn't ... his payment for such insubordination is not being included, even if it's for show." He stopped. Alison and I looked at each other. "Anyway, colour doesn't concern me, I am rich. So, frankly, I have nothing to complain about ... and I won't," he concluded, pleased with himself.

Feeling the urge to enlighten this African who did not care for the plight of Africans in the diaspora, I added my two cents. "How can you call yourself African if you do not care for the plight of the black man?"

"Are you talking to me?" he asked looking around perplexed as he downed his beer.

"There is only one African here who doesn't care for his darker-skinned brothers ... which is fine," I insisted before he could protest and say something like, *I have black friends.* "Going off what you said, my supposition is that your idea of the B in BAME isn't black but rather brown. And once they're filling that quota of appointing a brown body instead of black to the Conservative Party, us blacks don't really matter?"

"That's not what I meant. I love my black brothers the same way I love myself," he managed to say embarrassed.

"I'm sure you do." Sarcasm dripped in my voice.

Jan who felt like getting his feet wet in the conversation stated, "just because they put Black in front of BAME does not mean they're for us. It is just a façade to pacify us since we are so gullible." The word "us" sounded strange coming from him. Nonetheless, I agreed with his thinking.

"As my father said, it is the application rather than the intent of something that matters ... Black people aren't being applied in the upper echelons of politics the same way as our Minority and Ethnic partners are."

"Coincidence?" I asked.

"No! Institutionalised racism," replied Jan.

Wanting to go back to her party, Alison interrupted the entire conversation. "Guys, enough of race and politics, it's my birthday. Let's turn the fuck up!"

We were all happy to oblige as the pianist finished her set and some loud and vibrant hip-hop music consumed the room.

Hands went up in the air, heads bopped, and alcohol got consumed ... quite irresponsibly if I may add. The salivating aromas of jollof rice, fried rice, chicken, and other gloriously delicious foods mingled in the air with expensive eau de parfum and cologne.

Some footballers and a couple of musicians entered the room, and the atmosphere became that much more electric. Everyone was having a blast. Camilla was yet to arrive.

Ten minutes later, she and Lisa turned up. We hugged and had a brief conversation before I was stolen away by Alison ... again.

"There is someone here to see you!" she squealed with excitement that translated as tipsiness to me.

"Who?"

"Just wait and see, Bridge."

Standing in front of the glass wall, intently watching the world below was Joshua Garvey. I recognised his physicality, even from his back.

My heart skipped a beat. Placing my hands to my chest I buzzed with giddiness. *Oh my God,* I mouthed at Alison who was even giddier than I was. *I know,* she mouthed back before leaving me with the man she, me, and Camilla all fancied at one point in our lives, while at university.

I moved my hand towards him then pulled it back. I was so nervous that I almost turned around to leave.

"Bridget White," he breathed, his voice doing things to me. I should have known he could see my reflection in the glass. He turned around, bit his lip ever so softly, smiled then pulled me into an embrace that made my entire body hot.

"Have I missed you," he murmured in my ear, kissing my neck. His lips sent gentle tremors through me, which caused me to exhale softly.

"I've missed you too," I whispered as we untied ourselves from our embrace. I had not seen Josh in four years and in those four years, I sometimes wondered what life would have been like if Camilla had never been my friend and Josh happened to be my David instead.

"You look even more beautiful than I remember, Bridge."

I smiled shyly. "Do not be modest, because I know that you know your beauty is all-encompassing!" he asserted.

Taking my hand in his, he raised it then kissed it, gently. His lips were warm, his breath warmer still. My mouth parted a little from the sensation. I almost whimpered before looking away from the fire of lust that was brewing inside his chocolate-brown gaze.

"I still think about us, you know," he whispered. "Do you think about us, Bridge?"

What kind of question was that, I thought? I was with David, well, kind of.

"Yes, I do," I admitted, unable to lie since he was right next to me.

"I cannot seem to summon the same profound feelings of euphoria I felt with you that night inside my parent's greenhouse with anyone else..." he exhaled. "That night, the way we touched, kissed, and stared into each other's eyes have etched themselves indelibly into my psyche."

"What are you trying to say, Josh."

"I am saying that I think I am in love with you, Bridget White, and try as I may, I'm incapable of falling out of it with you."

His words fell on me like plush red rose petals. I felt naked as if he were touching me. His words were almost orgasm-inducing. I leaned in closer to him, our lips almost touching. His lips were incredibly inviting. I wanted to bite them before devouring them with my full red lips. The raging look of desperation in his stare told me he wanted me to do those exact same things. However, I did not. I could not. Instead, I said, "I'm sorry Josh, I have a boyfriend, his name is David and I think I'm still in love with him."

31

WEDNESDAY, MARCH 25

It was 5.02 pm. I was in a taxi to my parents.

Yesterday, I had fled Alison's party. It was imperative that I rushed from her penthouse because its four walls cocooned the person that is Joshua Garvey. Though I had told him I loved David, my heart refused to completely believe my words, deciding instead to play with the idea that perhaps I also had feelings for Josh. And from the way my heart pulsated whenever mine and Joshua's gazes met, I think it too may have believed there were still feelings there.

* * * *

In the taxi home from Alison's, I had called David. He was at work, valiantly fighting the virus. The NHS was in desperate need of medical professionals. And David, having only turned consultant a year and a half prior at such a young age was eager to prove his worth. He was very busy. However, for me, he was able to spare a few minutes.

"Hello, my love," he spoke through the mask of his hazmat suit. "I am so happy to hear your voice," he said. His voice sounded a little weary.

"What's wrong, baby?"

Sighing, he replied, "I just feel so overworked and overstretched today." He breathed heavily. "People are dying, baby," his voice ever so inconspicuously broke. A deep sadness for him struck me. It did not for a second escape me how rigorously David and his colleagues were working in hospitals across the country. I was in awe of his selflessness. David did not need to be on ground zero fighting to save lives. He could have simply stayed in his all-too-comfortable role as a consultant at a private hospital. But he did not. He had willingly volunteered his expertise to the NHS, joining their health professionals in the fight against the virus.

Nevertheless, for all his initial bravado and eagerness, I could not help but notice that the virus was at last starting to take its toll on him.

"I am so sorry, my love. Is there anything I can do to ease your day?"

"Love me, Bridget Celine White. All I ask is that you love me." And love him I did. So much so, that Joshua Garvey and any other man would always be an afterthought to David.

"With me knowing you love me, I can conquer every mountain. Even this one I'm currently facing."

"I love you with everything that makes me human, David King. I love you deeper than the oceans. I love you higher than the sky and I love you further than the galaxies," I said, wondering - since I loved him so much - if I should tell him about my encounter with Joshua at Alison's party.

"Thank you, Bridge. You are everything to me. My entire world."

I decided I needed to confess.

"I have something to tell you."

"What is it?"

"It's Joshua."

Silence drummed inside the phone. I had once told

David about Joshua. Then he had laughed and said the girls and I were silly to all like the same boy. Now there was no humour in his voice.

"What is it about him you wish to tell me?" The rational part of me said, do not tell him. However, my heart could not lie to the man I love.

"We almost kissed..."

That was all David needed to hear. Without warning, he told me he had to go, then he locked off the phone.

That night after work and after having got over his initial shock at my statement, he called me. He was upset, so much so, the call which should have been amicable turned into an argument, which meant he and I were no longer on speaking terms.

So much for telling the truth, Bridget.

* * * *

"Take a right, please," I told the driver.

Two minutes later, he said, "We are here." My hand pressed the card onto the contactless reader.

"Thank you." I got out. My mother and father were in the last week of their two-week annual leave. They were meant to have been on a cruise in the Caribbean. But the virus would not allow their already paid-for trip to go ahead. So, they had decided to stay at home in London instead.

My parent's driveway was decorated with two Range Rovers and a vintage Aston Martin that oozed with style - its sole purpose to oblige the old man's thirst for speed. Around the perimeters of the driveway were tall, beautiful plants that bloomed with vibrant luminosity.

The interior of my parents' home was prosperous. It oozed class and a quiet opulence which proclaimed the owners to be consultants. On the wall on the right hung my cheesy gift that read 'Consultants live here'. Father was a consultant surgeon and Mother a consultant psychiatrist. I tried not to let their success dictate or diminish me, but at times it was only human to feel like a disappointment.

While my eyes focused on Winner's, mine and Tariq's many photographs adorning the walls, my mother's soft and beautiful scent cascaded towards me. I had bought her some fancy perfume for Mother's Day. Like an angel, she floated down the stairs, grabbed my hand and squeezed it with both of hers. This show of affection unbalanced me ... just a little. I smiled.

"Good afternoon, darling," she said.

My lips made contact with her cheek, it was soft and smooth like velvet. "Good afternoon, Mother. Looking pristinely beautiful as per usual, you minx," I teased.

She blushed a little, placed a phantom strand of hair behind her ear and said, "Thank you, darling." Then she looked at me and whispered, "I love you," with all the sincerity in the world. I wasn't sure why, but my eyes moistened a little. Mother's love for me was at times mentioned en passant. Something along the lines of "Bridget knows I love her", not "I love you, Bridget". It was a phrase as opposed to a feeling. Yet this time it felt like an emotion; something real and tangible, something she felt for me (which I know she did, but sometimes it felt like she hid it due to me being somewhat of a disappointment). I pulled her in and hugged her. "I love you too," I said freely, without restraint or from fear that she would not say it back.

My focus fell on her face. The amount of beauty and near perfection Mother possessed was aggressive. Which was why, perhaps, she saw imperfections in others.

Mother was as dark as a night sky in the brightest of

summers or snow reflecting the sky in winter. Her blackness shone as if luminous beings and stars were playing in and around her skin. Her face was a romantic night, bright and round like the extra-terrestrial body of the moon. She was the most beautiful human my eyes have ever had the pleasure, and displeasure when I'm being compared to her, of observing.

Father always joked that "two beautiful beings cannot co-exist peacefully", which was why Mother and I sometimes bumped heads. Perhaps he was right.

Mother's eyes were bright and awake, sometimes too awake if you asked me, and her cheeks were plump. Black indeed did not crack when it came to her.

In the distance, Winner screeched in different tunes of toddler joy while Father engaged him by flipping him in the air, tickling him and pretending he was the Black Panther. I wanted to run into his arms and kiss Winner's chubby little cheeks. However, I allowed him to revel in the love of his grandfather some more while I made my way through the grand corridor.

Where Winner was playing by the translucent pink and white roses, a red-breasted European Robin flew by. It perched on the plumpest and softest pink rose and then busied itself with sweet sounds that sent a silky feeling through my ears. Winner pointed, "Grandpa!"

"Yes, baby, beautiful, isn't it?"

He nodded "uh huh" then ran after the bird boisterously, yelling, "Don't fly away, come back."

To my left, the words "Alexander White and Cecelia Blanc live here" were written on a canvas hung on the wall. It was ironic that my mother and father had the same last name. Mother's birth name is Blanc, Father's is White. Cecelia Blanc and Alexander White.

Mother and Father showed me that black love was not broken, it was not a struggle, nor was it a remnant of what we perceive white love to be. Black love was whole and electrifyingly pure like lightning.

Through the years, I watched my parents evolve into one another. I loved the philosophy of her practising the sacred art of black love with him.

On the table beneath the vintage mirror from Milan, Father's latest read, *Medical Apartheid* by Harriet A. Washington, lay inside its leather exterior. Next to it were some notes on his current project. Father - along with his contemporaries - was working on an anthology that described illnesses affecting those with black and brown skin that were not listed in the medical journals in circulation. And for such lack of information, black bodies were misdiagnosed or underdiagnosed, leading to senseless complications and deaths. The medical journals were filled with white bodies and white symptoms. That was what black and Asian doctors had to work with. They studied for the first eight years not on bodies that looked like theirs but like those of the white man.

Nevertheless, Father was fair. He did not blame the white man. After all, it was only white bodies that they knew. Nor did he blame the black man, because prestigious medical institutions like the ones he studied at did not teach the black man about his own body. All he could do was recount and rectify the issue.

Before finally making my way to the garden, I decided to take a sneak peek inside the library, for the smell, of course. That wonderful smell of leather, mahogany, and books. My parents' library was filled with leather-bound books and smelled of rich mahogany. Books on British Black Panthers. Books on prominent black Brits. Fred Hampton's Biography, first edition. Multiples books on Mary Seacole, who Mother deeply admired, Stokely Carmichael, Dr Harold Moody, John Edmonstone - teacher of Darwin. My mum, it seemed, detested teachers, yet she had bought a book on his life. Kwame Nkrumah, Ghana's first president. Daphne Steele, the first black Matron in the NHS. My dad had a book of which there were only three in the world that he got from an auction, the aptly titled *Persona Non Grata Activists*. All the names and partial histories of civil rights activists from both sides of the pond and across the world were in it.

Growing up, I did not know Britain's colonial history and the atrocities committed in her name. All I knew about were her glories and the lies that she crossed the seven narrow seas to liberate a people that already lived in their own liberation. America took the blame for its big cousin. But it was she, Grand Britannia who was the queen of the slaves. I only learnt these facts from Father's expensive first and limited-edition books. What some of the books also taught me was that Britain at one point was indeed great. The sheer audacity of an island to rule the world is pretty impressive. In hindsight, it also showed that certain black leaders were lacking in the ingenuity that some of the Europeans had then. Some of my parents' books also showed me that some black people, when it came to white bodies, are so unbelieving of their own powers. Surely If the voodoo men of Benin can stop the rain from pouring from the heavens, then the kinfolk of those same men can change the worlds in which they lived. But I am not African, I am British, which is perhaps why I think like this. It was possible that the African was thinking of more important things than taking over the world (after all, man was not made to have dominion over other men), though I could not envision what was more important than that.

As I stepped back into the hallway, the bell rang.

It was David.

My heart stopped. Was he here because of Joshua? Did he wish to continue the argument at my parents' house? I felt delirious. He smiled then leaned forward and kissed me ... on the lips. "Bridge," he whispered beside my ear in that deep, tense voice of his.

Perhaps he had come to his senses and realised that I did not want anyone else besides him. His kiss on my lips alluded to this.

My eyes looked back and behind me was my mother beaming with delight.

"David, my darling," she squealed darting me a look that said: *Behave and be nice to him, Bridget.* I laughed quietly.

Mother made it appear as if it were a brief visit, where she had asked him to pass by and get a takeaway bowl and kiss his son. In reality, however, I felt she was playing matchmaker. Pulling Mother aside, I hissed, "Forgive me if this is an inopportune moment, but why was I not told beforehand that David was coming?"

"Because he called your father and me and told us he loves you and wishes to see you, as you weren't answering his calls because you had an argument. We told him to come over today since you were also going to be here." She shrugged with a cheeky grin.

My heart skipped with joy, shouting, *he loves me, he loves me.* Mother wanted me with a black man. And mostly, I wanted a black man too. Yet, there was David. Part oppressor, part oppressed. It sometimes intrigued me that with all mother's intellect, she still possessed biases. She felt the half-black was somehow unstable because of his duality.

Yes, initially my mother had not been keen on David. It was only when she realised that he brought stability into my somewhat unstable life that she developed a profound likeness for him. The icing on the cake that he was Winner's father made her love him.

Mother directed us to the kitchen.

Father was a lucky man. Not only was his wife beautiful and intelligent, but her hands were also blessed. Mother's food was unmatched by the Michelin chefs themselves.

David inhaled the food while my mother and I watched him hawk-eyed with tiny smirks imprinted around our mouths. "Enjoying the food, I see," I said, bringing the fork to a halt in front of his mouth.

Sensing our eyes, he stopped the fork before it could deliver the food into his mouth. "I'm eating too much, aren't I?" he chuckled, wiping his mouth with the back of his hand.

"Your father's calling, Bridge..." interrupted Mother before I could tell David that I loved the way he ate.

In the garden, my father, Alexander the Great, was sitting on the wicker settee. He motioned for me to come over. As I flew into his arms, he kissed me and showered me with praise. "Sit," he tapped the space next to him, his eyes all the while glued to David. "I will not wish you to capitulate, my love," Father smiled, winking as he did so. Which made me laugh. Because for all of his greatness, his winking, which he only reserved for me, made him appear cross-eyed. "Love is for you to experience and I..." he cleared his throat, his slightly dimpled cheek exposing itself. "Your mother and I regard David as a fine man for you to experience it with. Do not try to excavate the past with him. Sometimes you must leave the hurt buried for the joy to sprout. Do not be a double helix of hate and resentment my dear child. But rather of love and understanding. You love him. I see it in your eyes. He hurt you, I feel it in your spirit. But it is your eyes I see, and I can only judge by what I see."

I was lost for words. Father had a way of doing that. "You must not conceptualise love nor must you compartmentalise it. Because if or when you do, it becomes diluted – and a diluted love is no love at all," Father considered. "Look at me when I'm talking to you," he commanded in that soft but strong voice he reserved for when I was being insolent. My eyes widened till they were two full balls of vision. Father wrapped his fingers in between mine, pulled my hands up to his mouth and gently kissed the back of them.

"My duty and my allegiance will always be to you, which is why I want you to forgive David. Your eyes dance and shine like fireflies whenever his name is mentioned and your lips crack into a smile brighter than the sun and stars combined." He smiled. "I am no fool to love, my child, nor do I wish you to be."

With great fondness I recalled the ways David held my hands. Always with tenderness, even if the world had aggrieved him. He made certain his quarrels with the outside world never soured our sacred love.

So when David broke my heart, I thought I would die of grief. I thought my heart would rip itself open.

But the laws created before earth herself, had ensured that it would not be love that killed but, rather, hate.

And because I loved him and knew that he still loved me, my grief became incapable of killing me, though some nights I felt it would go against the rule of law and break me completely.

Back in my parents' kitchen as I watched David eating a second plate of my mother's food, the tsunami of hate and never-ending oceans of love I've always had for him all drowned me.

Warm liquid trickled down my face. At first his eyes did not see the abstract lines. But as soon as he realised what was happening, he pulled me close, kissed my forehead ever so softly and whispered, "If I have to spend eternity reaffirming my love for you, Bridget White," the tip of his finger lifted my chin so I stared up at him, "I will."

With all my heart I believed him, and it was at that moment I realised he was worthy of my forgiveness - 100 per cent of it.

Love sometimes was not meant to be straightforward.

"I am seeing someone, Father," I said as David walked over to my dad.

"Who?" he asked while I went over and placed a soft kiss on David's lips. "Your grandson's father." We all laughed.

With David, love always eclipsed hate, try as I might for it to be otherwise.

32

As night drew near, with David having gone home to rest, the lights came on. Soft jazz breezed through the air. The tantalising smell of champagne, the intoxicating aroma of cognac, the delicate scent of roses and the spiciness of cigars - because Uncle Khan refused to "completely give up smoking" - wafted through the atmosphere.

Father is an only child of an only child. So, my uncles by default were mostly men to whom I wasn't biologically related.

Sitting in the garden drinking cognac were my two favourite uncles - my most beloved of the two being Uncle Khan.

Uncle Unisa Ansuma, my second favourite, stood up and motioned me over. "Come here, darling," he said in that refined cross between an African intellectual and a Cambridge academic. I loved his accent. One that was not removed from its Africanness but had also adapted to parts of its Britishness.

"Hi, Uncle" I smiled curling under his embrace.

"Good afternoon, princess." He gently pinched my cheek.

Uncle Khan who had to finish his glass before addressing me, stood up. I flew into his arms. "There she is," he laughed as my weight unsettled his balance, "the most beautiful girl in the world."

"You flatter me too well," I said as he jokingly tried to lift me off the floor. "What have you been eating young lady?" he teased.

"Well, there is this special thing that we humans consume named food." I poked his small yet untoned belly. Uncle Unisa joined us in laughter.

A few moments later, Father stepped out and, like three little boys, they began sniggering. At what? I was unsure. However, it was so infectious I joined in.

They were the three musketeers and I for what it was worth was beyond elated to always be their fourth wheel. Though at times they dismissed me, listened to my point of view and refused to take it in or, worst of all, treated me like their child. Nevertheless, I loved their company. I learnt about the world in a million ways whenever they spoke. They reminded me of the Socratic trio of Aristotle, Plato, and Socrates.

Uncle Khan, like Father, was also a consultant and Uncle Unisa was Head of African Studies at Cambridge.

"Sit," they motioned to me in unison, Uncle Khan pushing the plush cushion out of the way.

In the middle of our seating area, glorious-smelling blood-red roses inside a transparent vase decorated the somewhat-bland wooden table which buzzed with the sound of a busy bee that Uncle Unisa swiftly shooed away.

"So..." Uncle Khan looked at Father, then at Uncle Unisa.

Oh, here we go, I scrunched up my face, knowing the direction in which his concerned voice was heading.

We watched one another, keenly, before he lifted his arms in a fake stretch. I watched him indifferently.

"Okay ... more drinks," he chuckled.

I laughed at their apprehensive faces. "Guys, I'm fine. Yes, my course has been indefinitely suspended but life carries on."

"This could be a blessing," interjected Uncle Khan with such swiftness the words nearly missed my ears. He looked away as I turned to him.

I let my eyes rest on him. I could sense his discomfort as they walked over him, stomping, and digging nails into him. "Alright, alright, stop looking at me like that. We love you and we don't want you wasting your life being a common-or-garden teacher."

"Speak for yourself, Jim," said Father, with Uncle Unisa nodding his head in agreement. Uncle's full name was Jamir Ahmed Khan. But he made sure no one ever called him that. His name was Jim or Jimmy to all who called him by his first name.

"Oh shush, Alex," he teased. Father was always incredibly well-prepared for verbal warfare with Uncle Khan. However, he allowed Jim to have this.

Father was great, yet he acted as if his greatness meant nothing to him. But it did. Father's greatness was a mountain which grew and remained steadfast in its greatness. Sometimes I felt guilty that it seemed I wasn't even trying to weave even a small thread of his greatness into my DNA. People probably thought my parents had adopted me given my career choice. And I was not stupid. I received all A's in my GCSEs and A-levels. Nor was I mentally incapacitated. So, I knew that the circles my parents moved in thought it odd that an exceptionally sane and intelligent individual like me would choose to teach ... and kids for that matter. Black upper-middle-class kids did not make decisions like mine. But upper-middle-class kids did not have a father like mine. A father who told me, "The wind is yours to bend and curve at your whim, not at mine."

While I was sitting with my elders, I could feel a piercing gaze. It was Uncle Khan's gaze. It felt omnipresent, taking in everything and anything about me.

"What worries you?" he questioned, his face gently frowning.

My mind contemplated an answer to the question. They all watched me impatiently.

I sighed. "I don't know," my shoulders shrugged. "My life. All my friends are successful with actual careers, and yet here I am...!" My voice broke slightly. Father pulled me in to him. "Oh, princess. It's not the end of the world you know."

"I know but why does it feel like it?" I stuck my bottom lip out and sulked. Father placed a soft, gentle kiss on my forehead. A blessing, an assurance, but more importantly an act of love. "You know the world is yours to manipulate at your whim, right? I will stand behind or in front of you whenever and however you need. Do not allow this current situation to affect you negatively, baby." Maybe it was the mist in the air but a cautious thread of liquid gently flowed down my cheek. Father seldom inserted himself in my affairs. He allowed me governance to rise and fall as I pleased, always conscious of the security that he was nearby. "I love you, Daddy," I cried, the liquid now gushing like waterfalls.

"Oh, my love. Aren't you the sweetest?" He lifted my chin and erased the traces of tears. "You know tomorrow is a new day. And I need you to exist and be your authentic self. Do not let the sanctimonious piety of ignorance affect you. This is not a fall but rather a misstep. All you can do is learn from it, not be discouraged. Never cry for a failure that isn't yours. Do not allow yourself to shrink. Can you not see you are the child of a titan and the mother of a champion?"

Alexander was truly the greatest. With just a few words he had sewn my torn pieces back together. I was no longer afraid of this unsure future that lay ahead. Instead, I was looking forward to it.

When the night fully bloomed, the fountain lit up, changing the flow of the water to a gentler more romantic pace. It felt like wonderland. The music now changing from easy-going jazz to soft piano keys.

My uncles and Father were now talking about race. It was as if race was now the new discussion of topic since all the talk of lockdown had hit the headlines. The premise of the conversation was gravely combustible. Yet they managed to never allow a wayward spark to blow up this somewhat civilised yet impassioned debate they were engaged in.

Uncle Unisa who had been relatively quiet as he kept going back for more of Mother's food, decided to find a space in the conversation. I admired Uncle and so too did my mother. She had told me on multiple occasions, as if I hadn't heard the first time, that "he is not a normal rich black man. He is the only black man I know who in his prime left a white woman for a black lady." Uncle was a hero in black conversations. A mythical being, an enlightened man who saw the truth and rightfully pursued it.

"Britain is more anti-black than the US. Don't let the fact that we aren't being shot recklessly on the streets like those in America fool you. Look at the media, the most basic and unbiased form of it," he said with his fingers doing quotation marks. "Do you see any black consultants or professors at the forefront of your news during this pandemic?" We shook our heads. "Yet I know black professors and consultants who know better than the white and Asian and Arab men and women who grace our news screens daily."

I had not thought about it. But he was right. During this whole pandemic, our brightest professors and medics had not been given the light to shine.

Every so often, when the table fell momentarily quiet,

you could hear the leaves rustling, a squirrel chirping then scrambling up a tree, or Mother humming a tune so gentle it felt like clouds tickling your ears.

Paradise.

Mother's garden was paradise.

After a minute's thought, Father decided to elaborate on Uncle's statement: "Even their vaccines and medicines work differently on black people than they do on our white counterparts. When trials are being tested they focus on the impact on Caucasians."

Being the devil's advocate, Uncle said, "Could it be that it's because they go to trials?"

"Yes, but we should acknowledge that fact with some caveat."

"What caveat?"

"The one that stipulates that the cure is for the preservation of white bodies. If it works for others, good. But the target audience isn't meant to look like me or you."

"I can partly agree with you, my brother. However, will you say that's by default or racism?"

"Perhaps both," I asserted, all eyes on me.

"Ahh, your child," Uncle looked at Father. "She speaks, Alex," teased Uncle Khan; the table erupted in laughter.

Uncle Khan was a contradiction that perplexed and excited me in equal measure.

He had a hooked nose and light hazel eyes. His skin was pale for an Asian. In the caste system of his fatherland, he was considered better than everyone and he made sure to tell anyone who'd listen. He surely carried himself as 'better-than'. Sometimes he reminded me of certain black men; that troubling desire to always prove himself or make people aware of who he was; his doctorate, his clinic, and that £95,000 speed machine he would zoom along in with his beautiful young wife.

When he and Father were younger, they decided to open a clinic together. Yet Uncle pulled out at the last minute. He had blamed his finances, but Father told me it was because Uncle felt owning a practice with a black doctor would not be good for business. A year later Uncle was in business with an Irish doctor named Cian O'Brien. The clinic went bust a year later. Now Father owns three clinics and Uncle owns one with Father being his main benefactor.

Nevertheless, I loved Uncle. When he was not busy goading or feverishly annoying people, he was the best uncle I had. He had three boys, which he was ecstatic about to start with. But when the fourth child who he'd prayed to be a girl left the womb a boy, a tinge of sadness settled in him. According to him, "Bridget White is the daughter I never had."

With how he loved me, one could certainly believe those words.

33

I walked past the crystal-clear water fountain which gushed with delight towards the heavens, dancing ever so softly as it embarked on its journey back to earth.

Mother had curated a magnificent space of nature.

Winner had long since left for bed. There was a quaint nursery downstairs which Mother had made before his birth. That was where he was sleeping tonight since everyone was also downstairs. So, I decided to go take a breather in his room upstairs which used to be mine when I was younger. My parents had since decorated the space in a myriad of cool blue shades. Chadwick Boseman's Black Panther loomed behind the door; protector of the realm. Winner's bed was a Lamborghini. Yes, my parents loved their grandson. In one corner of the room, there was a porcelain planter where a glossy green Peace Lily bloomed. A plant the same age as Winner, since I bought it the day he was born. By the window, there was a world-class telescope which Father used to show Winner the celestial beings. Then up on the ceiling, tiny sparkling stars surrounded the fluorescent words 'Winner lives here!' The room was pure. It smelled of black-boy joy. So whenever I was in there, I felt black-girl joy.

However, once in a while, this room flooded me with memories of black-girl misery.

Though Mother never compared our parenting in words, I always had this feeling she overcompensated with Winner. There were moments. Fleeting moments, may I add, in which I wished to upend my life and make it into the one Mother envisioned. Mother never compared me to other people's children publicly. But behind closed doors they were winners and I was barely competing. I would hear her whispering to my father and he rightfully shushing her, telling her, "She's our daughter, have some faith, she will prevail." She would give me back-handed compliments as if I were a second-class citizen to her friend's first-class kids. I pretended, I always pretended, that I did not notice or that her words did not dip my ego into the sulphurs of Hades. But they did. They bruised and burnt me each time. It was only thanks to my melanin that the exterior of my physicality is opaque to the world. Mother's intelligence was terrifying. When I was a young child, she would mould me into shape with it. So, I guess it must have broken her heart when I chose to distort that shape.

Mother and I had a fairly ambivalent relationship. While I was growing up, she was firm. She had no room for dissent. Sometimes I thought, perhaps it was me, I was the problem. Perhaps it was my fault that she did not love me wholly. After all, every mother wants a child who listens; I was rebellious. She said A, I said Z; she said blue, I said red; she said, "Be great," while I from the looks of it said, "No, I'll settle for mediocrity." Perhaps it was these things that cut away at her love for me. And why should they not? It had not been an easy feat for my parents to succeed as immensely as they did. It took hard work, dedication, and sheer drive. So as an only child of such great humans, greatness should not just be expected of me, surely it should be a given, I realised, as the errors of my ways dawned upon me.

Finally, it all made sense. I wanted the best for Winner. At that moment, I was certain it was that same 'best' that Mother wanted for me. The same 'best' we all wanted for Tariq as he too had been an only child.

Suddenly, I began to sob – quiet, discreet sobs. At first, I did not know who my sadness was for.

Nevertheless, the more feverish my sobs became, the more I realised it was for all of us. For my mother, for myself, and for my brother, Tariq. When we were younger he'd say ever so playfully, "Don't make Aunty sad, you know she'll die for you, right?" I'd laugh and reply "whatever", but even then, I knew he was right. He was always right. Younger than me, but smarter, more rational, more loving, more caring, more brilliant, like a billion stars: a bright star.

I wanted to hug him, to tell him that now I had Winner, I knew exactly what he meant by "your mother only wants the best for you because you deserve the best". I wanted to tell him that Winner was the spitting image of him. I wanted to tell him that my heart broke into tiny pieces when I thought about how violently he was ripped away from me. I wanted to tell him that because of him I was happy that I never had another sibling - because I could never love them the way I love him. I wanted to tell him that though Winner illuminated my entire world, his absence left a darkness I could never erase. I wanted to tell him that, even if it took my last breath, I promised to unhood his killer.

Above all, I wanted to tell him the truest of truths: that I loved him eternally.

After my epiphany, I knew without a doubt that I needed to speak to my mother. When everyone had left, I went to the kitchen to assist my mum. I took a brief peek outside. Father was in the back with an old newspaper in hand, and the lyrics "Christopher Columbus is a damn blasted liar" by Burning Spear were playing in the background. *Interesting*, I thought. What a timely song.

Mother had all the qualities of a kingmaker. However, I was busy being a princess. Something I reckon pained her both secretly and explicitly. I was meant to be at the top ... always. Yet, I was somewhere playing catch-up in the middle.

My mother looked angelic. Though her face was deep in concentration, it had a gentle softness to it. I was in awe of her: her poise, her beauty, her sense of style, her exquisitely styled soft short copper hair. She was truly a work of art. A hint of a smile sat on my face as she handed me the last piece of cutlery to dry.

Finally, she was able to fully look my way. My eyes sat inside hers, so she could see my sincerity. "Mummy," I whispered, the word feeling strange yet sweet on my tongue since it belonged to an era where I was young and the love of her life. She smiled as though the word brought fond memories to her mind. Taking her soft hand which had barely noticeable green and purple veins laced inside, I continued, "Mummy, you remember when I gave birth and Father and David went out of the delivery room, congratulating each other, crying and hugging as if they were the ones who'd just pushed out Winner?" She nodded and chuckled heartily, the expression a beautiful sound in my ear, so I too followed and giggled. "That was the best day of my life, not only because I had given birth to Winner, but because of you–" her eyes widened. Shock, I assumed it to be.

"Me?" she looked at my face intently

Smiling, I replied, "Yes you, Mummy." She did not ask outright, but her eyes and the slight forward lean of anticipation told me she wanted to know why. "You remember when from nowhere I began crying violently, afraid of motherhood, what it meant and what it would entail ... and you took my hand," my voice broke as I held her hands tighter. "It was just you and me, and our baby Winner. You wrapped me in a cocoon of love and said–"

"You've got this, princess. The world is yours. It has always been yours, Bridget Celine White," she murmured, repeating the exact words she had said that night. The pieces I was desperately trying to hold together broke, and I burst into tears.

"Please be my champion again, Mummy." She pulled me into her slim frame. "Let us go back to that delivery room and stay there. Stay in that moment when you believed in me, and I felt believed in ... Please," I whimpered, a tiny trail of my snot glistening on her finely pressed shirt.

She held me tighter, and though she did not say a word, I knew this was the beginning of something new.

It may not have been Mother's Day 2020 any longer, as it had been three days prior, but it certainly felt like Mother's Day to me.

34

"Get in, bad boy."

"Gladly," said David, his eyes sparking with wildness. Mischievously, I laughed as he hopped inside Father's Aston Martin which I had borrowed or stolen, depending on whether or not you were Father.

David, having left the comfort of his bed to go on a joyride with me at my request was filled with excitement. After my mother and I had our moment in the kitchen, David was the only person I wanted to talk to about how euphoric it felt to hear her say she loved me unconditionally.

He had parked his car a couple of houses down the road so as not to rouse my parents' suspicion.

"Shh," I had giggled uncontrollably as I tiptoed out of my parents' house and straight into him, causing us to convulse with unrestrained laughter and joy.

"I love you, Bridge."

"I love you too, David. With all my heart I do," I had replied as we sped off into the night.

As we zipped along the motorway with my hand rubbing his knee, he raised a questioning eyebrow my way. "Are you intending to have your filthy way with me, Bridge?" he pulled my hand further up his leg.

"Oh, you bet, King David."

I had not told David that the professor wished to see me. After the way he had reacted to me telling him about Joshua, I knew he would take the news of the professor much worse. I did not tell him because I knew he would try to stop me from seeing the man he believed had a crush on me. Despite this, with the way the professor sounded, it did not feel as if what he had to say had anything to do with how he felt about me. I had the horrible feeling that it might be something to do with my brother, Tariq. So, for that reason, I would sit, even with the devil, to ascertain the truth about what happened on that fateful night.

However, if it was indeed that the professor wanted to elaborate on his feelings for me, then it was only right that I made crazy love to my man before going to see Matthew. That way it would be impossible for him to seduce me.

"Where are you taking me?" asked David, keen for us to stop and get down to business. Taking a deep breath, I veered sharply left, spinning the car till I was finally parked in the designated spot in the dark, quiet car park.

Before I could utter a word, David threw off his seatbelt, and pulled me to him, our lips almost touching. His breathing was ragged, and his breath smelled of coffee.

I wanted to kiss him so badly, but he was teasing me and, much to my surprise, it was turning me on beyond reason.

"Oh, you want to play games, huh? I reclined his seat and then slowly straddled my legs across him, my hands pinning his down. He moaned a little, the muscle in his pants growing. Hungrily, with all the pent-up tension his teasing had built in me, my mouth consumed his lips with frenzy. He groaned, then grunted, taken aback by the brazen animal he had brought out in me.

"You like that?" I goaded him a little. Pulling me harder onto his now fully-grown erection, I got my answer.

He was driving me wild with anticipation. His teeth lightly grazed my lips. "Bridge I love you so much," he whispered, holding my face so I could stare straight into eyes which were a little wet with emotion, "I am so sorry if I ever hurt you." He gently kissed my forehead. "I cannot see life without you, and I do not want to see life without you, Bridget White, and I promise that I, David King, will love you this lifetime, the next, and every other after it."

I did not think I could have been happier if I tried. "I love you too, King David," I said with yearning. "Now shut up and kiss me!"

His sweaty palm pressed against the roof of the car while his free hand unhooked my bra. With my back arched and resting on the dashboard, I unbuttoned my shorts, with my legs in between his shoulders. Gently he pulled off my shorts, his lips kissing here and there as they finally came off.

"Wow, you are perfect," he reflected, his eyes sexily taking in all of me. Leaning forward, he touched my stomach with his lips. I gave a sharp intake of breath while his tongue circled my belly button, biting whenever I arched my back. David allowed his tongue to trail further down, stopping just where the flimsy thong I was wearing began.

Our eyes met, he smiled; I laughed, consumed by a fever of lust.

"I think I want to taste you," he exhaled, the warmth of his breath burning me with desire. Spreading my legs, he gently moved his mouth up my thighs.

"Oh my," I shuddered as his gloriously full lips made contact with mine down below.

A few minutes later, I was on my knees, talking off his belt, pulling down his pants, my mouth returning the favour.

Making love to David was like creating art. No two pictures we painted with our bodies were ever the same.

After my body refused to take any more of his mind-blowing artistry, I collapsed on top of him, panting, the muscles inside me contracting with sweet, sweet, delirious pleasure.

Oh, did I love David King.

Putting back on our clothes, David said, "Can I ask you something?"

"Sure. Anything."

"Will you be my lady ... again?" he asked, after we had straddled the lines between lovers and foes for over two years. Granted he had asked this same question a few times during those two years. Nevertheless, I had never given an answer. Yet here he was. Trying once more to make me his.

"Yes I will," I replied without hesitation.

We now officially and exclusively belonged to each other ... again.

35

Some Things About Matthew Wylde

THURSDAY, MARCH 26 - First Day of Lockdown

In his dreams, he was with her. Matthew Wylde was always with Bridget White!

It was 1.30 pm. Lockdown had begun half an hour earlier. Today was the day he was going to see Bridget alone. Matthew was in London at his parents' holiday home. He had left the city of dreaming spires a week prior due to the closure of universities across the country. Initially, people had been bending the rules as they were not yet legally implemented. Now that they were, however, looking outside his living room window, Matthew could see that the rules were being diligently followed. Everyone was indoors. It appeared that the scaremongering implemented by the news and the politicians had worked. Outside, the one or two individuals who ventured outdoors for necessary travel were dressed as if in a post-apocalyptic scene. There was a man walking his dog. He had on a mask and thick latex gloves even though the sun outside was oddly scorching for this time of the year. He was walking his dog. The dog also had on a tiny mask and gloves. Matthew could not help but laugh while increasing the cool temperature of his home's air conditioning. In the distance, a woman carrying a grocery shopping bag kept stopping every so often to sanitise her hands. She had on two masks instead of one.

The world has gone crazy, he concluded.

The country was adapting to the UK government's legally enforceable rules of lockdown: maintain a two-metre gap in public spaces and only leave home for the following four reasons:

- To buy food

- To exercise once a day alone or with members of the same household

- Medical need or to provide care for a vulnerable person

- To travel to and from work that cannot be done from home.

It was the first time in Matthew's thirty years of existence that he had witnessed the world come to a standstill. Lockdown was at once scary and exciting. It would not, however, in the future, escape Matthew's notice that although some made their fortunes during the pandemic, plenty also lost their businesses, their livelihoods and their lives to the virus, COVID-19.

Back to early evening on the first day of lockdown. Matthew had fallen asleep. He was dreaming. Bridget was in his dream.

* * * *

In his last dream before they meet alone - he stares at her head, trying to pick her brain, wondering if there are any crazy thoughts flowing through it as she lies on his chest, sleeping.

There is something about her, something peculiar that he wants her to reveal to him. There is a darkness in her that intrigues him and compels him to desire her. She doesn't want to show it to him, but he knows it is there.

He lies with her, his breathing slow and hard, as his conscience looks upon him with scepticism. He is plagued with guilt, regret, and remorse ... for Tariq.

He looks at Bridget, her beautiful face and how happy she seems with him, and it makes him feel that he needs to tell her the truth about what happened to Tariq.

They lie, motionless, content, and free, even though he knows that a great storm is brewing, and quickly heading their way. Her chest heaves up and down, perhaps in anticipation of the storm. Matthew's heartbeat starts to escalate, eyes wide and hollow, staring at the ceiling, wishing for it to open up and reveal some light to him. But it doesn't, it keeps him stuck in the cocoon, holding him until the storm arrives.

Ring, ring, ring, screamed his telephone removing him from his dream.

The storm had arrived.

The storm was Bridget White!

* * * *

As Matthew walked to the place where he and Bridget were to meet, he felt fear and carried it like an infection that spread with every passing second.

Images of Tariq flashed in his mind.

America was the land of the free. What a great irony that it had now banished him for exercising that freedom in the form of free speech.

If there were ever a self-contradictory country, surely it had to be the United States of America, he thought angrily.

For five years, Matthew had been chewing it over, wondering if he should tell Bridget the truth. This secret he held plagued him, burning him inside out, and on Saturday, that day he saw her at Tunde's, he knew he needed to tell her. She may have appeared genial and appeased, but he knew those same flames he saw in her at Harvard were still consuming her five years later.

36

The cloud bloomed in the gloom, doomed for rain.

The streets were frighteningly deserted. On the phone, I had told David I was stepping out briefly for some fresh air.

It was a lie.

Closing the door to my father's speed machine (which I had yet to return), I stepped out into the open. I was the only living being walking that lonely road towards the park that late into the night. Lockdown had begun. We were meant to be inside. Yet I was outside. *What the hell is wrong with me*? I thought, almost turning back. But what if what the professor wanted to tell me so desperately was about my cousin Tariq? What then?

It was that *what then* that moved my feet all the way into the deep, dark park.

Someone was following me. I looked back. They were gone. Disintegrating into the sea of nothingness.

What the fuck has Matthew got me into? I thought, my mind fighting my body's urge to flee. Before I could decide on whether I should stay or run, it began to rain.

In the distance, there was a door. A grey, haggard, and lonely door. I ran towards it - its misery, like a wretched being, enticing me. Standing in front of it, my feet felt eager to enter, but my mind told me otherwise. I closed my eyes. A cool breeze passed, but it did not steady my thoughts. I needed more time to think, but my hand did not allow me as it turned the knob and opened the door. My body projected itself forth, and like a bad omen, the door slammed shut, holding me prisoner within its four walls.

I could feel something, or perhaps someone. Someone or something was watching me. Its stare was so potent, it felt like a steel blade piercing me.

My eyes looked up and beheld him.

The professor's crazed look pierced into me. A raging fire was ablaze in the blue balls of his eyes.

A cold chill touched me.

This time, unlike the night at Tunde's, there was no beating of hearts or eyes that brewed with desire. He peered about wild-eyed. "Is anyone with you?"

"No," I answered, glancing around. "Why do you ask?" He did not answer; instead, he continued watching me with eyes that were eerily vacant and almost filled with malice. Towards whom, I was uncertain.

An ominous shiver slithered up my spine.

"What's wrong?" I felt compelled to touch his hand, which he swiftly pulled away.

Fear fell from above and landed on top of me. My breathing, though shallow, quickened. Even at Harvard, Matthew's animus had not been this sinister.

Something was terribly wrong. His demeanour was hostile.

"Do you remember my lecture at Harvard?"

In every detail, I thought. "Yes, I do, why?"

"Do you recall the man with red hair who sat to the left of you?"

"Yes, he came up to me at the end and offered his sympathies for Tariq's murder. He said, 'I pray the person who killed him is caught someday.'"

In an almost inaudible voice, Matthew said, "He is the one who killed Tariq!"

Time stopped.

I needed to steady my heart rate or else it might explode.

A bitter chill ran through me, freezing me dead in my tracks. There were so many questions filling my mouth. However, all I could do was stare back at him. I stared at Matthew, his face flushed crimson. He forced a strained smile, but all I could see was a man on fire, suffering as the flames engulfed him like a funeral pyre. I wanted to reach out to him and ease his pain, but my pain was more acute, or at least, so I believed; I refused to console him.

A sinister thought crossed my mind. *What if he hates the exact same thing as me*? Yes, surely, he hated the killer as much as I did. But why now, why reveal this now? Why not five years earlier? In that room, where for all that made me human, I would have exercised the law of an eye for an eye and a tooth for a tooth.

Using my acumen, I continued to watch him. My eyes followed his as they peered around the room. The walls were cold and grey, marred with black veins, lifeless like a corpse. The only window in the room was fantastically flawed; the air, humid, and the floor, rigid, as if we were standing on daggers.

I wanted to say something, but words failed me. All I could do was stand still as the flames of Matthew's revelation burned wildly.

Without warning, Matthew began to speak. "I walk around with this guilt each waking day. Like a malignant disease, it eats away at me, ripping into the very sinews of my humanity," his mouth quivered. "To see a man dying is not easy. It fucks with..." his hands strayed in the air, searching for the right words, "it fucks with your soul." His voice broke violently: “I should have done something. I should have done something,” the weight of his torment finally falling on him, releasing a deluge of hot, searing fluid down his face.

37

As the professor spoke, memories gradually began to creep out of the crevices of my mind. Memories I thought I had buried, padlocked, and whose keys I thought I had thrown away due to the grave torment they always brought me.

However, the words I KNOW WHAT HAPPENED TO TARIQ immediately forced me to transport myself back to all those memories once more.

Tariq's parents had asked that I accompany them to go identify his body. Up until now, it is the hardest ask anyone has ever requested of me. Nonetheless, I knew I had to do it. I had to go. I had to see him.

"We're here," stated my uncle, Roger White, as we all looked at the mortuary with heavy, heavy hearts.

It was an overwhelmingly ominous day. A day I wish had not existed.

I had gone to America for a three-week tour of the legendary United States. I had gone to have fun and party. Most importantly, however, I had gone to see my cousin whom I called my brother and bright star: Tariq. His father and my father were first cousins. As an only child, there was always that one cousin who became your sibling by default. Tariq was such a cousin to me. He was more than my brother. He was a part of my beating heart.

* * * *

The first time Tariq and I ever met was during the summer of August 2001. He was three, I was six.

Exiting the Arrival gate at Heathrow, he was wearing blue chequered shorts, a white polo shirt and baby Ray Ban shades. "Wow, he's so cool," I had blurted out excitedly to my father, my face brimming with delight at this fashionable American who was swaggering towards us with his parents in tow. "That's your cousin," Father replied, "and he is pretty dapper, isn't he!" Father agreed as Tariq and his parents finally closed the space between them and us.

Tariq, handsome as could be, stopped, removed his shades, looked back at his parents and asked, "Is this Uncle Alex, Aunty Cecelia and Cousin Bridget?"

"Yes, baby," his parents grinned at their wonderfully idiosyncratic child.

Filled to the brim with awe at my baby cousin, I squealed, "Oh my God, he's so cute, Daddy," before lifting him off the floor, spinning him in the air and showering him with kisses. The boy, a little taken aback, smiled then politely asked, "Cousin Bridget, can you please put me down?"

The adults laughed.

Standing back on firm ground, he motioned to me with his forefinger. As I kneeled before him, almost at his same height, he leaned in and placed a kiss as soft as clouds on my cheek. Butterflies of happiness fluttered their wings throughout my body. "My name is Tariq White..." He spoke in the most wonderful and brilliant American accent I had ever heard. Unable to contain my extreme delight, I pulled him in for another hug before he could complete his sentence. He giggled with delight at this undiluted showering of love.

"My name is Bridget White," I said, holding him back to admire this person some more. "I know," he replied, "and although we are cousins, I think you should be my sister and I, your brother...”

That was the first time I knew what it meant to love someone without boundaries. Tariq was love to me and love to me was Tariq.

* * * *

Uncle Roger parked his jeep in front of a tall, dark, and overwhelmingly sinister building, which hovered over us like the Grim Reaper himself.

The patriarch of the family got out and opened the car doors for his wife and me.

Brutal concrete greeted us, its colour dead grey, with poison ivy living around it, hugging, and caressing the rough and rigid surface of the building. *An odd dichotomy indeed,* I thought, *that life could so casually live among death.* The building had an aura about it. It was tangible. It felt as though death itself was greeting us, saying, C*ome, come, and see the work of my hands!*

As we got closer, I saw that the building was covered in sores; even the poison ivy could not hide its hideousness. It was an atmosphere of pestilence that greeted us as we stepped inside the grey doors of the mortuary.

A gentle breeze rustled in, giving off an eerie feeling. My aunt edged closer to her husband. I walked behind, steadfast, and alone in my stride.

The medical examiner rushed towards us. “Good morning,” he said, taking my uncle’s hand and shaking it. “I am so sorry about this,” he said, bowing his head. “Please,” said the medical examiner as he started walking, “Follow me.” He motioned to the end of the corridor. We followed ever so quietly, ever so cautiously, ever so solemnly.

The medical examiner ushered us into a room

adorned with death's regalia. As we entered, the door slammed, and a cold breeze arrested me. "Are you alright, baby?" asked my Aunt Natalie.

I nodded.

In the centre of the room stood a steel table with a black body covered in a white sheet.

A profound sense of silence loomed over us. The medical examiner coughed. "Shall we?" he asked, as we all walked forward, my heart all the while drumming with unyielding violence. I wanted to scream. I wanted to cry. I wanted the heavens to hear my anguish and somehow turn it to relief by making my brother wake from the slumber he was in on the steel table. However, I must have known no such miracles were to happen, so I walked slowly, slowly behind my aunt and uncle towards the body.

While I stood back, my whole being shaking with devastating grief yet my body somehow still, the medical examiner spoke with my aunt and uncle. He asked a few questions which were answered with voices filled with restrained emotion. I wanted to cry for them, for their pain, which must have felt like a million arrows to their fragile hearts. Yet I could not. I could not summon my tears. For I was cried out. Yet my heart hurt. All its sinews had been ripped apart, that I knew because the pain I felt was tangible.

The medical examiner looked at us with undisguised sympathy, then peeled his gaze from us and removed the cover from the body's face.

Aunt Natalie screamed then stumbled back. I rushed to her side, holding her convulsing body, which somehow brought me consolation. It showed I was not the only one living in this great anguish that the passing of our bright star Tariq had caused.

Uncle Roger stayed quiet, seemingly unmoved, yet I

could sense his body was alive and agile with great pain.

"Is that him?" the medical examiner asked, his voice quiet, almost inaudible.

My eyes watched my uncle. He was a man on fire. My heart broke a million times for him as I watched him look at his dead son. I tried to inhale, to exhale, to chant words of resistance in my head. But resistance was futile as I gave a sharp, pained groan that travelled around the room like a sad, sad tune.

Uncle Roger, summoning all the courage in the world to not fall apart, clenched his jaw, closed his eyes, and replied, "Yes, that is my son," positively identifying the body of Tariq White.

* * * *

Tariq and I saw each other for the last time three days earlier. Before then I had seen him countless times. In my dreams, on my screen saver, on FaceTime, and multiple times in London and America. From the first time we met, I knew he was going to be great; a beacon of and for change. His actions proved this to be so. He produced straight A's in every academic task given to him. He was a sports star, chair of the debating team, adored by all the girls and admired by all the boys, and the following year he was to be valedictorian at his high school graduation.

Life was one big sphere of happiness with Tariq. He revelled in his black-boy joy. Life was in love with him, and he in return was undilutedly in love with life.

On that day, the last day we were to be in each other's company, Tariq had wowed me like he always did. "Sis," he had said, his hand behind his back with his signature cheeky boyish grin printed on his lips. I could not help but smile, smile at his beauty, his aura, everything about him just made the world seem a better place. He had a way of making you feel all was right with the world.

"What do you have behind your back," I had asked as he fidgeted behind him. "Nothing," he replied, his grin growing bigger.

Jumping up from my seat, we began wrestling, and because he was bigger and stronger, he allowed me to win and retrieve the paper that was in the hand behind his back.

"Ah hah, what do we have here ... a love letter?" I teased as he sat on the couch defeated.

Getting up, he replied, "More a poem, but about love, yes."

"Can I read it?"

Swiping the paper from my hand, he quickly said, "No, let me read it instead. I think it'll have a better ring to it coming from the admirer," he joked, wrapping my neck under his arm and rubbing my head.

"I'm your older sister, little boy."

"Yeah, yeah, whatever, Grandma," he joked, gently nudging me onto the couch.

Standing back, he unfolded the piece of paper and cleared his throat. I chuckled. "Stop it, sis." He burst into a mean fit of boyish laughter, which made me laugh even more. Each time he tried to read out the contents of the paper, we looked at each other like two best friends who could not stop laughing at something only they found funny. The room was filled with profound laughter that neither of us could control. Once we could no longer breathe from laughing, he managed to say through staggered breaths, "Come on, Bridge, this poem is important; let me read it."

"Well, if you stopped giggling, perhaps I would too."

"Okay." He took a deep breath. I copied him. The room fell quiet. Our eyes met and I could feel the laughter bursting to come out. His face squinted with restraint. I exhaled feverishly, fighting to contain my laughter.

"Okay, okay, okay, read the poem, bro," I urged, my voice tinged with hysterics. He covered his mouth and laughed into the cave of his hand. I covered my eyes, gritted my teeth and laughed inside my head.

"Okay, okay, I am going to read it now."

"1, 2, 3, go!" we shouted simultaneously.

"My Bridge Over Troubled Waters, a poem by Tariq White," he grinned, proud of his introduction.

"You're so silly," I teased, chucking a cushion at him. He caught it, winked at me then chucked it back. "Alright let's be serious now. Let me read." Putting my hands up in submission I motioned for him to continue.

When I'm unnoticeable, you see me...

like a billion suns.

When the world tries to demonise bodies like mine

you storm through the streets of Babylon, professing,

preaching that I am the only angel you know...

When my humanity is debated, you paint me nothing but...

Human!

When there seems no way

you create a bridge

My bridge ... always!

A soft gentle thread of liquid flowed down my cheek. That is the most beautiful poem I've ever heard, I wanted to say, but emotion choked my voice. Tariq came up to me, knelt and signalled me to lean forward the same way he had at Heathrow Airport when he was three and I six, then gently, lovingly kissed my cheek, whispering, “In case I forget to tell you, you will be my sister and best friend in every lifetime, Bridge, and I will love you equally with all my heart in all of them...” He hugged me, then left ... never to return.

* * * *

With something I could not put a name to that moved with each step I took, I edged forward and stared at my brother’s corpse unflinchingly. It was no time for fear. I had left that outside the building, in the car, where my palms had been sweaty, and my heart had pulsated like war drums.

It was a weird feeling because earlier, inside that mortuary, I had felt tormented, anguished and far from at peace. Yet as I stood in the room in front of my brother, I felt tranquil, calm, and oddly happy. I felt happy to see his handsome face which death refused to spoil. I smiled at his beauty, though my heart ached.

“Can I touch him?” I asked.

The medical examiner did not know what to say. He did not answer. I turned around and looked into his vacant eyes. He looked away.

“Do you know who killed my baby brother?” I asked.

“... erm,” he swallowed, looking around for help, “I, I...”

Uncle Roger stepped in, “Bridget, baby, no one knows what happened. It was an accident.”

“When did you become so naïve?” I quipped, my voice haughty, vexed at his gullibility.

“What did you say to me, young lady?”

“You are a financier, for fuck’s sake. Surely you should know that this doesn’t add up?” I snapped, two wild eyes gazing into the cold, grieving and bitter eyes of my father's cousin. "When did you become so naïve?" I questioned once more, while edging closer to him. He stepped back. His breathing was hard and heavy, as was mine.

"This is cold-blooded murder!" I roared turning around and walking over to the body. "Someone killed him," I shrieked, angrily throwing the white cloth which covered the black body to the floor, revealing the countless bullet holes it was riddled with.

My aunt shrieked in horror and ran out of the room, wailing.

"I'll go after her," replied the medical examiner, glad to be leaving.

It was only my uncle, the head of the pride and his two cubs that remained in the room. My gaze was like a dagger, and I could feel it cutting deep into my uncle's heart. His rage was too subdued for my aching being. I wanted - no, I needed him to feel my inexplicable pain, all of it, until it made him react. A father should not try to rationalise the murder of his black son out of worry that society might paint him as an angry black man if he revealed the extent of his hurt.

Uncle tried to match my ferocity, but he could not. He looked away. "What do you want me to do, baby?" he asked, eyes low.

"I want you to feel."

"Feel what?!" he bellowed, as he moved closer to me, this time his rage growing like I had wanted it to.

I pushed back. "I want you to feel the same hell that I'm in," I whimpered.

He tried to pull me close. "Don't!" I snapped, walking back to the body and assessing it.

Tariq's face was not rigid in agony, nor was his mouth gaping or shrieking in pain. His cheeks were not sunken; rather they were full in the bloom of youth; plump and firm. Slowly I lowered my head, closed my eyes, and kissed his cheek. As my face continued to touch his, it felt like we were the last two people on earth. I did not want to let go. "Come back, please, my baby, please come back, bro." I sniffed, and for the briefest of moments, I thought I might have felt warmth transfer from his flesh to my lips. It was as if he were alive, and in those brief moments when our flesh touched, he felt alive.

"We have got to go, baby," urged Uncle Roger.

Removing my lips from his cheek, it was then I felt the cold. He was cold, and as dead as I was alive. My eyes opened, and the realisation that Tariq was definitively dead stabbed me deep in the heart like a thousand daggers. I gasped for air, but it choked me. My hands trembled as I tried to touch him. I could not. Instead, I staggered backwards and let out a sinful shriek. "Noooo!"

Uncle Roger rushed to my side, stopping midway, as my palm opened and motioned to him to 'stay back'.

"I will not settle for living in this misery, Uncle." I lost control of the muscles in my face as my lips blubbered and my expression contorted in misery. Whether I wanted it or not, my uncle held on steadfastly to my fragile self, just like a father would. "I won't. I can't. If I do I will run mad, and I can't, I just can't," I snivelled, hot and heavy tears flooding down my face. "I can't breathe, Uncle; he's dead," my finger shakily pointed at the body. "They've murdered my baby brother." My weakened frame fell into my uncle's arms, accepting its comfort.

I never knew that hearts could literally break. However, on that day, in that room, my heart broke. Though Winner and David had put most of its broken pieces back together, it could never be fully repaired.

Unless ... his killer was to be brought to justice. That would be the only thing that could unbreak my heart.

38

As the gravity of Matthew's confession dawned on Bridget, he took it upon himself to explain how he stumbled upon the murder of Tariq and the action he almost took to avenge her cousin that fateful night.

* * * *

It was dead quiet inside a car on the fifth boulevard, Madison Avenue, Massachusetts. A dark figure was sitting inside, soundlessly lamenting the grave event he had just witnessed.

His name was Matthew. Professor Matthew Wylde.

His breathing was calm and regular. He appeared cool as ice. The storm outside, however, was hot, heavy, and downright vulgar. Earlier, the oracle on the weather channel had foretold a storm, prophesying heavy rains accompanied by deafening sounds of thunder with blinding bolts of lightning. Matthew had thrown caution to the wind. He did not believe in fortune tellers. "Perhaps I should have listened." He almost smiled.

He had smoked only once in his life, at university, age sixteen, a prodigy, under much pressure, seeking calm. Cannabis had provided this for him. He craved the sedative once more, but only a stick of cigar presented itself. Tucked away, deep in the glove compartment, a gift from an old girlfriend who had visited Cuba, and who felt he would be impressed by her choice.

The cigar had to suffice. Its tobacco was finely cured, fermented, and aged, encased in a sun-grown wrapper which had been hand rolled. He lit it and took a pull then puffed. He did not appreciate its flavour or excellence. The Cuban cigar did not impress him, just like his ex. Nonetheless, he continued to smoke it. He needed to. It was his only means of relief.

He was trying to forget. He had not meant to see what he had seen. He was not supposed to see what he had seen. Nonetheless, he had, and he knew that it could never be unseen.

He wished he had not stepped out. He had been at home, alone, bored, and disengaged. Sunday evening was driving him to the point of oblivion. He had not gone to a place of worship earlier in the day. He was not much of a religious man, but he believed in God, a higher Almighty being. And for that reason, he tried to do good, to be good when circumstances permitted. This was why, when he had earlier encountered a man on the road, who had riled his blood, he did good by letting him go. Something he regretted, as he sat pulling the life out of the cigar.

The man, Anthony Harris, who Matthew had considered to be mad, as no sane person would possess the audacity to approach him so boldly, had intrigued him. The man had rushed out of his car consumed by a pseudo-bravado which quickly faltered when Matthew had stood up to him in a more menacing manner.

Who was Anthony Harris? What in his nature gave him the impunity to do as he pleased?

It was those questions, which burned in Matthew's mind, that caused him to follow a trail of death.

Parked a distance away and camouflaged by the dark, Matthew watched Anthony, out of sight.

At the first shot, his breath caught in his throat. The second and subsequent shots made his heart lurch forward, as though he were the one feeling the impact of the bullets spraying into the young boy. A black boy. Tariq

White.

Anthony Harris was blood drunk. Fiendish in his killing. His ginger hair, red with rage.

A true connoisseur of death.

Matthew edged forward, almost revealing himself, but not quite. Anthony Harris must have sensed him, as there was no way he could have heard him. The man looked back as if he had seen him, but he knew that he could not be seen. It was impossible. He possessed the guile of a fox! Too cunning for the killer.

Anthony shouted, "Hey, hey, hey," as he ran towards Matthew. However, Matthew was long gone before the killer could catch up with him.

Finally, Matthew pulled the last breath from the cigar and flicked the carcass out to drown.

In front of him stood a house. A very normal house, with no special features or attributes. Like the rest of the houses lined up, it was bland and unassuming. Its inhabitants, however, were special, most especially the man. The man who had just killed another human.

He followed the man in the house with his eyes, as he paced back and forth in his bedroom. The glass and curtain stopped him from seeing the man himself, but the way his shadow floundered behind the glass showed him that the man had blood on his hands.

A revolver lay by Matthew's side, a fiery companion inside the coldness of his car. His fingers gently caressed the metal flesh. He wondered if the neighbours would wake if he took aim and fired, killing the man with blood on his hands. He had always liked the idea of an eye for an eye and a tooth for a tooth. The man in the mirror opened the curtain, looked deep into the distance, and stared directly at his car. But he could not see inside. He imagined the man's eyes squinting, fighting to see if anyone was watching him. Irrationality almost compelled him to remove his body from the vehicle and reveal himself. But rationality kept him seated, a phantom, watching as his nemesis searched for him in the middle of nothingness. The man behind the glass closed the curtains, leaving his shadow to take his place.

Matthew smirked. The man in the glass was tormented. He saw his demons standing beside him inside the glass, and even they smirked. The other man's torment possessed an uncanny ability to raise humour in Matthew. However, he was not there for jokes. He was there to avenge something; someone he knew nothing about but felt everything for. He took an unassuming peek at the revolver once more. He felt his mind hesitating, saying don't do it, but it was a false alarm. He knew he had to do it, if not for anything but for his sanity. He put on some dark gloves, and finally stepped out of his vehicle. Rain fell on him like tiny arrows. The winds rushed him, pushing him back, imploring him to abort mission, but he refused. He stood firm, steadfast, unmovable. He strolled soundlessly to the front door. There was no life there. He went around the building, scoped the place. There was light. There was life downstairs inside the living room. The silhouette of a woman grabbed his attention. He stood in plain view of the window, watching, stalking, vying to be seen, but she saw nothing. She was fast asleep. He removed a glove, touched the glass, leaving baleful impressions. He smiled and walked back to a distance where he was privy to a view of the man inside the glass.

He studied his prey, raised his weapon, steadied his aim, and fired, *bang, bang, bang*. The man in the glass did not die, even though Matthew's aim was infallible.

He would have made the shot; it would have hit the target, straight in the heart. But there were no bullets. A bullet kills a man. But he did not just simply want to kill.

He wanted a show and shooting a man through a window was not a show, it was cowardice, and he was no coward.

"Today is not your day to die," he smiled. "Sweet dreams," he whispered to the man in the window as the winds carried away his words.

And like a thief, he got back into his car and sped away. Leaving Anthony Harris alone with his demons.

39

Genesis - Five Years Earlier - Anthony Harris

Anthony Harris was a man of habit. His habits were as profane and as sacred as one could imagine.

He went to church every Sunday, gave his tithe, and made sure to never miss a service. Yet, on every other day, his actions were so riddled with sin, even the devil questioned his morality.

It was Sunday evening. The television was on, but no one was watching, not even his wife. Their attention was fixated on their mobile phones. He took a sly peek in her direction, but she was far too indulged with her phone to notice. She smiled, at what, he was unaware, and it tore at his heartstrings.

Her lack of acknowledgement for him agitated his entire being, so much so that his flesh broke out in crimson patches as his anger grew, hot. However, he had long vowed to keep the peace in his home on Sundays. But that Sunday was an odd one. He was fighting with himself to contain his rage, pain, resentment, and hurt.

His wife had done the unthinkable.

She had ripped out his beating heart. She had killed his hopes and dreams. And the fact that she thought he would never find out cut him like a knife.

She had aborted their unborn child, framing it as a miscarriage instead. But he knew, he knew what she had done. Why, was what he did not know.

He was visibly wounded. He needed cannabis to

calm his nerves. However, it was Sunday, so he decided against it. He raised his head to watch her. She stayed resolute in her disregard for him. His heart throbbed. He closed his eyes, shook his head, and allowed his mouth to slice in two, forming a thin, frail, and loathsome smile.

His green eyes opened, and they were fully in bloom with hate. He never knew a woman could be so contemptuous.

His pistol flashed in the distance. His eyes followed the glint of the metal. It lay obediently on the glass table, small yet mighty. It had an unsettling beauty about it. It was his most prized possession. Anthony Harris admired his third eye, as he called it, from afar. As his eyes looked away from the weapon, they met his wife's gaze. She had been looking at him the entire time. Her eyes were cold, dark, and vacant, and they said, *I know what you're thinking, Anthony,* before reverting to her phone.

His gaze narrowed*, don't do it,* pleaded the conscience he seldom used when it came to her.

He sighed with frustration, and yet still his wife paid no mind to his turmoil.

Leave, said the inner voice calmly, *before you commit bloody murder,* it continued, almost jokingly. But both the voice and Anthony Harris knew it was no laughing matter.

"I'll be back," he mumbled, as his wife raised her head and looked at him as if he were the devil himself.

"Okay," she shrugged.

Okay, she says, he roared in his head, as he politely gave her a wry smile. If he could strangle her, and get away with it, he would have; perhaps, he should have. But it was Sunday, so he chose to leave instead, and keep the peace.

She would pay for her crime another day, he

promised.

Anthony grabbed his pistol and left.

Outside, the sky was filled with gloom, the moon was inconspicuous, but he felt its presence nonetheless, as if it were secretly watching him, zooming in on him. So, in order to evade the suspicious gaze of the otherworldly body, he jumped into his car and sped through the arterial streets.

His thoughts were flawed, tainted with dark images. Something was tormenting him, but he could not touch the heart of it. He wished he could, so he could rip it out and stop it from beating inside his own heart, which drummed as if magma were in its core.

He felt himself burning, burning, burning ... as if he were cocooned in the bosom of Hades.

Respite was what he needed, so he sought it, by stopping the car in the middle of the road, removing himself from within it and fanning his flesh as the flames subsided. Anthony Harris was a man in turmoil at that particular moment. He appeared as a caricature of his former self. At that very moment, he was not himself, and he wasn't who he wanted to be. He felt weak. He was weak. He was simply Mr Harris, and he loathed it. He needed to revert to Police Sergeant Anthony Harris. The man who had the licence to do anything he pleased ... without any repercussions. That is the man he was, that is the man he had grown into. That is the man he loved being.

He had evolved, from a once lonely, lowly, and disillusioned teenager to a man who evoked and demanded fear in countless individuals on innumerable occasions, including his wife, who he knew would feel his wrath after Sunday passed.

He was an officer of the law, a police sergeant for that

matter, a man of valour, accomplishments, and awards and rewards. The more he gathered those things about himself, the more he became who he was.

A man above the law!

He loved the authority that being an officer afforded him. He loved the feeling of power he exuded over people who, without the badge, without the title, would look down on him.

Yes, Police Sergeant Harris loved being who he was, and on that fateful day, he decided that he was not going to change that for anyone or anything. He loved being at the vanguard of inciting fear, or order – as he would call it.

So, he sat back in his car and sped off as Police Sergeant Harris, a man of the law, as opposed to civilian Anthony Harris. The arterial roads he had taken earlier and felt tormented by, proved straight and direct ... as if they were leading him towards something ... perhaps even someone.

As he was chewing over the anger he felt towards his wife, another driver unceremoniously sped past him, which angered him some more. For in his mind, what the other driver had done was disrespectful, and he was not going to let it slide. He revved up his engine some more and overtook the unruly vehicle, violently stalling his car in the middle of the road. His brakes slammed, spraying dust and gravel like bad omens. He waited for the man in the other vehicle to crash into him. But he did not. Fortune was on the man's side, because if he had, he would be spending the night in jail. Officer Harris was determined to make sure of it, and he did not care if the fault was his or not. In his mind, that's what being a police sergeant meant; he could get away with anything and blame someone else for it – if need be, that was.

The other car swiftly stopped about a centimetre away from the officer's vehicle. Officer Harris stepped out, rushed to the other car, and banged on the window, demanding that the man inside "bring your fucking ass out, now!" The man stayed calm. His coolness heated Officer Harris's blood. "Out!" he ordered again, this time proceeding to yank the door open, almost pulling it off its hinges.

"Is there a problem?" questioned the man, as he raised his cold, arctic, blue eyes to meet Officer Harris's. There was venom in the other man's stare. It was unadulterated, white-hot, and raging, and the sergeant felt it.

"Yes, there is a problem, arsehole!" he yelled, his cheeks taut with anger. Red and bruised like a gash. Gently, he consoled his flesh and rubbed it, much to the subtle amusement of the other man.

"You seem upset, why?" questioned the man, his gaze gauging the officer like a rifle would a target.

Officer Harris did not answer. Rather, his hand reached for something hidden. He expected the man to flinch. He did not. The slightest concept of fear was not apparent in him. So, Officer Harris released his hand from his side. His blood boiled as he felt himself shudder imperceptibly. The man was audacious, causing anger, rage, and contempt to grow within Sergeant Harris, at an altitude that he could not fathom.

The man looked at him in such a manner that Officer Harris felt insignificant. No one had ever made him feel that way before, and it pained him. It pained him that the man viewed him as a mere mortal.

Slowly, the man stepped out of the vehicle. Officer Harris stepped back, instinctively. And though they were about the same height, Officer Harris felt the other man growing, taller, taller, taller until he was looking down on him.

He wanted to show his badge, bring the man back down, but something told him that this particular man was not afraid of ... anything!

Officer Harris laughed; the man grinned. And for the first time, the sergeant felt a crippling incompetence.

"I'll see you around," he mustered.

"No," paused the man, as he took a step towards the sergeant, who flinched, "I'll see you around," he vowed, so calmly and honestly that Officer Harris felt gravely uneasy, as though roles had been switched and the man was both police and hunter, and he the prey.

And like a thief, the man got back into his car and stole into the deep black night.

The man was Matthew Wylde.

Sergeant Harris was riled up. Matthew Wylde had deeply offended him, and for that, someone else would have to pay. He would make it his mission to restore his bruised ego.

He drove around for a while, aimlessly, until he got to a quiet road.

In the distance, he saw lights, smoke, and ghoul-like figures who danced insidiously inside the smoke. They appeared, disappeared, and reappeared, as if calling, seeking, and begging for his presence.

His investigative mind urged him to see who the shapes belonged to. But his civilian mind sought otherwise. Nonetheless, Anthony Harris threw caution to the wind. Sergeant Harris had a way of suppressing his civilian self.

He needed to be discreet. In front of him was a car

and in front of that another, so he used both cars as cover to drive past the lights, smoke, and shapeless figures who'd been dancing mysteriously.

As he cautiously drove past, something caught his eye, it flashed at him like lightning: bright and swift. He thought it was a blade, or a gun perhaps. He was not sure. Uncertainty shrouded him. Whatever it was, something within him told him to leave it alone. Maybe he should have driven off. Maybe he should have turned a blind eye, but Police Sergeant Harris would not allow Mr Harris to do such a thing. So, he parked in the distance, took out his concealed weapon, reaffirmed the position of Police Sergeant Harris and aimed to trigger fear.

As he got closer, the lights became brighter and the scent of the smoke stronger. Cannabis was rampant, weeding out the air, choking it and the officer at the same time. He coughed and it immediately startled the shape that had materialised in front of him. It was formed of blood, bone, and flesh.

A young and innocent-looking black face turned and stared at the thirty-something-year-old white man. Like a deer caught in headlights, the young man appeared paralysed with apprehension ... fear ... but ultimately dread at the white face with a vexed expression that stared back at him.

The very young man was Tariq White.

Tariq looked at the sergeant as if his expression offended him. Harris slightly bowed his head, perhaps in shame that the young man saw him for exactly who he was.

For a moment, it seemed the devil was staring at an angel, and Officer Harris was inclined to feel as if he were the former rather than the latter. His heart raced as if the feet of a thousand slaves were stampeding through it.

A peculiar and somewhat otherworldly feeling tied

itself around him like a noose. Fear tried to creep up on him unceremoniously, so he took a quick peek at his weapon, showing fear who was master. Tariq's eyes followed his, and immediately his demeanour changed.

"Who are you?" stammered Tariq.

"I'm a police sergeant," he smiled, deviancy etched on his lips.

A strange look of horror immediately formed on the young boy's face.

A white cop and an unarmed black boy: a deadly combination indeed, crossed the minds of both the officer and the boy.

Tariq's body stiffened, mouth fell slightly open, as a gulp of saliva tried to snake its way past his Adam's apple. However, it was his eyes that captured and captivated the sergeant. They were wet, as if oceans were growing inside and, in the centre of both, balls of perpetual blackness grew, dark, darker, and blacker still. Excitement fired up within the officer. He smiled unintentionally, giddy from the thrill that came from the young man's dread.

Sergeant Harris's fingers casually rummaged through his hair, an odd and futile attempt to try to understand the situation he was in. Nonetheless, insight into how he wound up in such a predicament eluded him. *Curiosity perhaps?* he thought.

He knew that curiosity had killed the cat, but Officer Harris believed he had nine lives.

He wanted to say something, but words failed him. So, he reverted to taking another peak at his weapon; the only master in the cat-and-mouse game that was being played. He thought that fear could not replicate itself, but he saw the boy's fear multiply a thousand-fold as his eyes once more followed the officer's as he looked towards his gun.

Sergeant Harris loved the look of fright that persisted in the young boy's eyes. Like a stalker taunting its prey, he slowly proceeded to encircle him, smelling his fear as if it were rotten flesh, pungent and decaying. The boy's breathing was shallow, cautious, and inaudible, yet still Officer Harris heard it loud and clear. For him, it was a symphony like the Egmont Overture; he heard and revelled in all its pain as if he were the executioner.

A drop of the ocean fell from the boy's eye.

"What do you want?" he squeaked, half-afraid, half-brave as another drop of the ocean escaped his other eye. Two lone tears on both cheeks, trailing down a most-innocent face curated in God's image.

Mr Harris knew that he should have felt pity for him. After all, he was a man of religion, principles, and values. But Sergeant Harris was, at times, an ungodly man, and no matter how hard Mr Harris tried to convince him otherwise, his efforts almost always proved futile.

"You know you shouldn't be smoking, boy," he spat, as he edged closer to the young man. Anthony Harris was not oblivious to his hypocrisy. For he had let off young white men in high school for harsher drugs like coke and meth without any consequence. Tariq shuffled, as if the hand the officer was dealing him was wrong.

"Can I help you, sir?" he pleaded, looking at the plain-clothes officer as if he were incarnate of the most unholy one.

It was a look that cut through Officer Harris like a steel blade. He knew evil lurked within him, but he always hated it when others could sense it, and the only other person who looked at him like that was his wife. The realisation caused his anger to grow tenfold.

"Can I help you, sir?" he repeated mockingly. "No!" he yelled. "No, you may not help me, boy." He snorted, as his hand went to touch his weapon.

Like a nosy neighbour, the moon pulled back its curtain of cloud and watched. Officer Harris noticed the intruder as the scene became luminous, and it was only in that illumination that he realised the boy across from him was actually human, not sub or less than, but fully human, perhaps even more human than he was. Not only was he human, he was but a boy, a teen, sixteen or seventeen, maybe even fifteen.

Mr Harris stepped back, ashamed of Officer Harris.

"I'm sorry," he whispered, eyes lowered as if he truly sought forgiveness.

The teen was taken aback, the once fearsome and ferocious white man who'd harassed him had turned into a timid and apologetic individual. The young man looked at Mr Harris as if he were mentally unstable. Because he was acting damn crazy!

For a moment, Tariq looked at Officer Harris like he might have some good in him. And that made Officer Harris also believe that he had some good in him.

However, it wasn't to last; Tariq swiftly reached into his car to retrieve something ...

Officer Harris, without warning, brought out his weapon and fired.

Bang!

He shot the child, once. The body stumbled, but it did not fall, the car had its back. The will to live was fired up in the teenager. An ocean of crimson flowed over the young man's hand as he clutched his chest. He managed to exhale a laboured and staggered gasp. His eyes widened, emboldened with adrenaline. He tried to gasp again, but the effort tortured his lungs. Officer Harris watched frozen, immobilised, and mesmerised as if in the presence of another-worldly being.

The act of dying was enthralling.

However, the act of trying to survive, to fight, further beguiled the officer. The body struggled as it descended to the ground, holding on to the door of the car, supported by hands that the officer could not see. Perhaps they were the hands of his ancestors, trying to help. Even so, whoever they were, their grip was not strong enough because the young man's entire weight finally made contact with the bloodied earth. He coughed and motioned to the driver's seat of his car.

Officer Harris watched, wondering what the teen was motioning to.

Though weakened the boy's fingers strained to reach something, something metal-like, something that could have been a weapon.

Something that caused the officer to react, swiftly.

Bang!

Bang, bang, bang ...

Whatever it was that the boy had tried to grab stayed in the car, forever elusive to the officer, as he unfroze from his trance and immediately fired two, three, four, five, countless shots, wildly, madly, as if intoxicated by blood lust.

He stopped.

The shots impaled Tariq to the car.

His legs jerked fiercely, then softly, and then they stopped altogether. It was Tariq's final act of dying.

His blood gently rained down and watered the earth, forming creaks, and rills and streams of crimson. Parts of his skin were charred, blackened by the impact of the bullets. Bits of his flesh lay splayed across the floor and on the car, like grotesque pieces of art.

His body was a mess.

His face, however, his handsome face remained untouched, beautiful, and unspoiled by death. It was calm, soft, as if engaged in peaceful slumber.

Officer Harris's heart quaked. He lifted his eyes to the heavens and roared with anguish. He had never killed a child before. It felt like infanticide, the worst type of murder. Perhaps he and his wife weren't so different after all.

A cold touch arrested the officer. His breathing quickened and his mind spun itself into a million thoughts. *What have you done?* screamed Mr Harris at the embattled officer.

"Shut up!" he roared, "Shut up," he insisted to the voice in his head. "Let me fucking think, damn it," he snapped.

Officer Harris went to the car, searched frantically, looking for it, whatever it was. Whatever Tariq was trying to retrieve. Whatever it was, he could not find it. It did not exist. It was all in his mind, a phantom, an epithet of the white man's fears, misconceptions, and biases towards the black boy he had just killed.

But what if it wasn't biases or misconceptions? queried a voice in his head. What if there was actually something the teen could have attacked the cop with? What if? The voice concluded.

Nonetheless, guilt immediately attacked him.

The only tangible thing he saw was the young man's mobile, which rang violently. He edged closer to the phone and the name 'Bridge', with a love heart beside it greeted him on the screen. He suddenly pulled back as if Bridge had seen him.

Officer Harris felt his heart pulsating, boom, boom, boom, trying to break through his ribcage.

He stood in the middle of oblivion, glowing, ghostlike, as the moon illuminated the lone white killer.

The air reeked of guilt ... and fear. He felt something: eyes. Though he could not see them, he felt them like daggers in his back, stabbing, poking, until he was forced to reach back and remove them.

Someone was watching Officer Harris. He looked back and the person was gone, camouflaged by the night. Never to be seen. He ran after the intruder, shouting, "hey, hey, hey," but no one could hear him. No one was there, except him and a dead body.

Perhaps it was his imagination, he tried to convince himself, as he cautiously walked back to the scene of the crime, looking around and acting shifty as if he were guilty of murder and not self-defence, as he tried to force himself to believe.

He had to call his comrades. He needed to speak with his cronies back at the station, men like himself, men that had the means and the power to disassociate him from the predicament he found himself in, or at the very least keep his name and his identity hidden ... forever.

America had again turned into a boiling pot of racial tensions.

Blacks hated whites, and whites hated blacks even more. Black America and some of America needed someone, anyone to hold to ransom, and Officer Harris had no intention of being a martyr for the cause.

He ran to his car. And as he did so, rain began to flood down from the heavens towards earth, beating him like a whip. The moon, though having lost its radiance, refused to leave its watch, as though it were crying at the atrocity it had witnessed. Officer Harris's heart beat chaotically, rugged in its rhythm. "Drive, damn it!" he roared at the vehicle as it failed to start smoothly. The car shook and trembled at the ferocity of the wind as its owner sped away with it. The road home was dark, frightening almost. But every now and then bolts of lightning flashed everywhere as if taking mugshots of the killer from each and every angle. It was a perilous journey for Officer Harris. His hands gripped the wheel, refused to let go until the car came to an abrupt halt in front of his home. He exhaled, indebted to whatever spirit it was that had allowed him to reach his destination in such ungodly conditions.

His fingers shook as they turned the key to his home. He looked back, half expecting the police to be behind him. However, there was no one. He saw nothing, other than his own guilt staring him dead in the eye.

He slammed the door and entered the hallway. The familiarity of his home made him feel odd.

Who was the stranger that had seen him?

What did they see?

Too many questions whizzed around his head, as he stood in the hallway, hoping, praying that his wife was asleep. However, something told him that she was not. There were mud stains on her rain boots. She had been out. Where? And why? From the wetness of the mud, he knew she had entered only a couple of minutes before him, and had rushed to get changed, which was why there was still mud on her boots.

Paranoia surrounded him, taunting him as he had taunted Tariq. He raised his hand to shoo it away, but it stayed, steadfast and unrelenting. He shivered, even though the mercury in his home was at an all-time high.

Slowly, he dragged his feet towards the door of his living room. He could hear his wife breathing. She was awake, she was waiting, and he was suspicious and nervous. He entered, not out of desire, but rather tactic.

"Hi, baby," she greeted.

Strange, he thought to himself. Strange indeed. She was far too happy to see him. She was never happy to see him, well, that is what he had long told himself. According to Officer Harris, Mrs Harris hated him more than he had grown to despise her.

"Hello," he smiled absently.

A judgemental look sat inside her eyes as she watched him, sentencing him without trial for a crime he hoped she knew nothing of.

Paranoia cackled at him.

Officer Harris left his wife downstairs and scurried upstairs to their bedroom. He needed to wash. He stunk of death, guilt, and regret. He ran the bath and waited for the water to fill.

For he had done many bad things in his life, but none of them had amounted to taking a child's life. He told himself that it was not murder. He tried to force himself to believe it was self-defence. He insisted that he had to shoot first and fast, fearing for his own life. *But not countless times,* added the voice within, *Mr Harris.* That was what he called the sensible part of himself.

Oh, how he wished Mr Harris was the only part of him. How he wished for that 5 per cent of him to have manifested itself into 100 per cent of him before he turned into a killer.

He submerged all of his flesh into the body of water, hoping, wishing it would absolve him of his sins. But he knew that his crimes had gone beyond forgiveness. So perhaps that was why, instead of absolving him, the water tried to drown him. The body of liquid pulled him under. He gasped for air, arms flaying, feet flapping, until he managed to break free from the water's grip.

He went to the sink; the man in the mirror grabbed his attention. His once abundant hairline had receded drastically over the years. His bright eyes had long dimmed, and his upside-down frown seemed perpetual as though he had been born with it. He washed his face, over and over and over again, hoping it would wash away the old and change it anew, to a better man, a godly man, a man other than himself.

He looked in the mirror once more, eyes red and glazed and for the first time, he realised that the devil was not black!

40

BACK TO THURSDAY, MARCH 26.

My eyes with unrelenting zeal looked at the pictures of my brother's killer. Matthew had taken three photos of Anthony Harris on three separate occasions. The first on the night he killed my brother, the second at his workplace, dressed in his police regalia, looking valiant and hero-like indeed. The third, and most ironic of all, at Harvard, of me and him engaged in conversation. There was a soft smile on his face, his white hands in mine, consoling me for my great loss. For what it was worth, Anthony Harris appeared as sincere as one could be.

My chest, with brutal violence, heaved! heaved! heaved!

A shrill squeal of horror expelled itself from my throat.

The professor, unsure of whether he should hold me or not, stepped forward ever so cautiously. His eyes were wet and red, burning with the same anguish that was eating me alive.

There was something holy between us in that moment. Two souls feeling justifiably pained by the murder of a bright star.

"I am so sorry, Bridget. Please forgive me for not doing enough, for not doing something ... anything," his lips quivered, incapable of mastering their composure.

I watched him, my eyes wide with raging intrigue. He wanted me to say something, probably a reply that would repel or minimise the flames that were burning him; but I could not, since those same flames had burnt the words in my mouth to ashes.

As we stood there; man and woman, black and white, feeling the same things a body that bleeds and loves feels, his tears began to flow.

At first, a soft angry sob shook him, causing him to lurch onto me. His weight like that of the world's fell on me, yet I was able to carry it as if it were my duty. My arms wrapped around him without restraint and held his convulsing body in place. He gave in to his agony as frenzied, shuddering spasms of grief raged through him. Still, I held him till his torment lost its fevered will to fight him any longer.

Slowly drawing back, his eyes now bloodied, our pained stares met. My palm gently touched his face which was red hot, like Hades.

He managed a slight smile, which cracked the rigid cement-like mask on my face.

Taking a step forward till our noses almost rubbed I placed my other palm on his other cheek.

He sniffled...

"What you have done is beyond enough, Matthew." Our noses, ever so faintly, touched. Like a spark, something lit up in both of us.

Our lips like two colliding galaxies grazed one another ... softly ... briefly ... sincerely.

"Not even the heavens and earth can appreciate the weight and significance of what you've done for me ... for my brother ... the brightest star whose brilliance I'll never see again..." my breath caught and for the first time in a long time a tear flowed for Tariq.

My eyes shot up to the black heavens, which

temporarily held in the rest of the hot liquid which was searing my eyeballs. Nevertheless, gravity was a powerful force, and it forcibly ripped threads of liquid which bled ferociously down my face.

Matthew without hesitation pulled me in and held me in a strong, ever-loving embrace.

"I'm sorry," he kept chanting, his voice broken yet steadfast as one of us needed to be strong for the other.

Slowly, I took a step out of his embrace. My heart still pounded but instead of only with torment there was gratitude dancing in it also.

Matthew's speech at Harvard had not only been a ploy to rile up the black man and get him to be more about action than words. It had also been an act of defiance against Anthony Harris. He knew Anthony was in that theatre. He was goading him to react. It was not a speech said to entirely anger the black man but rather to compel Anthony to act and reveal himself. Something he did not do. However, he did not need to. Matthew had him right where he needed him, in plain sight sitting directly next to me.

It was at that moment that all the puzzle pieces of Matthew Wylde's speech came together, showing me the masterpiece he had created.

Yes, he could have shot Anthony that night, but it appeared he wanted vengeance to be exacted by the black man or maybe woman.

"In this life and any that may come after it..." my eyes fell with gratitude on his beautiful, beautiful face, "you Matthew Wylde will be my hero..."

His face softened, sparking the piercing brilliance of his eyes. "For this..." I sniffled, my eyes studying this white man who'd initially appeared an enemy but was far from that, “this great act of kindness – I, Bridget Celine White, will love you till the oceans are dry. Till the sun freezes and till this heart of mine,” I took his hand and placed it on my chest, “beats no more.”

A lone tear melted down his rosy cheek.

It was as if no one had said such true, pure, and profound words to him before.

“Thank you, Bridget,” he murmured, a steadfast oasis of happiness swimming inside his wet blue eyes.

“I hope you will now be able to get justice for Tariq.”

“Oh, I will” I promised, so calmly and sincerely I frightened myself.

41

SATURDAY, APRIL 4

Matthew's revelation had felt like eight earths had been placed on top of me, and I was forced to carry them. A feat even Atlas could not achieve. Yet, carry them I did. For eight days I barricaded myself inside my flat. Stepping out only to go see Winner and my parents who were in my support bubble. The world was fighting isolation. However, I craved it. I needed it to function after such a disclosure.

For eight days and eight nights, I obsessed over the contents of Matthew's words. For eight days and eight nights, I sought vengeance - drawing up plans, disposing of them, and then drawing up new ones all over again. For eight days and eight nights, I was not Bridget Celine White - I was the storm that Anthony Harris did not know would inevitably drown him.

* * * *

David lived in east central. Prime London. Liverpool Street, to be specific.

His building was filled with foreign buyers from Hong Kong, Malaysia, Saudi Arabia, the USA and her nemesis China. Many did not live in the country but had bought properties nonetheless, because ... money talks.

It was 9 am. Lockdown was now fully upon us.

I had tried to sleep in my bed the night before but, sleep eluded me as images of Tariq, Anthony Harris, and the professor kept painting themselves in my mind's eye.

Feeling lonely and troubled, I had called David, who picked me up and took me to his, ensuring I got some much-needed sleep while cuddled in his warm embrace. I still hadn't told him that I had met up with the professor or of the conversation we had had. I wanted to tell him, desperately. But I could not. I did not want him to ruin the plan I had set into motion.

This was why on that Saturday morning, sitting in David's dining room drinking a cup of coffee, I had consciously decided to remove my mind from the contents of the professor's confession until the time was right. And when that time was right, Officer Harris would surely feel the wrath of this woman, Bridget White.

"Let's go for a walk," David proposed as we both finished our cups of coffee.

Stepping outside, the streets were isolated. For the first time, it struck me that nature actually lived in these parts of town.

In the distance, The Shard greeted us from a not-so-far yet not-too-close position. A gush of fleeting spring breeze lingered on my skin before dispersing in different directions.

David wrapped his cashmere jumper around me, placed a kiss on my neck and asked, "Better?"

I smiled, kissing the back of his hand. "Yes, better."

In the distance, The Gherkin made itself known. It was as if all the tall buildings in that part of town were vying for our attention as we turned a little to the right to witness the Heron Tower waving vigorously.

David pulled me into him. There was a mischievous look in his soft gaze. "Does the Princess Bridge of Hackney Town seek a morning adventure?"

"You are so silly," I laughed with fervour.

"Only for you Bridge, only for you."

"Yes, I would love a morning adventure," I beamed as he pulled me into a gentle jog.

Some minutes later, we were at the main gates of a small and quaint, hidden outdoor market. It was the second weekend of the lockdown that the government had imposed on us. We expected the market to be a ghost town. However, a dozen or so people were waiting two metres apart in the queue. My guess was that cabin fever was kicking in after having been locked indoors for over a week, and these people like myself needed a respite which came in the shape of this market.

In front of the gate were two stations of sanitiser, which we all had to use before and after entry.

We waited for a red-cheeked, buoyant character with a top hat and a kilt to approach. Silence fell on us as the man with the kilt turned the last click on the thick double-padded lock. A crescendo of woos erupted.

"Welcome," his huge voice boomed at us. In his hand was an infrared thermometer which took our temperature before entry was permitted.

"Thank you, man," David said, much to the kilted one's delight.

"You are welcome."

The delicious aromas of continental foods tickled my taste buds. But we weren't there for food. Taking my hand David led me to a florist.

"Oh, wow, what a gloriously beautiful couple," said the florist, stopping to look up at us. I smiled, a little shyly. David said thanks on behalf of both of us.

"Now, tell me have you ever seen a real-life princess before?"

"No."

"Well today, you are in luck"

"Oh, my," the florist half-squealed, putting down her pruning shears and the flowers she was arranging. Carefully, she removed her gloves, dusted her hands and cautiously reached out a hand to me with a slight curtesy. David winked my way. "It is such an honour to behold your presence, Princess..."

"Princess Bridget of the Ashanti Empire of the Gold Coast." David inserted. It took all my restraint and will to not burst out laughing at this well-orchestrated fable of my origins.

"Wow," she mused, her lashes fluttering as if I truly had blue blood. "Please, Princess, what can I get you? Anything at all, I am here to serve."

"Thank you."

"Three dozen roses for the Princess, please."

The florist, eager to treat me with reverence, went over to the fancy cupcake stall and borrowed two of their chairs. Placing them down she cleaned them thoroughly with some disinfectant wipes. "Please sit."

Ten or so minutes later the florist had prepared a large and wonderful boxed bouquet of red, white, and pink roses.

"For you, Princess of the Gold Coast."

I smiled, impressed by the full-blooming roses. "Thank you so much."

Before she could say the price, David removed four red notes from his wallet and gently placed them in her outstretched hands. Her face beamed with joy. "Oh, this is too much - thank you, thank you."

"No, thank you," he said, smiling a smile that

probably made her feel like the only girl in the world.

Making our way back to his, I stole furtive glances at David. It had not dawned on me before, but now it did. He reminded me of Tariq to some extent.

It was uncanny how all the great men in my life reminded me of this singular entity – Tariq White.

42

Moments in April 2020

As I was making myself food, which I did not need for nutrition but rather comfort, my phone began to ping endlessly in the background.

I hissed, "Arrgh, who the hell is that?"

I was determined that I would finish making my ham and cheese sandwich before I went anywhere near the phone. "You look so pretty," I said to the sandwich as I took a large bite out of it. I poured myself a glass of orange juice and headed to the living room.

The pings were incessant. "Oh shut up!" I yelled. I picked up the phone and the pings calmed down, as if the sender knew that I was upset with them.

The messages were all from my PGCE WhatsApp group, which was aptly named: PGCE WhatsApp group. There were only fourteen students in the English class as it seemed most would-be teachers fancied the Maths and Sciences more. Who knows, perhaps it was because they were awarded higher bursaries, but that was none of my business. My English class of fourteen was dwarfed by the other courses in the Initial Teacher Education department. However, I liked it like that. It meant that we were closer than the other subjects, and it was easier to talk to fourteen people than it was to eighty or ninety people. I mean, can you imagine that many people messaging you all at once? One would surely go tone-deaf.

My class was made up of some interesting characters. There was Sabrina who spoke ever so lightly and ever so calmly, so that we all had to lean in to hear what she was saying. Then we had Aaron, he was the lad's lad of the group. Each time we were at university, after the last seminar of the day, he would propose we go to the pub to treat ourselves for completing one more day of our hectic course. "Who's up for drinks?" he would say. I would laugh then say, "Thanks for the invite, but I have to get home." He would then look at the rest of the group who would move away from him as if he were contagious. He'd chuckle then say, "Only me then," and go off on his jolly way. I liked his outlook on life, though it seemed he was half-drunk half of the time. We also had Alisha, the talkative one who raised her hands in lectures, in seminars, and even in the queue at the café. Then, last but not least, we had Leo ... my favourite.

Everyone in the WhatsApp group had a lot to say about ... something ... nothing ... and everything in-between, which is why I purposely put my group on mute for weeks on end, only checking it at my leisure and not because incessant pings were forcing me to ... like now. Clearly, the weekly mute cap I had applied to my PGCE group had expired, which was why all the messages were trying to be heard all at the same damn time – until I put it on mute again.

Upon opening the group chat, it was one message after another, after another, after another. I decided to type a message: *Hi guys. I hope everyone is well and keeping safe, and applying social-distancing measures.*

For a minute or so, no one replied. I was used to it. It was my punishment for not interacting with the group as much as I should have. But then after five minutes of playing mean girls and boys, one 'hello' and 'hi' after another started coming in. I laughed. They may not have known it, but I quite enjoyed their bullying tactics to entice me to become more involved with them. In their case, it showed they cared and that they valued my opinions and insight. The reason I knew that was because, whenever I spoke or mentioned something, everyone would listen and take it on board and message me privately for more information if they needed it.

Guys, I am sorry I've not been engaging with the group recently, I wrote, feeling a little bad.

It's fine ... no worries ... we know you're busy with Winner ... and *are you sure*? were some of the replies that followed my message.

Yes, I am sure, Leo, I replied.

Hmm, he replied with an emoji.

Leo was my only actual friend in the class. Firstly, because we were the only two with kids, and secondly, we were the oldest. Yes, when you are in a class filled with twenty-one-year-olds and a twenty-two-year-old who was only a year late because he wanted to take a gap year, twenty-five was considered old. I was the second oldest in the class after Leo. The twenty-one-year-olds looked at him as if he were ancient. A fossil. Or an antique.

On the first day in class, the twenty-one-year-olds thought I was the same age as them because ... 'black does not crack'. But as soon I said I was twenty-five, they started speaking slowly using monosyllabic words as if I was hard of hearing.

Leo was forty-eight, so he was ancient. And it was his ancientness that drew me to him. He believed that we should call our lecturer 'Sir', even though he was only twenty-nine and told us to call him Ian – because that was his name, and in the UK, university students called their lecturers by their first names. But Leo was from a different era and country. So, I suppose it must have been a culture shock for him to be sitting in a class with people who had been teenagers barely two years earlier.

Leo was the unofficial patriarch of the group. We went to him to seek advice as well as get our daily dose of laughter. He had the funniest stories to tell, and whenever he spoke, we listened. And sometimes Leo spoke so much that Ian, our lecturer, would have no choice but to listen. I think sometimes Leo, though respectful of Ian, forgot who the lecturer was. The class would giggle as Leo lectured us and the lecturer. And, though at times we would finish class without going through all the intended topics, our lecturer took it in his stride. He was understanding, Ian. There were times when I would come in late because Winner was being moody or I had a rough night, and after class he would pull me aside, ask if I were okay and tell me that I was doing a good job, looking after a child and completing a course such as a PGCE which required me to be at school or uni five days a week.

For a young lecturer, Ian was near amazing. And even Leo agreed, though he would sometimes say, "That boy needs to teach like a man and not allow you kids to be on your phones all the time." Only Leo in Leo's mind was allowed to go on his phone during lectures as he maintained that he was doing research whenever he used his phone, while he felt that us 'kids' were on Instagram, Snapchat, and 'faze-book' as he called it. I would laugh at his theories, not because they were untrue, but because they had some truth to them.

I took another bite of my sandwich. *Leo my friend, how are you today?* I wrote in the group chat.

I am fine ... just bored AF!

I chuckled, *lol* I typed. Leo was trying to use the kids' lingo. Even he had to laugh. *Lol ... AF means as f**k, right?*

Yes. We all typed, adding the laughing emoji.

Good ... because since lockdown everything now has

AF in it ... hungry AF ...tired AF ... bored AF ... sad AF ... lonely AF ... depressed AF ...

Something was wrong. Leo never spoke like that. He always saw the glass as half-full. But the words he was using showed that his glass was half-empty.

I exited the group chat and called him on a normal call.

A message from David came in: *Good morning, beautiful*, it read. I swiped up. I would have to reply to him later.

The phone rang ... once ... twice ... thrice ... and on the fourth ring Leo picked up.

In his thick Italian accent, he said, "Good morning, Bridget," he was the only one in the group who called me Bridget.

"Morning, big bro ...how are you?"

"I'm alright."

"Are you sure?"

"Yes," he paused ... "No," he corrected. "I miss my kids, and even their dragon of a mother."

Leo had received a scholarship from the university he had been attending in Milan to complete a PGCE at our university and was in London on a student visa. He had left his two kids, Bella and Leo Jr, with their mother so he could pursue a brighter future for them. Leo had once owned his own pizzeria, but the business had hit rough times and he could no longer maintain it, so he'd had to lock up shop. And that was when he decided to be a teacher. In his village he was the only one who could speak English well, so he started giving free English lessons to the kids in the area and perfecting his own English in his spare time. He studied hard and took some online courses, which resulted in actual certificates. He took those certificates as proof of having the drive to become a teacher to the university in Milan and applied as a mature student. He got a job at the student café as a waiter and finished his undergrad as manager of the café and, most importantly, with a first-class degree which gave him a scholarship that took him straight to one of the best universities in the UK to complete a PGCE, leaving his kids and family behind.

So, when he told me that he missed them, his words touched me like a sad song. "I'm sorry, Leo ... can't you go and visit them?"

He sighed. "All flights in and out of Italy have been suspended."

Ahh, yes. Italy was now the epicentre of the virus in Europe, so the aviation companies were only applying safety measures, I supposed.

"Okay ... I need you to do something for me, Leo." I paused. "... Are you listening"

"Yes, Bridget, I am listening."

"Good ... now get up from where you are sitting ... are you getting up?"

"Yes, I am up."

I took a sip of orange juice. "Now, make your way to the kitchen."

"The kitchen?" he questioned.

"Yes ... the kitchen."

"I am there."

"What do you see?"

He half laughed. "I see my kitchen, Bridget."

"Sure, you see your kitchen ... but what is that you see outside the window of your kitchen? What do you truly see?"

"I see the canal..."

"Yes..." I urged.

"And I see the thick and trimmed bushes ... and I see the birds ... no ... I hear the birds ... I hear them, they are singing a symphony, as if it were composed by Giovanni Battista Sammartini, and I also hear the stream..."

When he fished telling me all the things he could see and hear, I asked, "Could you see and hear those before?"

He smiled. "Nature is coming alive, Bridget..." he paused.

"Yes, it is ... and for every day that you feel down, I want you to look outside your kitchen window and imagine it to be Venice. Imagine the lake as the grand canal, and the birds as the Italian sparrow or flamingos. Imagine the beauty without pollution, where you can see all the fish of the canal and hear all the songs of the birds ... That is the view behind your window ... that is your little Italy, Leo..."

"Yes ... yes, it is," he said. At that moment I could picture him immersed in the little Italy behind his English home. "Thank you," he said.

I smiled. "Now I want you to do one last thing for me."

"If it is as glorious as little Italy, then anything."

"It may not feel like little Italy initially, but give it five minutes and it'll feel like big Italy," I said, laughing quietly. Leo had once described the setup of the house in which he stayed with four other students. He told me there was a dirty, muddy lake behind the kitchen, and he also told me that the birds near his home sang as if they were drunkards. And he was the one who told me he kept his favourite bottle of alcohol in the top cupboard on the right with a note that read: "Do not touch or I will eat your heart alive."

"Get a glass."

"Okay."

"Open the cupboard on the right, take out Hennessy the heart eater and pour a shot for me."

He once told me that Hennessy was his favourite drink. So, I was certain he would at least have a bottle somewhere.

"Done."

"Now drink it. This isn't something I would advise you to do on a daily basis," I said, though I drank a bit, but the idea was to do as I say not as I do. "But you can do it once in a while ... for the moments when you may need a bit of escapism. Okay?"

He laughed. "Alright, Miss."

"Salute," I said as I gulped my orange juice.

"Salute," said Leo as he downed the shot.

We spoke a little while longer until he noticed his kids were calling. I told him to answer.

Before he locked off, he said, "Thank you so much for today; sei una principessa, Bridget!"

43

The month of March which in its embryonic stages had bloomed with luminous green convictions of hope, promising to melt away the dark and gloom of February, swiftly aborted its mission. The birds no longer breezed through the sunlit heavens singing glorious melodies and the incandescent pastel leaves withered and died, leaving remnants of blackened-brown leaves in their wake.

We were now in April.

Across the seven seas, in the land of the free, the psychosis of white supremacy reared its ungodly head once more. It was the hunger games with Team White hunting Team Black. A father and son duo from Team White hunted and gunned down a jogger from the opposing faction. The referees saw no foul until the masses from both teams demanded justice, claiming the rules did not include murder.

Somehow, affairs stateside reminded me of Tariq, which in turn reminded me of the professor, which in turn reminded me of Tariq's killer; an entity who was now unmasked.

March had deceived us all. And, as for me, she had hung me out to dry at the peak of an unforgivingly cold mountain.

But salvation was on the horizon. Inside my television screen on BBC1, to be precise.

My once-upon-a-time undying foe, Principal Greaves, was standing on a podium, his long thin frame imposing and tactile. There was an ugly charisma about him. He embodied the allure of a man you admired, not for his looks but for his virtuosity. He made a gesture with his hands and the bodies near him departed like flies. He took a deep sigh and looked at the camera with something that one could only interpret as an attempt to look half-human.

I gulped the glass of water in my hand and focused on the screen. "What the hell is he up to now?" I muttered, still incensed at the foul dust he had sprinkled on me during my final day at his school.

The principal was adorned in battle regalia. An armour of self-confidence, the sword of egotism, and a helmet of intellect. I would be lying if I said I was not, at that precise moment, mesmerised by him. He commanded attention, and he had mine, undivided.

He cracked a smile that almost split my screen in two.

"Jackson..." our prime minister "... and his fleet of enfeebled advisors have declared war on our education system." He paused, his demeanour defiant and unapologetic. "They've lambasted and denigrated the importance of the state school, and as a result, uprooted the livelihoods of its most vulnerable party: the students..." he continued.

The principal admonished Jackson in a fashion that took one's breath away. His words were agile and succinct, with their arrows skilfully flying off the bow and hitting their target every time. His grandeur harboured an acutely guarded brilliance accessible only to a few. At times, the verbiage of his eloquent diatribe was a matter for reproach. But I continued to listen, nonetheless. For I was anticipating a wondrous climax. And the principal did not disappoint.

Principal Greaves was right. There is never a probable cause for ceasing education. The principal may have been older than time itself, but his words were not outdated or archaic. Rather, they were present and modern.

Compulsory state-run education, which had been hailed as the shining beacon of Western civilisation, seldom did much to produce critical and curious minds. At times, it diverted fact to fiction. Intellectual curiosity was defunct, and some students used school as a social club till the age of sixteen. Indefinite periods of distance and remote learning were not for such students. The private and grammar school caucus will manage, but not the state school children. For some of them, the dominant medium of information was social media. Go figure what staying at home for months would do to their intellect. "I will not allow such an unethical act for my students..." the principal bellowed.

It was a particularly fierce diatribe against the government and the DfE. The principal's grandfather was a duke and a distant cousin to the throne. Again, with all that privilege, I was dumbfounded as to why he chose the job he chose, at the school he chose. Perhaps it was the white-saviour complex, or perhaps it was the pure desire to create change. Whatever it was, he was passionate about it, which was apparent by the way his fingers gripped the mic. His attack on Jackson was an act of white-on-white violence. And for some strange reason, it excited me and most of England who were watching the news that day. The principal, with a more refined enunciation of the received pronunciation vernacular, bared his fangs and ripped into Jackson and co. I imagined Jackson inside the fortified walls of No 10 breaking everything and yelling, "You fucking wanker!" at the TV while Principal Greaves spoke. The image made me laugh deliriously.

The principal did not identify with impulsivity, and he saw the hurried decision to close schools as such.

"The doors of Lady Liberty High will not close." His words, though simple, were warheads directly aimed at you, me, us and everyone watching the news that fateful day. It was a bold act of defiance. Challenging the powers that be to censor him. They did not. They could not, because, by the time the principal stepped off the podium, social media had assembled the hashtag #badboygreaves. Within minutes, the vampire had been thrown into the limelight. He could either disintegrate under the bright lights or further shine them on his principles. He did the latter. And I imagined Jackson ripping out every thread of his blonde locks, flipping the bird and yelling, "Wanker!" once more.

* * * *

Sitting on Winner's chair mulling over the principal's tirade coming from inside my TV earlier in the day, I smiled back at the photo of Tariq on the wall in Winner's bedroom. How I wished he had met Winner.

Winner was at his grandparents, which was why I was sitting in his chair. David was at the hospital valiantly fighting the virus and the professor, like an Achilles heel, was always afoot, creeping into the crevices of my thoughts alongside Tariq and Anthony Harris.

With my life still in tatters, my mind wandered to the profession I had chosen.

The teaching profession was a funny one. It proclaimed autonomy. But teachers were so restricted it felt like pseudo-slavery. You are told "you have authority" in the classroom, but you couldn't tell a student to shut up when they were being obscenely rude to you or their classmate. You couldn't slap the little shits when they aggravated you. Autonomy my arse! Commandeering a class was like going on a failed mission each day, with troops who were gravely demotivated, obnoxious, and mind-bogglingly childish. Yet somehow it was thrilling.

Not knowing what the school day held in store was thrilling.

My first placement school was deep in the dark, dark wilderness of white working-class folks. Understandably, I had come to acquire biases and stereotypes that I had placed, unbalanced, on white shoulders. Nonetheless, life was a bastard or a truth serum depending on what side a tossed coin landed.

The night before my first day had been turbulent. Sleep arrested and released me in equal measure, and by the time I woke, the sun was so wide awake that I thought I was in a dream of a dream. But my alarm, the differentiator between the realm of make-believe and reality, buzzed incessantly, inciting me to practise what would be my morning ritual for the next three months. Twenty-five minutes in the shower, ten for me and fifteen for Winner who liked to sit in the bath playing with his ducks while belting out Pinkfong's, Baby Shark, seven minutes moisturising and dressing for us both, and ten minutes for breakfast before I dropped him at nursery then made my three-minute sprint to the train station.

At Tottenham Hale station, the black bodies vanished into the Victoria line or onto the buses parked outside. The few that were left led their suitcases by the collar and walked or ran with their four-wheeled pets onto the Stansted Express.

My train was for Cheshunt, Hertfordshire.

The stereotypes I had about predominantly white schools were to be violently debunked. There were no wealthy or highly intellectual or smart kids in this white land I was heading towards on the train.

The media did not report the disparaging statistics of predominantly white schools. Especially when they were in such close proximity to London. The bad schools in

London were sardined with foreigners whose mother tongues were Bengali, Urdu, varieties of Eastern European and African languages. Those were the badly performing schools in the minds of the masses. So, imagine my great shock-horror at seeing blonde, ginger, and light-brown-haired kids not fitting the narrative.

I was shocked. The rate of poverty was astounding. Children on free meals. Learning difficulties.

The media never showed that side of white schools. It was the gang violence in South London they highlighted. Yet this school I was going to had more than half its students on pupil premium or free school meals. Special Educational Needs, looked-after children. And a very limited amount of gifted and talented students, who ironically happened to be three black girls and two Asian boys with a single white boy, and education welfare officers were littered all across the school.

On my first day, a boy with violently red hair brought cocaine and a knife to school, I was bloody shocked.

Needless to say, it was at that school where my mentor and I bumped heads. Their disregard for my PGCE was astonishing. During my first three weeks, I had to teach the classes by myself. At the end of my placement, only one of my mentors signed my documents; the other white woman (the ITE coordinator) refused, even after endless emails from me and my lecturer.

I think we all know why.

Furthermore, it was at this school that I found out that Years 10 and 11 did not know what GCSE meant.

"I hope you're all ready for your General Certificate of Secondary Education?" I had asked the Year 11s. And everyone had asked in unison, "What's that, Miss?"

I was stunned.

It was at that school I became aware of the great divide in education that the media did not highlight.

44

Growing up, I was British.

It was during adulthood I became black British. Even 'just black' to a degree.

I loved being British. I loved the currency; that mighty pound that could be exchanged for plenty in foreign lands. I loved the education system; the oldest and most prestigious in the world if the history books by old white men were anything to go by. I loved the people. I even loved the soggy piece of fish that was accompanied by even soggier chips aptly named "fish and chips". I loved it all. Great Britain was home. A beautiful one at that.

Growing up, I was not black. I was simply British. I knew what black meant but now, in hindsight, I had no bloody clue.

I suppose attending one of the most prestigious private schools somewhat blinkered me or rather gave me the privilege, or lack thereof, of not seeing race but rather money. Money, prestige, and pedigree were the great determiners, growing up in my world. And fortunately for me, the wealthiest donor of my private school was black. Like black-black. And his child, who attended the school, was also black-black. He was wealthier than the Jewish, American, and British billionaires who poured money into the school as if they were fetching it from the Atlantic Ocean.

It was not loud, black money that he had. He had wealth; "generational wealth", he had once told my father, who appeared to be a non-believer, while we ate dinner in his gargantuan dining room which was teeming with servants who attended to our every whim. He had the kind of money that was so inconspicuous you knew its amount had to be enormously profane. It was the kind of money that had his globe-shaped, copper-toned face plastered across the school grounds like a prophet. A prophet of money, that is. He made it possible for blackness to be cool in my school the same way whiteness was cool across the world. It was because of him the words "money talks!" were coined. He made the Caucasians and other fairer-shaded folks feel black. And it was only in adulthood that I knew what a massive achievement that was.

He was a hero without a cape, and most importantly, father to my best friend, Alison.

Alison's parents, alongside my own, played a massive part in me not acknowledging how the world would ultimately see me when I left the cocoon I had been bundled in for my school years.

I was most likely the poorest of the black students at my school. That is if you consider my parents making £175k each per annum poor at the time. Even so, in my school that was considered poor compared to the other black students. Yet relatively richer than plenty of white students. My parents were not senators or ex and current heads of state nor were they "entrepreneurs" like every other black student's parents.

However, what other parents had in money, mine had in prestige and pedigree - the prestige and pedigree of my parents being world-renowned consultants and leaders in their medical fields. Like the principal, Dr Bernard once said, "Your parents are the greatest." And he was right. My parents are the greatest, apart from my mother who, at times, competed with the devil to see who could boil my blood the most. Nonetheless, that was then. Now, Mother and I are like best friends.

Then, however, Mother preferred the world to

revolve in the directions she proposed. Any other route was damn-near sacrilegious. I was seldom allowed to leave the bubble in which, according to her, she had lovingly placed me in, because according to her perception of the world, her prognosis was that "it was a cruel place".

Ironically, she was right.

So, it was on those rare occasions when I was allowed to visit my cousins, whose parents were not intelligent enough and had the misfortune of not being doctors or lawyers, that I began to see the world Mother spoke of. It was during those illicit adventures with the less-refined folks that my blackness revealed itself to me. It was my cousin Aaliyah who first called me "brown skin". And it was her boyfriend Tyrone who first said, "Wow!" his eyes mesmerised by me. "You're pretty for a black girl." That was because she was mixed and he did not expect me to be prettier than her, but I was. Not that I cared. But he did, and I noticed. His incognisance both humoured and shocked me. I was alarmed that he did not see that aliens like me were also bestowed, much more than the others if you asked me, with the gift of beauty. Especially seeing as he was part of my alien tribe. Which begged the question did he not see beauty in himself?

Because I saw it. His skin, black as tar, and his teeth, white like clouds.

Going to Brixton was the first time I noticed black-on-black violence. A Jamaican boy slapped an African boy and said, "Go back to your country, you freshie." The fact that one was Jamaican and another African was only made apparent when my cousin elaborated that the modern Caribbeans felt some type of superiority over the Africans because they made it to the island of Britain first. Though it was the Africans who were more successful. It made no sense to me, but I was deeply fascinated because in my home, black was black. It never occurred to me that I could tell someone else to go back to where they belonged. The cool kids in my school were Africans. There was only one Caribbean pupil, and he was there on a scholarship. So, the disgust that the Jamaican boy harboured for the African boy was alien to me. A form of self-hate that became pronounced every time I left my cocoon in Hampstead and explored the London my mother despised with my cousin.

I began noticing things that had not been apparent in the majority-white cocoon that my parents kept me in. Not because they choose to, but because their pedigree and their prestige placed them in white surroundings that ironically only a few white English people had the privilege to be part of, contrary to popular belief.

What I liked about prestige and pedigree was that it was not easy to attain. It did not allow uneducated, uncultured, and uncouth white people in. And I liked that. I liked that hard work needed to be done on both sides, even though I was consciously aware that whites did not work as hard as blacks.

We studied Swahili at my school. Which now seems mind-boggling. Our teacher was a white South African. Which is now even more mind-boggling than the fact we studied Swahili. He would say things like: "I am an African man to the bone," which made me think "liar." Yet, whenever we visited his class, we left feeling cultured, muttering Swahili phrases in the different accents that we all possessed.

When I was growing up, most of my friends were rich and white. I was aware that I was rich and black. But I was also aware that we were equal, which made colour obsolete, to a degree. Our skin complexion at the time was simply a rainbow, different hues in a singular body.

As I grew up, however, that rainbow became scattered, splitting itself into separate spectrums, refusing to amalgamate back to its former single unit. Showing me that the world was indeed black and white. And no matter how hard we tried, white conversations about black and vice versa would always occur. They will occur at home, at school, in the workplace and especially during the middle of a worldwide pandemic.

45

Three Months Later – July

I had decided not to pursue a career in teaching.

My mother's prayers had been answered.

Although I had completed my PGCE with flying colours, received my certificate and participated in the online graduation held for my course, I was no longer filled with a yearning to enter the classroom come September. Although in April the principal had vowed that Liberty High would stay open – it did not. The powers that be were to allow no such thing to occur. This meant that the rest of my course was done online. With each passing day, meeting on Zoom or Google Meet, my desire for the profession dwindled. Until one day I decided that although I would complete the course, as I did not like to leave things half-done, I was not to utilise the certificate it came with.

I wanted to move away from England and do a Master's in one of the courses that Mother preferred.

* * * *

With my palms clammy and my heart racing erratically, I asked David as earnestly as I could, "Move to America with me?"

He looked at me, bemused, an uncertain grin on his face which was suddenly transformed into a snort. This made me laugh; the way he snorted, which was seldom, always made me laugh.

For a moment time stopped, my chest drummed

while his ice-cool gaze lay in my burning brown one. *Please don't say no, please don't say no,* I kept hearing my heart plead.

Sitting between his legs was the champion, Winner, blissfully eating a slice of cheesy pizza while inquiring why his father had just stopped playing the game inside the television.

"Daddy, press X," he insisted, taking the PlayStation console, as it seemed David had frozen in time.

I swallowed, hoping the action would water the desert that had formed inside my throat.

"Say something ... please."

Winner, feeling the tension that had settled in the room like a thick fog, looked at me, then his father.

"Daddy answer. Say something," insisted Winner, annoyed that the lack of an answer from his father's end was taking time away from their game.

I could imagine all the thoughts flowing through his mind. Why? Why did I wish to move so suddenly?

I would tell him the truth. Just not that day. On that day all I needed was his devotion, to follow me, anywhere, everywhere, even if it be to the ends of the earth.

His eyes skimmed the ceiling, then the game inside the TV, which was not on pause, so the avatar kept repeating the same movement over and over again. Perhaps it was my mind playing tricks but the tiny figure looked just as pissed off as Winner at the lack of activity from the controller.

"Oh, Daddy, Spidey is bored," grumbled Winner as he finally decided to snatch the controller from David, find his own seat and play the game all by himself with a sulky look embedded on his face.

David kissed his head. "I'm sorry baby," he said, taking my hand and leading me to the balcony.

Incredulous, he hissed, "What?"

"Move to America with me!"

He wants to ask, to gain insight into such a request. But he does not. Instead, he gauges me with his eyes, then cool as ice says, "For you, Bridge, I will travel to the ends of the earth."

During the first lockdown, economy flights were completely unavailable. You could only buy business and first-class tickets. Private jets were running rampant, but that privilege was reserved for the super-rich. The poor weren't allowed freedom of movement. They were forced to stay in the country and in their homes. Only being allowed to venture to supermarkets and outdoor markets to purchase essential items. The rich, however, could go wherever they pleased. The segregation between rich and poor was happening right before our eyes. And though I liked the company of people on or above my level, it did not for a second escape me how unfair the conditions of lockdown were.

David bought three first-class tickets. I had told him to purchase business class instead. However, he had teased me, saying, "Surely, we cannot move countries on business-class seats. We have to travel in style, baby."

* * * *

I hadn't thought about where we were going to live, what cars we'd be driving, or where Winner would be starting school when we settled.

All I had thought about was Anthony Harris. I was obsessed with him.

Anthony Harris was the only moving, breathing thing that consumed my thoughts day in, day out.

David, however, had thought about where we would live, and the cars we would drive. He had made all the arrangements for our move to the States even though it was my idea. It was as if he knew I needed him to tie up all the loose ends. He may not have said it, but I felt he knew I was in America for a purpose. A purpose that I could only reveal to him after its achievement.

* * * *

At last, I was happy. Well as happy as could be, that was.

David and I were finally a family. I had forgiven him for Camilla-gate. The true reason for my forgiveness was because Camilla had confessed. She confessed that she was the one who had kissed him and that he had rejected her so forcefully, she had been ashamed to admit to me that David had firmly turned her down. I had also forgiven her. Because I could only imagine how hard it must've been for her to admit such to me, finally. Needless to say, our friendship would not be the same. But I had forgiven her and that was what mattered. However, the truest reason for my forgiveness of David was love. I loved him like I loved no other. I loved him like I loved myself. And he loved me more than he loved himself. Such a man deserved my forgiveness, so I gave it to him with all my heart.

My mother and I were no longer at an impasse. She was who she was always meant to be to me: my hero! She and Father, Alexander the Great, would be visiting us in December, and I could not wait as I, alongside David and Winner, had been missing her cooking ... greatly. For all my talents I could never match Mother's skills in the kitchen. The woman was blessed all around.

46

August

It was a glorious Sunday morning in August. Winner was dressed. David was dressed. I was watching myself in the mirror, getting dressed.

I did not frequent a place of worship. But the spirit of benevolence was apparent in me. I knew God was real. I spoke with him daily. I asked him for protection, mainly for Winner, David, and my parents. I also asked him to protect others, others like the professor.

"Hurry up, babe. We don't want to be late."

David was right. I did not want to be late. I wanted to be there for the entire press conference. It was imperative that my family and I were there to pay homage to my brother Tariq and the other fallen black bodies, then and now.

The ingrained attitude of police forces across the US and the UK could only be changed with training and workshops that aimed to remedy the institutionalised racism and ideology that black bodies did not require rational thinking or patience from the men in blue. Many of the rotten apples in the force regarded black men as titans whose godly and mighty physiques - which provoked resentment in lesser men - could only be tamed by metal. The police as an institution needed to regard the male black body as human, not otherworldly.

As humans it is indelibly ingrained in our nature to conquer what we are physically threatened by or what we feel could ultimately be mightier than ourselves. The black man is such an emblem. A physical symbol of might. And in the art of war, the greatest of men have been known to always target the strongest of their kind. It is the ultimate symbol of power: to conquer what might appear unconquerable. The difference with the black man is that he isn't only a symbol but rather a literal manifestation. You see, symbols die, in time they do. But the black man is eternal so his fight is eternal. And that is the problem. His immortality.

Constantinople, Rome, Egypt, The Benin Empire, Genghis Khan, Mehmed the Conqueror, Alexander the Great, Malcolm X, Martin Luther King Jr: all conquered by one thing or the other. Yet the black man as an emblem remains, even after being subjected to the cruellest of lives.

I was happy this service was taking place to commemorate Tariq. I was glad that steps were being taken, however small they were. It is said Rome was not built in a day. Surely, the shackles of the black man couldn't be removed in a day. Also, it was essential I noted that some of us weren't too eager to remove our shackles. We were enslaved by our lack of self-worth and desire to do better and be better as a collective –thinking that others would help us, even though they were busy helping themselves.

"I am ready," I said to much jubilation from David and Winner.

"Finally, Mummy," sulked the champion with a cheeky smile.

David kissed me on the cheek, then my lips. "I love you, Bridget White."

"I love you too, David King."

"Yuck" giggled Winner, who was swiftly swept off his feet and smothered with kisses by his father.

In the car, my small family and I bobbed our heads to the latest hip-hop, dance music and classical beats. All the while, Winner was multi-tasking, playing on his tablet, pointing out fascinating architecture and weird American things like the spelling of words such as 'color'.

I was happy. My heart was full.

I could not have asked for a more perfect Sunday.

"We're here ... we're here" chanted the champion, who swiftly removed his seatbelt and impatiently waited for his father to open his door.

During the drive, I had asked once or twice "Are we there yet?" with excited anticipation. Now that we were there I could not help but feel heavy of heart. A deluge of Tariq's memories flooded me. *You must be strong*, I told myself. I must've been listening to my subconscious because the memories fled from me and I was left feeling invigorated as if the genesis and revelation of something predestined was about to happen.

"Shall we?" David took my hand and led me inside the building.

My eyes wandered around the room. Taking in the sea of bodies swimming inside it.

That was when I saw him. Alive and with hair as red as can be.

My heart dropped. My hand held on to David's a little tighter. He looked at me, a little perplexed. My eyes might have given away my internal anguish because without saying a word, he suddenly kissed me on my forehead and held my hand tighter.

Guilt ate away at me. Here was a man who had willingly uprooted his life just to make me happy. Yet I had not told him the truth.

I had not told David about my night with Matthew all

those months back in the park. I had not told him how Matthew had revealed Tariq's killer to me. I had not told him the 100 per cent truth about why I had uprooted his almost perfect life in London and implored him to move to America with me.

I had not told him that I had just seen Anthony Harris, the man who murdered my bright star, Tariq.

47

The intensity of his red hair piqued my interest. It was as if it had been amalgamated with blood. He must've caught me looking. I am not sure what he saw aflame in my gaze. Whatever it was, it evidently burnt him because he swiftly turned and walked away.

I needed to keep an eye on him. I could not afford to lose him. There was just something about him. I wanted to talk to him. Ask him about Tariq. Ask him whether he thought about him as much as I did.

"Let us take our seats, my love." David ushered us to our seats. Winner sat between us. Next to me was a man with dark brown hair and his family. In between him and his wife was their son, a young boy a year or two older than Winner. The boys, who instantly connected, began giggling and showing off their superhero toys to each other. David and the other man laughed with pride at their sons. I was too busy trying to pinpoint where the man with the blood-red hair was among the crowd. The man beside me must have noticed my gaze.

"Quite an interesting character, isn't he?" he said, his eyes also watching the red-haired man in the distance.

For the first time since we had sat down, I finally looked at him.

He smiled a most beautiful smile, while his eyes were still glued to redhead.

"Bridget." I reached out my hand to him. As he turned his face to the side, our eyes met.

"A pleasure to meet you, Bridget." His hand reached

for mine.

He was as cool as ice.

"You have a lovely family," I waved towards his lady and his son.

"Thank you."

Turning to David and Winner, I said, "This is my boyfriend, David, and my son Winner."

"What a befitting name for a champ," he smiled.

The press conference began. The chief of police stood on the podium, his voice booming. He kept going on about how he would be the one to bring about the change that was much needed in his organisation. He spoke about having a black great-great-great-grandfather, though by looking at him you'd be forgiven for thinking there was no blackness in his lineage. This blackness that he was now claiming was, according to him, the main catalyst for his desire to bring about change because, he claimed, if he did not act, his great-great-great-grandfather would roll over in his grave. I was part listening and part keeping my eyes on redhead.

The man next to me kept trying to make small talk, much to my annoyance. There was something about him that I did not like.

David was intently listening to the various speakers who graced the podium. Winner was busy chatting about Black Panther with his new friend. The little boy was cute. His mother – a pretty young lady – looked at me and gave that smile mothers give each other when they're happy their child has made a new friend. I smiled back, feeling the same as her.

We were all sitting there seeking our separate pieces of enlightenment I supposed. However, I wondered what the man with the child and his lady were seeking in that room. They did not look like they or anyone close to them had suffered any type of police brutality. They were a bit of an eyesore in the row in which we were sitting. There were plenty of white people in the room. Nevertheless, the black and Hispanic bodies seemed endless.

"So, why are you here?" I asked the man whose eyes were focused on the speaker on the podium.

At first, he did not say a word. His gaze fell on me a little too long. I wondered what was going through his mind. Maybe I was wrong. Perhaps he too, just like me and my family knew what police brutality felt like. "If I'm being honest, my wife forced me to come," he said cool as ice, his head swiftly snapping back to the podium.

From the corner of my eye, I could see a glimmer of red. My heart drummed. It was the man with the red hair who I did not want to notice me. He was walking towards our row. There was a lone seat at the end of the row. He sat. I could feel his eyes digging into me. I wanted to look into his eyes. But I was afraid. Afraid that he would know it was me, Bridget White, Tariq's cousin.

Needing a distraction, I decided to ask the man sitting next to me another question. "What would you do if someone murdered the person you loved the most in cold blood?"

He replied insouciantly: "An eye for an eye I'd say."

As I continued to clandestinely watch the redhead, an eerie coldness settled next to me like a living, breathing thing.

Out of nowhere, the man with the family commanded, "Let's go guys," and yanked the arm of his son who looked upset by this move but could not protest as he and his mother followed the head of the pack all the way to the front of the room.

David, finally noticing something was amiss, asked, “What happened?”

“I think the testimonies of the survivors of those killed was all too much for him.” I guessed, shrugging, even though in my gut I felt it was something else.

The conference had come to an end. I was in a hurry to go and look for the man with the child. I needed to talk to him.

He was lost in the crowd. My eyes swam over the heads of people as I tried to locate him.

A hand touched me.

“Hi Bridget,” said Brian, the redheaded man I had been trying to avoid. He used to be Tariq’s friend. They played basketball together. It was him that Tariq had been going to pick up for basketball practice that evening he was killed. I had blamed him for Tariq’s death even though it was no fault of his. Ever since, he had been trying to reach me, to beg my forgiveness even though there was nothing to be forgiven.

Before I could say a word, he rushed at me, hugging me ever so tightly. “I am so sorry that I wasn’t there with him that night...” he stopped, sniffling. “Perhaps if I was there, he would still be alive.” It was a simple statement, yet I knew the weight it carried. Sometimes, in America, the difference between life and death when encountering a cop while black is having a white friend beside you. “I miss him so much,” he said, his voice breaking, his arms still around me.

“I know. I miss him too, Brian.” I snuck out of his embrace to properly see him. He had grown into his tall, lanky teenage frame. Now he was a young man of twenty-two. I wondered what Tariq would look like at such an age if he were still alive. My hands curled around Brian and held him tight. He was the only tangible reminder I had of Tariq at that moment. "I am so sorry if I blamed you for his death all those years ago, for I know how you loved him and how he was like a brother to you."

The way he looked at me, it felt as if my words had just removed the tonne of guilt he had been carrying all along.

He wanted to talk. He desperately wanted to talk ... But I had to find the man with the child. "I'm so sorry, but I have to go ... let's keep in touch," I shouted, already walking away from him.

* * * *

I could hear the sound of blood pumping in my heart. For months I had thought about how my revenge on Anthony Harris would look. What it would feel like. Would I in the end be satisfied? What would satisfaction feel or look like? I imagined my revenge to be raging, ferocious and downright ungodly. But I was never that person. I had never been that person. In the end I hoped, I concluded, that my revenge would be a quiet and intimate affair. Nothing filled with fireworks. Only filled with that soft, yet burning sense of pure, unadulterated satisfaction.

That was my hope. The hope that in the end, it would be a girl, the professor and a bright star who won, not Anthony Harris!

The man with the family was outside, smoking. He was sitting in the middle of the huge steps which led to the museum the press conference had been held in. Most of the crowd had left, were leaving or just about to leave.

"Still here?" I said, taking a seat beside him. He did not look at me. He simply shrugged. "Can I have one?" I asked pointing to his cigarette, though I had never smoked one in my life. He gave me a stick, lighting it as it burned between my fingers.

"Can I tell you a story?"

"Sure. Go ahead," he finally spoke, while lighting another cigarette for himself.

"There was once a man who had it all. A wife, a kid and a career. But still, he was not happy..." I paused, my eyes searching his face which was looking far into the distance, while he pulled vigorously on the cigarette. "This man was not happy because, in his past, he killed someone." I paused yet again. The stick between his fingers fell to the ground. Tiny beads of sweat began to form on his forehead. He shook his head as though a grave realisation had just occurred to him. I continued: "The man had changed his home, changed his wife. He had even changed his hair..."

That was when it finally dawned on him. He knew who I was, the same way I knew who he was. "You see, you can dye your hair, you can change your location. You can even change who you once were. But you can never change the fact that you are a killer, Anthony Harris."

Paralysed from shock, his breathing which for the most part had been steady, became erratic. He stared, wide-eyed into the distance as more bodies kept going past us. I knew his world was breaking, crumbling around him as I assessed the nuances of his fragility through his facial expressions as he took in my words. "Surely you did not think you would get away with killing Tariq, did you?" He could not answer.

It was 12.05 pm. The sun was shining, a cool breeze was blowing and below us came the distant, yet seemingly close, sound of sirens that were fast approaching. The plan I had spent all those months so painstakingly devising was finally materialising.

The sounds of the sirens were a grand, grand symphony to me.

My hand, reaching into my bag, tried to retrieve something. Officer Harris, quick as lightning stood up, brandishing his pistol.

I had only wanted to show him the photo of us shaking hands at Harvard. I was going to say to him, "Isn't it uncanny ... to now know that you were shaking the hand of the woman who would avenge Tariq White."

"Don't move," he shouted at me, pointing the weapon wildly at me, at the public and at his colleagues who had now arrived and were shouting, "Drop your weapon!" But it was too late.

Bang!

Bang!

Bang!

His comrades shot at him ... fearing for their lives.

48

The summer of 2020 was one for the ages ... lifetimes if you ask me!

Darkness consumed the light. In retaliation, the light swallowed the darkness whole. A replication of such biblical proportions illuminated the human condition deeper than ever before.

The virus was at an impasse with its human targets. We brought forth our best warriors who waved vaccines as if they were swords forged from the heavens themselves.

In England, a self-loathing woman was running immigration. It was brilliant how the white man used the non-white woman to get rid of those who looked like her and others darker than her. Her name might have been pretty, but her ways were downright ugly.

In the United States, white supremacy, now at its height, began to falter like a lofty tower as black voices rose, rose, and rose.

The professor's denigration of the black man was five years ago. He had said they were fools who were all talk and no action against their predicament. Five years later it appears the black men he was speaking about no longer wished to be serrated - they were consciously sharp and all about action.

Black women, who for centuries were known to religiously defend and protect black men in every way and shape possible without sometimes receiving the same love back decided to go against the grain.

It was July 2020. Protests were rising in every corner of the world; from black rights, countered by white and blue rights, to human rights, to women's rights, which were then countered by men's rights. All across the board, rights were being countered by the Right and Left.

Twitter, the town square of the world, was inflamed with opinions and theories about the virus, Black Lives Matter and, most prominently, a black man who did not value black women.

He was a black American who lived in Waco, Texas and, was known across social media for spewing hate against women whose flesh mimicked the same hue as his mother's skin for mainly white entertainment. He would get on Twitter, Facebook or Instagram and post his one-minute videos degrading and desecrating the holy body of the black female form. *They are bitter ... they're not even that pretty ... they're overweight ... I wouldn't date one for free ... and if I were to die, I'd hope none came to my funeral ...* he would say.

The likes and comments ascended as if his words were descended from heaven itself. His notoriety was blossoming like a thorny rose. Whether you hated or loved him, you could not help but watch and listen to him.

And though I hated him I was one of the people who watched him, maybe hoping that someday he would find deliverance from his self-loathing.

One day while watching his videos, which I hate to admit were intriguing, I laughed. Not because I was entertained but because I was taking in his surroundings. He was cooped up in a small room with a bed in the background. It appeared to be a single bed and by the bedside table were dead cigarettes, cheap beer bottles and coins. On top of his bed was a half-naked poster of a blonde with writing, which I assumed to be his own, scribbled across her chest. A curtain that resembled a flimsy cloth more than it did a curtain blocked the world outside. Nonetheless, because the curtain was so flimsy, my eyes could make out parts of the world he tried to conceal from his audience. While I sat there, a drink in my hand as that was the only condition in which I could stomach his bile, I noticed that there was a silhouette moving in slow motion behind the window. As one body disappeared from view, another appeared. Straining my neck forward it suddenly struck me that these shapes were either gangsters or police.

"Oh, shit," I murmured. I did not like him, but he was one of us.

My fingers typed furiously ... *I think there are people with guns surrounding you. Get out now!!!*

Either he did not see my message, or he saw my black face on the avatar and refused to take heed. Whatever it was, it appeared a black woman was not destined to save him.

A door broke open. "Get on the ground now!" barked some hefty-sounding men.

The man, unable to react quickly, gave a wry smirk before the camera smashed onto the floor.

A scream was heard.

Some rigorous scuffling followed the scream.

Then silence.

The following day, it was reported on all the news outlets on social media that this particular man had died in police custody.

There was no major uproar over his death. A few non-black folks and some black men feinted anger.

I, for one, was apathetic. How do I feel pity for a man who shunned the sanctity of my being? How? Yet he was still part of my being no matter how hard I tried to ignore this fact.

The hashtag #justice began floating around that same day the news spread across continents like wildfire.

As it was the year of countering, another hashtag #wedontcare grew roots and began sprouting that same day. To match the vexation of the latter hashtag the former decided to organise a march to demand justice.

The man had said that if he died, black women should not be aggrieved. We were not. What he did not realise was that except for people like him, most black men followed where the black woman goes. So, because we did not march or protest on his behalf, black men refused to march and protest for him also. Seeing this, white people too refused to march and protest his killing. He had not considered that people will be your biggest fans online, but reality was a whole different realm.

He had not realised that without the backing of black women, every fight for the black man will fail. Which was why his killer was never brought to justice.

Black women had finally refused to support those who did not support them.

* * * *

That summer, my hairdresser, Aunty, made a small fortune from fixing and braiding hair in her tiny one-bed apartment. It was big enough to upgrade to a two-bed outside London and most importantly to buy tickets for her sons so that they could come and visit her after lockdown was temporarily lifted. In addition, luck had smiled upon her. The Home Office had finally, after all those years, given her indefinite leave to remain in the United Kingdom.

The first time I called her, while in the US, she had

screamed with excitement, "My daughter, Bridget, I am so happy to hear from you."

"Me too, Aunty."

"You won't believe it," her voice choked, "but they have given me my papers." She sniffled, "After all these years, they have given me, Eniola, my indefinite leave to remain." My eyes moistened. I wanted to hug her because I knew that the storm she had endured all this while had finally resulted in her landing on dry ground. Now, instead of fighting the waves she could finally walk, or run. My heart somersaulted with undiluted joy for her.

"Oh, and guess what else?"

"What?" I inquired excitedly.

"This lockdown has been a goldmine for me."

I was thrilled for her good fortune. Aunty deserved it. "How so?"

"Well, it seems men and women care a lot about their hair, even during a pandemic," she laughed. "I was getting customers left, right and centre. And it is all because of you."

"Me. How?" I inquired, dumbfounded.

"Do you remember when I called you during lockdown saying, 'I do not know how I am going to survive this pandemic since the salon was closed and working there, doing hair, was my only source of income'?" I now remembered. "Do you recall you sent me £500 that instant?"

"Which you profusely refused to accept until I said I would shave off all the hair you had spent years helping me grow." We laughed.

"You this girl, you wanted to give me heart attack then." She said of me threatening to go bald if she did not accept my help. “Anyway, it is that money you gave me, which I used £50 from, to pay the son of one of my customers who was in his first year studying graphics design to create a business page for me and connect it to my Facebook account, just before lockdown was lifted. From there on everyone was booking appointments. I had four or five slots per day and they were booked out days, sometimes weeks, beforehand with a non-refundable deposit.” I was proud of Aunty’s ingenuity.

“I am so happy for you, Aunty. You deserve all the good that comes your way.”

“Thank you, Bridget.” She stopped, her voice tinged with emotion. “I know you sometimes say that I am your hero. The truth, however, is that it is you, Bridget White; you are my hero.”

* * * *

That summer, for the first time since Tariq was murdered I knew what it felt like to be truly at peace. David was mine and I his, and Winner was ours. We were my perfect little family.

I never knew that no longer seeking revenge healed one’s wounded soul. I never knew that no longer seeking revenge gave one the best night’s sleep. But above all, I never knew that no longer seeking revenge makes you love and allows you to be loved.

That summer, Winner blossomed into a billion stars. The more he illuminated, the more he reminded me of Tariq. Maybe the heavens and The Almighty knew how much I missed and craved to see Tariq again, so grace was offered me in the form of a most magnificent human: Winner, who in some capacity was the continuation of Tariq.

Every time I turned around and looked back at Winner, a new star was born. Surprisingly the old star didn't die, it only morphed into the new one with brighter eyes, a newer voice with quicker feet and hands, but most importantly a grander heart with a wider smile. I could not love another human more if I tried!

Being in the presence of Winner was like witnessing a perpetual miracle morphing and merging into more wondrous and glorious miracles the closer I got to him.

Just like his Uncle Tariq, he was indeed my bright star.

49

Harvard was buzzing with the lives of new and old students. A tangible feeling of excitement moved feverishly through the air. Behind me, a group of postgraduates were complaining about their professor who derived great pleasure from giving 10,000-word essays every fortnight. "He's such a jerk," groaned a voice that I assumed belonged to the leader of the pack. His tone was filled with disdain.

"Isn't he just!" insisted another member of the group who sounded older than the leader.

I turned back to take a brief peek at them.

"Oh my God, you're Bridget White," beamed the student whom I'd assumed to be older but looked about twenty-three.

"Oh, wow, it is," confirmed the leader.

I was not aware till now that I'd turned into a mini-celebrity at Harvard. My face was on a couple of posters in praise of trailblazers. Next to my name were the words, A Bridge You Mustn't Cross!

Cheesy, yes. But I liked cheesy Harvard. It had a ring to it.

"Can we take a pic with you?" inquired the quietest of the group, his feet moving to my side before my voice could find an answer.

They all filed around me. Three mobile cameras flashed at me. Plastering a smile on my face, my fingers split into the peace sign.

Around us some students stopped and took photos of me from a distance, wooing as they did so. The statements: "You're so cool," "We need more heroines like you," and the one that sounded clearest in my ear, "... Your brother will be so proud of you," filled me with happiness.

Chuckling, I waved goodbye and squeezed my body through the sea of people to my first law lecture.

During the cessation of my PGCE, it had dawned upon me that teaching may not have been my calling. It appeared I had a penchant for exacting justice more so than being an English teacher. In addition, I had come to the realisation that my mother deserved to see me at my best. The daughter of Alexander and Cecelia White deserved to be the greatest criminal lawyer there was.

As I entered the lecture room, bodies were raised from their seats as a deluge of overwhelming applause drowned my thoughts.

I was the recipient of this adulation. Lowering my head in gratitude, I placed my hands on my chest.

One of the law professors was at hand to welcome me to the group.

"The inimitable Bridget White, ladies and gents..."

Someone even threw a bouquet of roses at me, which made us all laugh.

"Thank you, rose thrower," I teased, much to the delighted face of a wonderfully quirky young black man.

"You're my hero,"

"I hope for you to be mine someday..."

"Marcus." He beamed.

Moving towards the mic, the head of the law department spoke, insisting that individuals like myself were the reason why Harvard would always produce the best lawyers in the world. Before ending his speech, he told us he had a surprise for us.

"Now, class of 2024, please welcome our guest speaker..."

We all looked around wondering who it was.

It was the one and only, Professor Matthew Wylde. The room erupted in thunderous applause.

"The last time I was here, I was quoted as saying the black man was a fool..." This was met by some good-natured boos.

"Now you might hate me for this. But I do not think I was wrong, well not entirely." He stopped, his eyes assessing us. No one disagreed, so he continued.

"What I should have said was the black woman is a genius. She is ... or rather she will be a saviour..." Before he could finish, the room exploded, booming with raucous applause. I wanted to be diplomatic in my agreement with his words. But how could one be diplomatic in the face of such truths? I joined all those others also standing in praise. An indulgent smile plastered itself on my face while my palms clapped until they were crimson.

"... Well, it's good to see an entire crowd agreeing with me for once," he winked - his eyes glued on me.

The room noticed.

Shyness consumed me.

I glanced up cautiously; his eyes did not remove their gaze from me. I could feel my cheeks burning as my eyes saw the sweet delight in his. I could feel the room excited by this unspoken game Matthew was playing with me.

The professor was just as animated as before. I guess

one could not just erase love for a being like me. For him, my shyness was his assurance that deep down I too felt something. Even if it'll never be as potent as what I feel for David.

There'll always be a spot for the professor somewhere in my heart that is soft - yet hard, sensual - yet bland, hot - yet cold. It'll always be there, and as I watched him on the screen of the projector's monitor, I realised this wasn't a bad thing ... after all, he will forever be that soft light in my life. Nothing like the light of the sun that David was to me, but a soft light that still shone brightly in the dark - and that was enough for him too, I suspected.

Acknowledgements

To Ezekiel, my son, the perpetual light in my life. Thank you for the hugs, the "I love you's", the "Mummy, you're my best superhero ever", before you proceed to kiss me and get back to Spiderman. Thank you for the insurmountable degree of light, love, happiness and hope you have brought into my life since your inception. I love you a billion times more than all the words in all the languages of the world could say. I will always be your superhero, my dearest, sweetest, kindest, and most loving boy.

To Rebecca Gandi, you are my rock mama. To every and anyone who has ever believed in me being a writer. Thank you for the big and/or small dose of confidence your belief injected in me. It meant and still means a lot to me.

Printed in Great Britain
by Amazon

36163016R00198